"I found the check my father tried to give you," Chelsea said, her voice barely a whisper.

"So that was it." Jack felt his jaw tighten.

"I didn't know, Jack."

He looked away, the pain fresh as a new wound, past her to the sports car parked by the chutes. Her sports car. He smiled bitterly. For a moment, just looking at her, listening to her, being so close to her, he'd forgotten. Now he looked from the car to her, recalling only too well everything he'd once felt for her—and all the reasons they had been wrong for each other.

"If you'd just told me," she said.

How many times had he questioned that decision? How many times had he thought about going back to try to straighten things out? But the memory of her father coming out that morning to the corrals with the check, the look in Ryder Jensen's eyes, the accusations, the contempt—all had kept him moving on down the road.

"It wouldn't have made a difference," he said.

"I don't believe it."

He turned away. He definitely didn't need this.

"Jack."

It came out a whisper, so familiar and so intimate, he stopped in his tracks, unable not to remember that soft sound, the feel of her breath on his skin....

"Believe it," he said, walking away from her, just as he had ten years ago.

Dear Reader,

I grew up on old Westerns, spending many a Saturday with Roy Rogers and Dale Evans, riding the range and rootin' for the good guys. Is it any wonder, after spending part of my youth in Texas and the rest in Montana, that I love cowboys—and rodeos?

They say that rodeo is a reaffirmation of the Old West, a celebration of life and a lifestyle that has all but passed away.

That's why I loved writing this book as part of the TRUEBLOOD, TEXAS series. I like to believe that somewhere in Texas right now Chelsea and Jack and their descendants are keeping the cowboy way of life alive. A life based on a love for the land—and each other.

B. J. Daniels

TRUEBLOOD, TEXAS

B.J. Daniels

Rodeo Daddy

HARLEQUIN®

TORONTO • NEW YORK • LONDON
AMSTERDAM • PARIS • SYDNEY • HAMBURG
STOCKHOLM • ATHENS • TOKYO • MILAN • MADRID
PRAGUE • WARSAW • BUDAPEST • AUCKLAND

B.J. Daniels is acknowledged
as the author of this work.

To Judy Kinnaman, a friend and fellow writer, who has been there from the beginning. Thanks for all your support and encouragement.

Acknowledgments:

With special thanks to bull riders Colby Yates of Azle, Texas, and Canadians Blade Young of Saskatchewan and Denton Edge of Alberta.

HARLEQUIN BOOKS
225 Duncan Mill Road, Don Mills,
Ontario, Canada M3B 3K9

ISBN 0-373-65087-6

RODEO DADDY

Visit us at www.eHarlequin.com

Printed in U.S.A.

TRUEBLOOD, TEXAS

THE TRUEBLOOD LEGACY

THE YEAR WAS 1918, and the Great War in Europe still raged, but Esau Porter was heading home to Texas.

The young sergeant arrived at his parents' ranch northwest of San Antonio on a Sunday night, only the celebration didn't go off as planned. Most of the townsfolk of Carmelita had come out to welcome Esau home, but when they saw the sorry condition of the boy, they gave their respects quickly and left.

The fever got so bad so fast that Mrs. Porter hardly knew what to do. By Monday night, before the doctor from San Antonio made it into town, Esau was dead.

The Porter family grieved. How could their son have survived the German peril, only to burn up and die in his own bed? It wasn't much of a surprise when Mrs. Porter took to her bed on Wednesday. But it was a hell of a shock when half the residents of Carmelita came down with the horrible illness. House after house was hit by death, and all the townspeople could do was pray for salvation.

None came. By the end of the year, over one hundred souls had perished. The influenza virus took those in the prime of life, leaving behind an unprecedented number of orphans. And the virus knew no boundaries. By the time the threat had passed, more than thirty-seven million people had succumbed worldwide.

But in one house, there was still hope.

Isabella Trueblood had come to Carmelita in the late 1800s with her father, blacksmith Saul Trueblood, and her mother, Teresa Collier Trueblood. The family had traveled from Indiana, leaving their Quaker roots behind.

Young Isabella grew up to be an intelligent woman who had a gift for healing and storytelling. Her dreams centered on the boy next door, Foster Carter, the son of Chester and Grace.

Just before the bad times came in 1918, Foster asked Isabella to be his wife, and the future of the Carter spread was secured. It was a happy union, and the future looked bright for the young couple.

Two years later, not one of their relatives was alive. How the young couple had survived was a miracle. And during the epidemic, Isabella and Foster had taken in more than twenty-two orphaned children from all over the county. They fed them, clothed them, taught them as if they were blood kin.

Then Isabella became pregnant, but there were complications. Love for her handsome son, Josiah, born in 1920, wasn't enough to stop her from growing weaker by the day. Knowing she couldn't leave her husband to tend to all the children if she died, she set out to find families for each one of her orphaned charges.

And so the Trueblood Foundation was born. Named in memory of Isabella's parents, it would become famous all over Texas. Some of the orphaned children went to strangers, but many were reunited with their families. After reading notices in newspapers and church bulletins, aunts, uncles, cousins and grandparents rushed to Carmelita to find the young ones they'd given up for dead.

Toward the end of Isabella's life, she'd brought together more than thirty families, and not just her orphans. Many others, old and young, made their way to her doorstep, and Isabella turned no one away.

At her death, the town's name was changed to Trueblood, in her honor. For years to come, her simple grave was adorned with flowers on the anniversary of her death, grateful tokens of appreciation from the families she had brought together.

Isabella's son, Josiah, grew into a fine rancher and married Rebecca Montgomery in 1938. They had a daughter, Elizabeth Trueblood Carter, in 1940. Elizabeth married her neighbor William Garrett in 1965, and gave birth to twins Lily and Dylan in 1971, and daughter Ashley a few years later. Home was the Double G ranch, about ten miles from Trueblood proper, and the Garrett children grew up listening to stories of their famous great-grandmother, Isabella. Because they were Truebloods, they knew that they, too, had a sacred duty to carry on the tradition passed down to them: finding lost souls and reuniting loved ones.

CHAPTER ONE

CHELSEA STOOD at the door, her hand poised over the knob. It had been more than a month since her father's death and yet she still didn't want to go into his den. Unlike the rest of the ranch, with its eclectic mix of furnishings collected over many years, Ryder Jensen's den mirrored the strong, determined man who had made the Wishing Tree one of the largest working ranches this side of the Pecos.

But it wasn't just the thought of seeing her father's neat, very masculine office and the memories it would evoke that made her hesitate at the door. It was his words just before his death. He'd been trying to tell her something. She felt a chill, although it was April and, in this part of Texas, already warm.

What had he taken to his grave? Something to do with her, that much was clear. And the answer, she feared, was on the other side of this door.

She steeled herself and opened the door. Instantly she was hit with the scent of leather and her father's tobacco. Tears welled in her eyes, and for a moment, she almost turned away. But if anything, she was her father's daughter. Whatever secret he might have been hiding, she would face it. Just as she'd had to face his death and the terrible sense of loss that came with it.

She went to the desk and slowly began going through the stack of papers resting on the surface. The heart attack had taken her father quickly. He'd had no time to put his affairs in order. It had been in the ambulance on the way to the hospital that he'd tried to tell her something. No, she thought, it was almost as if he'd tried to *warn* her about something. But she'd been unable to understand him and she'd never gotten another chance.

The Wishing Tree felt empty without him, as if the heart of the ranch were gone. While she had friends who'd supported her and let her talk about her father and his death, her older brother Cody had shut her out, refusing to even mention Ryder's name. Cody's way of dealing with his grief was work. She hardly ever saw him these days, and that made her loss even greater.

She couldn't remember her mother, who'd died when she was two. Her father and brother had always been the center of her life and now she felt abandoned, adrift.

To her surprise, the papers on the desk all had notes on them, reminders of things her father needed to get done, all personal. Had he known about his illness and just not told Cody and her?

Her fingers slowed as she worked her way through the pile of papers, a cold chill coming over her. He must have known! Why hadn't he told them, prepared them for this?

As she neared the bottom of the pile, she was almost relieved when she still hadn't found anything pertaining to her. Then she saw it. *Tell Chelsea before it's too late.* It was written in her father's clipped, slanted script, and attached to the note was a check.

Tell Chelsea *what?* Fingers shaking, she pulled the check from behind the note. Her heart took off at a gallop when she saw who it was made out to. Jack Shane.

Memories blindsided her, a deadly mix of pleasure and pain, love and betrayal. Why had her father kept one of

Jack's old paychecks from the time he was a ranch hand on the Wishing Tree? It had been almost ten years.

She started to wad the check up and throw it away, wondering what her father could have possibly wanted to tell her. Jack Shane was old news.

Her eye caught the amount of the check. She froze. Ten thousand dollars! Her gaze flew to the date. It was the same day Jack had left the Wishing Tree. The same day he'd broken her heart, his note short and to the point: *I can't do this, Chelsea. I'm sorry. It's for the best. Goodbye, Jack.*

She dropped into her father's chair, her hands shaking so badly that the check slipped from her fingers, fluttering to the floor.

Her father had bought off Jack! She couldn't believe it. She felt sick. That was what he had been trying to tell her. How could he have interfered in her life like that? She and Jack had loved each other. They'd planned to marry. Ryder Jensen thought she was too young to know her own mind, not yet eighteen, and tried to convince her she was wrong about Jack. But to pay Jack to leave?

Her anger at her father was eclipsed by the realization that Jack had betrayed her. He'd taken the money. Ten thousand dollars to turn his back on their love.

Fury brought her to her feet. He'd settled for peanuts. He could have gotten so much more. He could have had her—and half of the Wishing Tree—if he'd stayed and stood up to her father. The coward.

With tears in her eyes, she knelt down to retrieve the check, incapable even now of forgetting her feelings for Jack. Her father had been wrong. She'd damned well known her own mind. She'd been in love with Jack. It *had* been the real thing. At least for her.

As she picked up the check and straightened, she saw

something that was destined to change her life forever—just as her father had thought he could change her destiny.

The check had never been cashed! There was no cancellation on the back. No signature. She stared at it, trying to make sense of what she was seeing. Jack hadn't taken the money.

She stood looking at the check for a long time, remembering, then she folded it carefully, put it in the pocket of her jeans and went out to saddle her horse.

THE MORNING AIR smelled of pine and sunshine as she set off on Scout. She loved this land, this life, as much as her father had. All she'd ever cared about was ranching and the Wishing Tree. Ryder had insisted she get a formal education, an education befitting a woman. But she'd always known where she belonged and had returned to the ranch to take over the financial end of it, while Cody saw to the day-to-day running of the place.

That arrangement allowed her to ride every day and continue to be the tomboy she'd always been, helping with calving and branding and even mending fences when she felt like it. But at the same time, she was the lady of the house and found that role also fit. Her father loved to entertain in the grand living room with the massive stone fireplace and the windows that looked out over a small lake and ranchland.

Her father had left her and Cody the Wishing Tree with the restriction that it could never be sold outside the family. Not that either of them would dream of such a thing. She planned to see her children raised here and her children's children.

She worked her way toward the south forty, riding Scout through the scrub pines and rock outcroppings until she spotted her brother with a handful of men repairing one of the corrals.

Cody looked up when he heard her approach. He frowned, but said nothing as she dismounted and, ground-tying Scout, walked toward him.

"I need to talk to you," she said, a few yards from the men.

Cody didn't seem surprised, just obviously not happy about the prospect.

"Now?" he asked pointedly.

"Now," she said, digging in her heels.

He looked worried, as if she'd ridden all this way to talk about their father's death. She knew people dealt with their grief in different ways, but Cody seemed to be running from it. She'd heard him up at all hours of the night, roaming the old ranch house, as lost as she was. If only he'd talk to her about it.

She desperately needed her big brother back, she thought as she watched him slowly move toward her. He was tall and broad-shouldered like their father, with slim hips and long legs. His handsome face was tanned, the lines strong, confident. She'd missed him. Worse, she could feel a distance between them that scared her and she feared what she had to say would only make matters worse.

But she was her father's daughter and didn't know any other way but to take the bull by the horns. "I'm sure you can spare a minute."

"I'm really busy right now," Cody said impatiently. "I'm sure whatever this is about can wait until—"

"It can't wait." She wished she'd tried harder to talk to him before this. She'd let him stew in his own juices for far too long.

With reluctance, he followed her over to a lone oak.

Once in the shade, she turned to face him. "I found something in Dad's den I need to talk to you about."

His expression instantly closed.

She pulled the check from her pocket and handed it to him.

He looked puzzled, but took it from her, unfolded the check, glanced at it, then handed it back.

"You knew about this!" She couldn't believe it. She thought this was just her father's doing. "You knew," she accused, angry and crushed that her brother had been part of it. "Damn it, Cody."

"No reason to start swearing like a cowhand, Chelsea." He shifted the weight from one dusty boot to the other, his gaze moving off to the west as if he wished he could go with it.

"You knew how much I loved Jack. You knew." She felt hot tears. "Why?"

"Isn't it obvious?" Cody asked.

"No." She brushed the wetness from her cheeks. She'd never been a crier and didn't intend to become one now. "All that's obvious is that the two of you tried to buy him off."

"You don't know the whole story," Cody said with a stubborn set of his jaw.

"Then you'd better tell me—" she planted her hands on her hips "—because we're not leaving this spot until you do. And don't think you can avoid me like you have for weeks and not discuss this."

"Let it go, sis," Cody warned. "It's all water under the bridge."

"Not for me." She'd never gotten over Jack Shane. Nor had she ever found another man who could fill his boots. It hadn't been just a schoolgirl crush, damn it.

Her brother looked down at the ground.

"Dad tried to tell me something in the ambulance," she said. "I found a note attached to the check, 'Tell Chelsea before it's too late.' It's obvious that Dad regretted what he did and wanted to make it right before he died."

Cody's head jerked up, his brown eyes darkening. "The only reason he'd have told you was to warn you," her brother snapped.

"*Warn* me?"

"Jack Shane wasn't the man you thought he was," Cody said, avoiding her gaze. "I'm sorry, sis, but he was only after the ranch."

"Like hell." She felt the tears again but fought them back. She'd loved Jack. And he'd loved her. A woman knew. Even a young woman who'd fallen in love for the first time. She couldn't have been wrong about Jack. *Oh yeah? Then why didn't he come to you with this? Why did he just leave a hurried note? And the big one, why hadn't he come back?*

She felt the check in her hand. "He didn't take the money. That proves what kind of man he was."

Cody chewed at his cheek for a moment, then slowly raised his gaze to meet hers again. "I never wanted to have to tell you this, but I know Dad was worried that Jack might show up again after... Dad planned to tell you himself...."

She stared at her brother. He'd known that their father was dying. She felt sick. Sick that her father hadn't told her. Sick that Cody had had to carry the burden of that knowledge alone.

It took a moment for his words to sink in. "Dad thought Jack would come back? Why would he think that?"

Cody looked away. "With Dad out of the way—"

"That's ridiculous," she snapped. "If Jack had wanted

the ranch, he'd have stayed and fought for me." If he'd
loved her enough…

"Not under the circumstances," Cody mumbled. "I
hate to be the one, but someone has to tell you."

Her heart thumped wildly in her chest and she held her
breath, suddenly afraid. "Tell me what?"

"We started losing cattle just after Jack hired on. Dad
and I didn't want to believe it was him, because from the
start we could see how you felt about him."

"Jack was rustling cattle?" she asked, her voice barely
a whisper. "I don't believe it."

"Well, it's true. Remember the night Ray Dale Farnsworth was killed?"

Ray Dale was the son of a neighboring farmer. Her
father had hired him as a favor to Angus Farnsworth, Ray
Dale's father. Ray Dale was a wild one, always in trouble,
but Ryder thought he could help the young man.

Then Ray Dale was found dead in Box Canyon at the
north end of the ranch. It appeared he'd fallen from his
horse and hit his head. Everyone had always wondered
what he'd been doing in the canyon that night.

The sheriff had wondered as well. She remembered
overhearing something about semi-truck tire prints along
a nearby road and a rumor of rustling. But rustling was
always something to worry about on a ranch the size of
the Wishing Tree, and when the sheriff ruled the death
accidental, that had been the end of the rustling talk.

"Ray Dale and Jack were rustling our cows," Cody
said quietly. "Dad and I had suspected it for some time."
He held up a hand. "It's the honest to God truth. I saw
Jack ride out after Ray Dale that night."

She couldn't believe her ears. "That proves nothing."

"The two had rounded up about fifty head in Box
Canyon," Cody continued, as if she hadn't spoken. "I

don't know what happened. There was a storm that night so maybe the lightning and thunder spooked the cows and they stampeded and Ray Dale got thrown from his horse." He shrugged. "But Jack was there. I followed him to the canyon, then I rode back to tell Dad."

She shook her head. "There has to be another explanation."

"Jack had a record, Chels. We found out that this wasn't his first brush with the law. He'd done some time in Juvenile Hall for stealing on other ranches where he'd worked."

She closed her eyes, remembering Jack telling her he'd gotten into some trouble when he was younger, made some mistakes. He'd grown up hard and hadn't had the advantages she and Cody had, but he'd been so determined to change his life.

"He wouldn't steal from us," she said adamantly, opening her eyes. "And if they really were rustling, then why didn't Dad have him arrested? Why didn't any of this come out at the time?"

"Isn't it obvious? Dad knew how you felt about Jack. He didn't want you to be hurt. Ray Dale was dead. The Farnsworths were going through enough, losing their only son, without adding the pain and embarrassment of knowing Ray Dale was rustling. Dad felt that the loss of a few cows and letting Jack Shane get away with it was better than hurting people he cared about."

She stared at her brother, missing her father all the more because what Cody said was true. That's exactly how Ryder Jensen would have handled the situation. But it wasn't like her father to try to buy off a thief and they both knew it. "Dad wouldn't offer ten thousand dollars to Jack if he really believed he was stealing from the ranch."

"Wouldn't he?" Cody said.

She didn't want to hear this. Didn't want to believe it.

"He did it to protect you," her brother continued. "I can't tell you how it hurt Dad to do it. He knew you'd be devastated if you learned the truth. By then, Jack knew we were on to him. That's why he took off the way he did."

"But why didn't he take the money?" she cried. "If money was all he cared about, why didn't he take it?"

Cody shook his head. "Maybe there is some honor among thieves. Or maybe he thought it was a trap." He reached out, encircled her neck with his arm and pulled her to him. "I'm sorry, sis," he said, hugging her. "Maybe now that you know the truth, you can finally get over Jack Shane once and for all, and Dad will be able to rest in peace."

Unable to hold back the tears, she hugged Cody, glad to have her big brother back. She'd give up crying tomorrow. At least now she knew why Jack left the Wishing Tree and hadn't looked back.

CHAPTER TWO

IN THE DAYS that followed, Chelsea rode Scout every morning, galloping through the cool dawn, the wind blowing back her hair, blowing back her tears.

On those rides, she questioned every aspect of her relationship with Jack, searching for some sign that she'd been dead wrong about him. That her love for him had blinded her to his faults, his weaknesses, his deceitfulness. Or that, like her father and brother believed, she really had been too young to see the truth.

She remembered everything about Jack Shane. The way he talked, the way he stood, the way he touched her. And the way he'd left her.

She'd been seventeen that summer, Jack twenty-two. He had a way about him. A quiet, gentle strength. She liked how he handled the horses she loved. She liked the tenderness that came into his dark eyes when he looked at her. She'd felt a pull to him, stronger than gravity, whenever she was near him.

She'd known he'd been hurt bad when he was young, and suffered poverty and neglect. She'd felt his pain, just looking at him. But she'd also seen his desire to overcome his past, his determination to succeed. He was a man willing to work for what he wanted. He hadn't been kicked down so much that he didn't still have dreams.

Maybe it was that hunger that had led him to steal.

It wasn't like she hadn't seen how overwhelmed he was

by the size of the Wishing Tree ranch, how envious he was of her family's closeness and how…uncomfortable he was with her wealth. He hadn't wanted to fall in love with her because of it, and told her as much.

Chelsea had never thought much about money. Probably because she'd never had to. Everything she'd ever needed was on the ranch. Her life was unbelievably rich in so many things she hadn't realized until she'd met Jack Shane. Money was only one of them.

Jack had never believed he would be accepted in the circles in which her family traveled, and because of that, he'd had trouble believing the two of them had a future.

He'd been right. She ached at the thought of how Jack must have felt when her father offered him ten thousand dollars to leave the Wishing Tree and her. She knew how much pride he had. In fact, he'd had little else.

That alone could explain why Jack had written the hurried note telling her it would never work out. Why he'd left without talking to her and why he'd never come back.

What if Cody was wrong? She kept thinking about the check and the fact that Jack hadn't taken the money. The more she thought about it, the more she believed Jack hadn't left out of guilt, but hurt and embarrassment. What if there was an explanation, just as she had originally thought, for Jack going to Box Canyon that night?

The more she considered it, the more she worried that Jack had been falsely accused. She couldn't have been that wrong about him. If she had been, she would never trust her heart again.

"I'm going to find Jack," she said one morning at breakfast, surprising herself as much as she did Cody. "I have to confront him. I have to know the truth."

"I *told* you the truth," Cody said contrarily.

"I believe you," she assured him. At least she believed that Cody believed it. "I just need to know why."

"For once in your life, just let it go, Chels," Cody said, pushing away his plate. "He's going to break your heart all over again."

"Try to understand," she pleaded, not wanting this to come between them. "I have to do this."

"The man is no good, Chels," her brother said hotly. "The worst thing you can do is dig all this back up. Think of Dad. This isn't what he would have wanted. If it comes out about the rustling, it's going to hurt everyone, especially the Farnsworths."

"This is just between me and Jack."

Cody threw down his napkin and pushed back his chair. "Why do you think Dad debated telling you for so long?" he demanded as he got to his feet. "Because he feared you'd do some fool thing like this. You always took in every stray cat or dog that wandered onto the ranch, thinking that with some food and love you could save them all. Well, you couldn't save Jack Shane but you would have died trying."

"It wasn't like that. Cody, please, try to understand. I've never been able to get over him. If you're right, then after I see him, I'll be able to move on. Finally."

"You think he'll admit the truth to you?" he demanded.

"Yes, I think he will."

Cody shook his head, his gaze softening. "Sis, I'm just afraid you're going to fall under this guy's spell again."

"I'm a big girl now, Cody. I'm not seventeen with stars in my eyes. If Jack lied to me, I'll know."

Cody was still shaking his head. "Dad made one hell of a mistake by running him off. He should have let Jack stay long enough to hang himself so you could see who he really was.''

"Yes, Dad should have," she agreed. "But since he didn't, I intend to see for myself. Support me on this, Cody. Trust me.''

"It isn't you I don't trust, Chels. It's Jack. I saw the way he stole your heart. He would have stolen this ranch just as quickly. You're making a mistake, one you're going to regret.''

"I guess it's my mistake to make," she said quietly.

"Then you're on your own." He swore as he turned and stomped out, grabbing his hat on the way. "Just don't say I didn't warn you.''

"I NEED YOU to find someone for me," Chelsea said the moment she stepped into the office of Finders Keepers a few hours later.

Dylan Garrett laughed at her abrupt entrance. "Chelsea. What a surprise!'' He got up to embrace her.

Dylan and her brother Cody were the same age and had been good friends since they were boys. The Garretts owned a ranch in the same area outside of San Antonio as the Jensens. She hadn't seen Dylan and his sisters Lily and Ashley since her father's funeral.

Dylan released her, holding her at arm's length to look at her. "How are you? I've been wanting to stop by to see Cody...."

She knew what he was asking. "Cody is doing...better. You saw how he was at the funeral. He fills his days with work. But I think he's sleeping more now and he's talking to me again.''

"Good," Dylan said, offering her a chair.

"That is, he was," she added.

Dylan raised a brow. Rather than go back behind his

desk, he took a chair across from her. Dylan had always been a strikingly good-looking man. At one time, Chelsea had had a terrible crush on him—his rugged, muscular build, his sun-streaked light-brown hair, always in need of a haircut, and those incredible blue eyes so like his father's.

But it was the laugh lines around his eyes and mouth and that little dimple in his left cheek when he smiled that used to get to her. That and the fact that he was a nice guy.

Unfortunately, he'd been her brother's friend, one of the reasons the crush hadn't lasted long. That and Jack Shane.

She took a deep breath and smiled, trying to calm down. She'd always been impetuous, but now that she was in Dylan's office she felt a little…scared. "How are you?"

He smiled. "Good."

"I've been following your wonderful success with Finders Keepers. I hope I get to see Lily while I'm here, and the baby. How old is Elizabeth now, almost a month?"

"She's the cutest thing," the proud uncle said, a sparkle in his eye.

It struck her what a great father Dylan would make. But so far, it seemed, no woman had caught his eye.

"So, who do you have to find this early in the morning?" he asked, no doubt sensing her need to get this settled and as quickly as possible.

She took a breath and braced herself, not sure how much he knew about all this. "Jack Shane."

He arched a brow. "Jack Shane?"

"He worked on the ranch about ten years ago."

She filled Dylan in on everything Cody had told her,

although she suspected he probably knew most of it. "I was in love with Jack," she confided.

"I remember," Dylan said quietly. "You went to Europe later that summer."

Her father had surprised her with that trip to Europe. Now she knew why. Obviously, he'd hoped it would help her get over Jack. Too bad it hadn't worked.

"Are you sure about this?" Dylan asked.

She'd never been more sure of anything. Or more afraid. "I have to know the truth."

Dylan looked skeptical. "More than likely, you'll never know the truth. If he conned you before, what's to prevent him from doing it again? I have to raise these questions, Chelsea. Jack Shane might be guilty. He might even be…dangerous. What then?"

She started to argue, but he stopped her.

"Did you ever think that he might not want to be found?"

She knew what Dylan meant: if Jack was guilty, seeing her turn up on his doorstep wasn't going to make his day.

"Or he might be in prison—or worse," Dylan added. "Ten years is a long time. And all things considered, there's more than a good chance you aren't going to like what you find."

She nodded. "Either way, I need to know and I need to hear it straight from Jack."

Dylan studied her for a moment. "Okay, I'll do my best to find him for you, but I have to tell you, it's against my better judgment."

"Thanks, Dylan," she said, opening her purse to pull out her checkbook.

He reached over to put a hand on hers. "Let's see what I find out, then we can talk about my fee. I'll give you a call.'' He got to his feet. "Lily is around—you have to see this baby. Stay here, and I'll be right back.''

Restless, Chelsea walked around the tastefully furnished office, too nervous to sit. She knew she wouldn't be good for anything until Dylan found Jack. Until she got this settled in her mind. And her heart.

She heard Lily's voice and turned to hear Dylan say, "Give me that baby, and come in here and say hello to Chelsea.''

"Chelsea? You didn't tell me she was here." Lily burst through the door and rushed to hug her as Dylan brought the baby in. Elizabeth was so tiny and adorable, Chelsea melted at the sight of her.

"Everything's all right, isn't it?" Lily asked with concern after Chelsea had made a fuss over the baby.

Chelsea nodded. She'd always felt close to Lily and her sister Ashley, but she couldn't bring herself to tell Lily about Jack. "Congratulations. Elizabeth is beautiful.''

Lily's face glowed with happiness as she nudged the blanket down with a finger so she could look at her baby cuddled in her brother's arms. Chelsea watched the expression on Lily's face and wondered if she would ever have a child of her own.

DYLAN WATCHED Chelsea leave, unable to shake off the bad feeling he had. Chelsea was like a little sister to him, and, like Cody, he felt protective of her.

"What's wrong?" Lily asked behind him.

He turned to look at her holding her precious infant daughter. Everything, he wanted to say. He envied his sister. She had Cole and now Elizabeth.

"I'm worried about Chelsea," he answered honestly.

"She's a headstrong woman," Lily agreed.

He had to laugh. "Like someone else I know.''

"Dylan, when I came in earlier, you were on the phone with Zach Logan. I couldn't help but overhear."

Zach had been Dylan's boss when he'd worked with the Dallas police. "Zach's just helping me with Julie's case," Dylan said. He didn't want to concern his sister any more than he already had. "Zach's involvement will help me settle it faster, that's all."

Julie. The woman he loved. The woman who had married his best friend, Sebastian Cooper.

It had only been a few months since Dylan had discovered Sebastian was up to his neck in the mob. Julie had learned of it even earlier and had taken off, pregnant.

That had been a year ago January—a long year in which Dylan had searched for Julie, finally locating her in the tiny Texas town of Cactus Creek. Julie was fearful for her life and that of her baby son, Thomas. She was convinced Sebastian meant to harm her, and after eavesdropping on Sebastian and mobster Luke Silva, Dylan knew her fears were grounded. He had put her in a safe house in Boot Hill until he could find enough evidence on Sebastian to send him to prison for life.

Dylan worried that he wasn't moving fast enough. That Sebastian was going to find Julie and Thomas before he could get what he needed on his old friend. He had tried to keep the fact that he'd found Julie a secret, but his twin sister Lily knew him too well—Lily and their ranch foreman, Max, who was like a brother to Dylan. They noticed Dylan had changed in the past few months and had guessed the reason. But Dylan trusted them to keep his discovery of Julie a secret. And even though he hated to inflict worry on his sister and Max, it had helped having them to confide in.

"I heard you tell Zach that you're planning to go see J. B. Crowe in prison to flush out Sebastian," she said, then lowered her voice, realizing she'd startled Elizabeth. She looked down at the infant, then back up at him. "J. B. Crowe is the head of the mob. You helped put him in prison—you know how dangerous he is." Dylan stepped over to his sister and rested his hand on her shoulder. "Believe me, I know. But for Julie's sake, I've got to find Sebastian before he finds her, and J. B. Crowe is going to help me. He just doesn't know it yet."

"You really love her, don't you?" Lily said. "Just do me a favor. Please be careful."

"Always." He kissed his sister on the forehead, then Elizabeth. "You just take care of my niece and don't worry." But he could tell that would be hard for her. It was another reason he had to find Sebastian. And soon.

IT WASN'T UNTIL the next evening that Dylan called. Chelsea had been waiting anxiously by the phone. Cody had cleared out of the house and was back in his distant, uncommunicative mood. Her attempts at conversation with him only elicited grunts until she'd finally just given up.

It broke her heart to lose him again. She could only hope he'd come around, because now that she'd gone this far, she wasn't turning back.

"Chelsea?" The sound of Dylan's voice made her heart begin to pound.

"You found Jack?" she whispered.

"He doesn't go by Jack Shane anymore," Dylan said. "He calls himself Jackson Robinson."

Why did that name sound familiar?

"He's a bull rider on the pro rodeo circuit," Dylan continued. "Shuns publicity but has made a name for himself by winning more than a few titles."

"You're sure it's Jack?" she asked, surprised the man she'd known would be riding bulls. Even more surprised he'd changed his name. But then according to Cody, she didn't know the man at all, and ten years ago he would have had good reason to try to drop out of sight.

"Unless someone else is using his social security number it's the Jack Shane who worked for your ranch ten years ago," Dylan said.

"Where can I find him?" she asked, more determined than ever to see if this Jackson Robinson was really her Jack.

"Hold on, now," Dylan said. "I've just started digging. I would strongly advise you to wait until I get more information on this guy before you confront him."

She couldn't bear the thought of waiting any longer. "Is he in Texas?"

"Yes."

She took a breath. "Is he…married?"

"I have no idea. Given more time—"

"Where is he in Texas?" she asked, determined to get her own answers—and quickly. "Dylan, I need to see him. Now."

"Cody will have my hide for this," Dylan said.

"You've always been able to hold your own with Cody," she returned. "Where, Dylan? You can't talk me out of this any more than Cody did, and believe me, he tried."

"I'm sure he did," Dylan said with a groan. "Jackson Robinson is riding in Lubbock tomorrow night."

Lubbock, Texas. That was only a day's drive away.

"That's perfect. Thanks, Dylan. You don't know what this means to me." She started to hang up.

"Chelsea, don't get your hopes up too high."

Too late for that.

"Why don't you take Cody with you?" Dylan suggested.

"Cody?" He had to be kidding. "I think not. Anyway, he has a ranch to run. I'll be fine. Really." She didn't need her big brother protecting her.

She hung up, her heart pounding. As impulsive as she'd always been, even she was shocked by what she planned to do. She was going to see Jack. Jackson. Whatever he called himself these days. She told herself that she'd know the truth the moment she looked into his dark eyes.

CHAPTER THREE

WHEN SHE GOT UP the next morning to leave, Cody was already gone. She loaded her bag into her car, scribbled a goodbye to her brother with the promise to call, and left.

The night before she'd packed hurriedly, shaking with just the thought of seeing Jack again. Maybe Dylan and Cody were right. Maybe this man *did* have some power over her. He'd certainly stayed in her thoughts all these years. And in her heart.

She hadn't known what to pack or for how long. A few days max. What should she wear? What any Texas-born cowgirl wore to a rodeo—jeans and boots.

But she threw in her favorite blue silk dress for good measure, just in case.

Just in case what? What did she hope was going to happen? She tried not to go there.

She'd just closed the bag when she heard a sound behind here.

"So you're really going to do this," Cody said from the doorway.

He no longer appeared angry, just concerned. She nodded.

"Could you at least tell me where you're going?" he asked.

"Lubbock. He's riding bulls with the rodeo circuit."

Cody nodded. He'd ridden a few bulls himself, and a few broncs.

She hadn't really wanted to tell him that Jack had changed his name, afraid Cody would only see it as more evidence of his guilt. "He's riding as Jackson Robinson."

"Is he?"

"Have you heard of him?" she'd asked, seeing something in her brother's look that worried her.

He hadn't answered. "You realize you might be the last person he wants to see."

She refused to even consider that possibility.

Cody had stood in the doorway for a moment. "I know better than to try to talk you out of this fool behavior."

"That's good," she'd agreed.

"Could you at least call and let me know you're not dead on the highway?"

"What good would calling do? You'll be out mending fence or chasing down some stray calf, acting like you work around here." He didn't seem to appreciate her sense of humor. But then he never had.

"I'll take the cell phone with me," he'd said after a moment. He'd made a disgusted face and looked even more put out with her. Cody hated cell phones and refused to carry the one she'd bought him.

"Then I'll call," she'd promised, and smiled. "Wish me luck?"

"You're going to need more than luck, little sister."

Last night she'd felt confident, but now that she was on the road, she was less sure of herself. What if she was wrong about Jack? What if he didn't want to see her? Or worse, what if he admitted he'd never cared, that he'd only been after her cattle—and her ranch?

That thought almost made her turn around. Almost.

She remembered the day Jack had arrived in an old red

pickup, rattling up the road in a cloud of Texas dust, look-ing for a job. He'd climbed out of the truck. Even at twenty-two he looked solid, as if he'd done a lot of man-ual labor. Had it been love at first sight? She'd always thought so.

A terrible thought struck her. What if Jack thought she'd known about the check?

She drove past San Antonio, took Highway 10 and headed west. At Sonora, she'd angle up 87 and on into Lubbock. She figured she'd be there before Jack rode.

Turning up the music, she put the top down on the Mercedes her father had given her for her twenty-fifth birthday. But she couldn't quit thinking about Jack. Or worrying that she might be wrong about him.

AFTER GETTING CAUGHT in road construction for hours, Chelsea was late reaching Lubbock, and suddenly, she wasn't so sure this was a good idea. She was twenty-eight, no longer a kid. And yet she was still chasing rainbows.

But she'd come this far. And if she didn't see Jack, she would always wonder, right?

A little voice in the back of her head that sounded un-cannily like her brother kept warning her this was a mis-take.

She glanced in the rearview mirror, shocked to realize she hardly recognized the woman behind the wheel. Cheeks flushed, eyes bright as stars, excitement radiating from her. And determination. She was a woman who liked to finish what she started, one way or the other.

By the time she found the rodeo grounds on the far side of town, the rodeo was over and the crowd had gone home.

She parked, raked her hand through her long, unruly

hair, wishing she'd had the sense not to put the top down on the car.

Getting out, she walked slowly toward the chutes at the rear of the arena, hoping that Jack would still be there.

She asked a cowboy loading his horse into a trailer where she could find Jackson Robinson. He pointed her in the direction of a dozen trailers, pickups and motor homes camped under a long row of old oaks—and one older model motor home in particular.

As Chelsea neared, she saw that the outside door was open and light was spilling out the screen door onto a piece of carpet in front of the metal pull-out step.

The evening was warm and filled with the fragrances of coming summer. Woven into the scents were the many different foods being cooked in the tiny community camped here, and the leftover smell of corn dogs, cotton candy and fried bread from the rodeo.

The lights, the warm breeze and the inviting aromas gave the encampment a cozy, homey feel. Horses whinnied in the corrals. Laughter drifted on the breeze from small groups of cowboys sitting outside their rigs in pools of golden light. There would be another rodeo tomorrow night, so it appeared most of the riders were staying for it.

As she approached the motor home, she thought she smelled something cooking inside. Then she heard a sound that stopped her cold. It drifted out the screen door. Light, lyrical, definitely female laughter.

She stopped walking, realizing just how rash she'd been. Had she expected Jack to pine away for her all these years as she had for him? Obviously she had.

Suddenly she was struck with a huge case of cold feet. She started to turn and stumbled, almost colliding with a child. The cowboy was small and slim, dressed in jeans, boots and a checked western shirt. His straw cowboy hat was pulled low over his eyes.

"Sorry," Chelsea murmured, feeling like a coward. Didn't she want to know the truth? If she couldn't face the fact that Jack had someone else, how could she face it if he'd lied to her, rustled her cattle and taken off with her heart? Which right now seemed damned likely.

"Are you looking for someone? I know everybody here."

"Oh you do, do you?" Chelsea asked with amusement. She'd thought the child a boy, but on closer inspection, she realized the cowboy was in fact a cowgirl of about eight or nine. And from the amount of dirt on her jeans and boots, Chelsea would say a tomboy. She recognized the look.

The screen door on the motor home banged open. Chelsea turned, afraid it would be Jack. Instead, a young woman dressed in western attire came out, still laughing and smiling back at whoever was inside. Her boots rang on the metal step of the motor home and her laughter echoed through the trees.

"See ya later, Jackson," the woman said, and swinging her hips, sauntered off.

The tomboy next to Chelsea made a rude noise. "Terri Lyn Kessler. She's a barrel racer."

Just then, a man stuck his head out the door of the motor home. "Samantha?" he called, but the retreating woman didn't turn around.

Chelsea's gaze swung back around to the motor home and Jack standing in the doorway. It seemed as if it had been only yesterday. She stood rooted to the spot at the sight of him in the light from the open door. A whirlwind of emotions swirled like a dust devil around her, engulfing her, taking her breath away. Some things didn't change— her reaction to Jack Shane one of them.

"Samantha?" he called again, his eyes seeming to adjust to the semidarkness.

Chelsea thought he was calling after the woman who'd just left. But to her surprise, it was the tomboy next to her who finally answered.

"Coming, Dad," the girl said with obvious reluctance. "I got to go," she told Chelsea. "It's dinnertime and I'm late as usual and in trouble." She sounded as if this was nothing new.

Chelsea watched the girl amble toward the motor home, kicking up dust with the scuffed toes of her worn boots.

Dad? Jack had a daughter.

Chelsea took a step back, ready to make a run for it, when she saw Jack's gaze lift from Samantha to her.

"Chelsea?"

JACK KNEW the moment he breathed the word, it betrayed him. For years after he'd left Chelsea and the Wishing Tree Ranch, he'd imagined seeing her again. He'd always known he would look up one day and there she'd be. For years he'd search the rodeo crowd for her face. Other times he would think he saw glimpses of her in passing. Or hear her voice and turn so quickly it gave him whiplash.

For a long while after he'd left the ranch, he'd expected her to come looking for him. Had hoped she would. But she never had, and he'd stopped expecting it. Still, he'd always known he'd see her again. And feared the day.

"Jack." She took a step toward him and stopped as if unsure what she was doing here. She wore a blue shirt that hugged her curves, designer jeans and boots.

What *was* she doing here? He shook his head, unable

to believe she was anything more than a mirage. As he stepped toward her, he feared the moment he was within touching distance, she would disappear.

Samantha stood watching the two of them, looking too curious for her own good.

"Go on in and wash up, Sam," he said as he passed her.

"But, Dad—"

"No buts," he said firmly, his gaze on Chelsea. What was she doing here? He'd seen in the paper where her father had died. There'd been a big write-up.

"Chelsea," he said again, just the sound of her name on his lips bringing back the old ache, reminding him of the feel of her in his arms.

She smiled tentatively. "Hello, Jack."

He stared at her, searching for words. It had just been too long, and he was feeling way too much right now.

"What are you doing here?" He hadn't meant to make it sound as if she were trespassing.

"I heard you were riding on the pro rodeo circuit and I just happened to be in the area," she said too quickly.

"You just happened to be in Lubbock?" he asked, eyeing her suspiciously. He'd known her well enough to know when she was lying. Also when she was nervous. Right now, she was both.

"It's been a long time," she said.

He nodded, shocked. He'd thought the years would have tempered the desire. Lessened the need, the gut-clenching ache inside him.

"Almost ten years," he said. "What are you doing here, Chelsea?" he asked again, his voice filled with the anguish he felt. *Whatever it is, just get it over with.*

"I had to see you," she said, her eyes shining, her voice cracking.

He swallowed hard, waiting for her to tell him what had made her drive all the way here just to see him. Nothing good, he would bet on that.

"I found the check my father tried to give you," she said, her voice barely a whisper.

So that was it. He felt his jaw tighten.

"I didn't know, Jack."

He looked away, the pain fresh as a new wound, looked past her to the sports car parked by the chutes. *Her* sports car. He smiled bitterly. For a moment, just looking at her, listening to her, he'd forgotten. Now he looked from the car to her, recalling only too well everything he'd once felt for her—and all the reasons they had been wrong for each other.

Just look at the two of them. Chelsea, standing there in boots that probably cost more than everything he owned. Him, wearing worn jeans and a T-shirt, stocking-footed, a day's growth of beard, and standing in front of a motor home that, like him, had seen better days.

He'd almost forgotten how inadequate her wealth made him feel. He stepped back, purposely putting some distance between them.

"Jack, if only you had—"

"Chelsea, all that was years ago." Only it felt like yesterday. He raked a hand through his hair. "I was sorry to hear about your dad," he said, hoping that would be the end of it.

"Why didn't you tell me?" she asked, her voice barely a whisper. She glanced around as if she didn't like talking out here in the open. Her gaze settled on his motor home, and she suddenly seemed at a loss for words.

He understood the feeling. Their lives had taken different paths, that was for sure. They were strangers now. No, he thought. He and Chelsea could never be strangers, not after everything they'd shared. That's what made this so damned painful.

"Chelsea." He shook his head, shaken by her sudden appearance and the feelings that had once more been forced to the surface.

"Dad?"

"I thought I told you to go wash up for dinner, Sam," he said quietly without turning around. He met Chelsea's gaze, could see the pain in her expression.

"If you'd just told me," she said.

How many times had he questioned that decision? How many times had he thought about going back to try to straighten things out? But what would have been the point? The memory of her father coming out that morning to the corrals with the check, the look in Ryder Jensen's eyes, the accusations, the contempt—all had kept him moving on down the road. Still kept him moving on.

"It wouldn't have made any difference," he said.

"You don't know that."

"Yes, Chelsea, I do."

"Dad?"

He swore under his breath. "Sam—"

"I'm interrupting your supper," Chelsea said, looking as if maybe she finally realized the mistake she'd made in coming here. "I should go." But she didn't move.

He figured she hadn't gotten what she'd come for.

"My brother told me about…" Her gaze locked with his and for a moment he couldn't breathe. *I'll be damned.* So she'd just found out about the rustling. The old man hadn't told her.

He waited, taking some perverse satisfaction in making her say the words. He watched her get up her courage. It was one thing Chelsea Jensen had never lacked, or so he'd thought.

"He told me about the missing cattle," she said.

Jack let out a snort. "I wondered how long it would take before one of them told you."

"I don't believe it," she said, only a slight break in her voice betraying her.

He turned away. He definitely didn't need this.

"Jack."

It come out a whisper, so familiar and so intimate he stopped in his tracks, remembering that soft sound, the feel of her breath on his skin, her lips—

He didn't need to be reminded. He'd tried for ten years to put it behind him. To put Chelsea and the Wishing Tree and all of it behind him. Damn her for coming here.

"Believe it," he said, walking away from her, just as he had ten years ago.

"I'm hungry," his daughter said, watching him intently from a short distance away. She'd obviously seen his reaction to Chelsea, if not overheard their conversation.

"Then why didn't you take the check?" Chelsea called after him.

He stopped and turned slowly. "Don't do this. Whatever it is you're looking for, you aren't going to find it here."

"Aren't you going to ask her to have dinner with us?" Sam asked loudly.

He gave his daughter a warning look. *Don't do this to me, Sam.*

"We have plenty, don't we, Dad?" Sam persisted, flashing him her best wide-eyed innocent smile and completely ignoring his warning look. "We have that *huge* casserole."

He ground his teeth. He knew what his daughter was up to and it wasn't going to work. Sam had seen Terri

Lyn bring over the casserole and now thought she'd found a way to kill two birds with one stone, so to speak.

"Don't you want to have dinner with us?" Sam asked Chelsea, as if it were only good manners to ask.

Jack closed his eyes and lowered his head. When he looked at Sam again, he could almost see the mischief dancing in her eyes.

"Please!" she pleaded. "We don't *ever* have company."

Last night he'd forced her to sit through a dinner with him and Terri Lyn. Sam had never liked any of the women who came around trying to mother her and cozy up to him, and did everything in her power to discourage them. She especially didn't like Terri Lyn for reasons he couldn't understand. But he'd made it clear last night that Sam wasn't going to pick who he dated. If he ever really got down to dating again.

This was payback and she wanted him to know it.

"Sam," he warned. The girl had no idea what a hornet's nest she was stirring up.

"I'm sure your mother—" Chelsea began.

"I don't have a mother," Sam said, cutting her off. She sounded so pathetic Jack almost laughed. "She left me on Dad's doorstep when I was just a baby."

Chelsea was appropriately startled.

"Sam," Jack warned, but there was no stopping Samantha tonight. Tomorrow he'd ground her little cowgirl behind. A few days doing extra homework in the motor home should take some of the sass out of her.

"My mother was a barrel racer and couldn't handle having a baby," Sam continued as if she hadn't heard his warning—just like all the other warnings she'd ignored. "I'm the product of a one-night stand. At least that's what Terri Lyn says."

Thanks a lot, Terri Lyn. Jack groaned as he saw Chelsea's shocked reaction. He watched her glance toward the motor home and hesitate—the last thing he wanted her to do.

"So your father's raised you alone all these years?" Chelsea sounded impressed, damn it.

Sam nodded. "Just the two of us."

"Sam," he said pointedly, "Chelsea needs to get going now—"

"No," Chelsea said, her dark gaze coming up to meet his. "I'm not in that much of a hurry. And anyway, I didn't get my questions answered."

He swore under his breath. It was obvious that Chelsea could see the spot Sam had put him in and she planned to take advantage of it. "I thought you knew the answer before you came here."

"I thought I did, too," she said, her gaze hard. "Now I'm not so sure." She looked down at Sam. "I'd love to stay and have dinner with you and your father."

Sam beamed. The little scamp.

He gritted his teeth, knowing that he should put an end to this before it went any further. But maybe Chelsea had to see how he lived, had to taste Terri Lyn's tuna casserole before she could leave. The two put together should have her hightailing it back to San Antonio in her expensive little sports car, thanking her lucky stars she was leaving it all behind.

"Fine," he said. "I hope you like tuna casserole."

"My favorite," Chelsea said.

We'll see about that, he thought.

"We can eat inside," Sam said brightly. "You can help me light the candles that go with the casserole," she told Chelsea. "Won't this be fun?"

He scowled at his daughter, but she pretended not to

notice. "Fun," he echoed, and followed the two toward the motor home. Wait until Terri Lyn heard what happened to the little romantic dinner she'd had planned for later. But first he had to sit through an entire meal with Chelsea. Why hadn't he just admitted to the rustling and sent her on her way?

CHAPTER FOUR

DAMN! So much for thinking one look in Jack's eyes would tell her everything she needed to know. All she'd seen so far was arrogance and anger.

Not true. She'd glimpsed something when he'd first seen her. Surprise. And something that had set her heart running off at a gallop. It was one of the reasons she'd agreed to stay for dinner. That and the fact that Jack had been so dead set against it.

She knew she should turn tail and run. Hadn't Jack pretty much told her everything she'd come to find out? What more did she want him to say? That he'd never loved her? That he'd used her? That he'd been stealing her cows while seducing her?

She felt tears rush her eyes. It seemed she was becoming a crier whether she liked it or not. She fought them back with the only weapon she had: anger. Damn Jack Shane—or whoever he was.

"So you changed your name?" she said. "Got tired of Shane, did you?"

He bristled but didn't seem surprised, as if he'd been waiting for this. "Jackson is my given name and Robinson's my mother's maiden name. When she divorced my stepfather, I went back to Robinson." He raised a brow as if to say, *Satisfied?*

She couldn't think of anything else to say. For the mo-

ment. She could feel Jack's gaze on her, hotter than a
Texas summer night.

She felt the hair stand up on her neck and turned, unable to shake the feeling that Jack wasn't the only one
watching her. At the edge of the darkness, she would have
sworn she saw a figure move, furtive as a cat, disappearing into the blackness beyond the camp.

"It's a little small," Jack was saying as he opened the
door to the motor home and stepped back for Sam and
Chelsea to enter.

Small was putting it mildly. The inside of the motor
home was neat and clean but incredibly tiny, everything
in miniature. How could she ever get through dinner in
here with Jack so near? She wouldn't be able to swallow
a bite.

"Go wash up, Sam," Jack ordered.

Sam seemed about to argue, but apparently changed her
mind. As she slipped past her father, Chelsea heard Jack
hiss something at his daughter.

Jack stepped toward the kitchen. Chelsea had to move
to give him enough space in the tiny living room. He
appeared as uncomfortable as she felt. "Look, I know you
didn't come here for dinner so—"

"No. I came for answers." A thought pierced her heart,
as unerring as an arrow. "Sam must be what? Nine?" she
asked under the sound of water running at the back of the
motor home.

He raised a brow as if that should have been answer
enough. "She'll be nine in July."

It didn't take an accountant to figure that one out. "You
didn't waste any time, did you?" she asked, turning her
back to him so he couldn't see her hurt. Damn the man.

Sam came back into the small kitchen, glancing back

and forth between the two of them, her gaze full of open curiosity.

"Aren't you going to set the table?" the girl asked her father.

He turned to open one of the cupboards. "I don't think eating inside is a good idea," she heard him tell Sam.

"The wind will blow out the candles if we eat outside," Sam said. "Do you want to help me light them?" she asked Chelsea.

Chelsea couldn't miss the look that passed between father and daughter. Sam seemed especially pleased with herself. Her father, on the other hand, looked just the opposite. Chelsea almost felt sorry for him. "We don't have to have candles if your father wants to eat outside."

"Sure we do," Sam said. "Dad *likes* candles."

Somehow that didn't seem likely. Chelsea wondered what was going on between the two of them as Jack began to set the table with more than a little racket. He was obviously upset—and not just because Sam had asked her for dinner.

That's when Chelsea noticed the foil-covered casserole resting on the stove and groaned inwardly. Next to it were two tapered candles and a bottle of wine. Someone had drawn a heart shape into the foil. The barrel racer! The woman had an intimate dinner planned and Sam was in the process of ruining it—with Chelsea's help. Things were starting to make sense.

As angry as she was with Jack, she actually felt a little guilty. "Jack, I'm interrupting your dinner plans—"

"Why don't you help Samantha light the candles?" he said, then gave a shrug. "Plans change."

"You're going to use the good plates, aren't you, Dad?" Sam asked.

"Of course. Does this mean you plan to remove your hat?"

Samantha let out an embarrassed laugh and pulled off her hat, a long reddish-brown braid tumbling out. She disappeared into the back of the motor home for a moment.

The table sat between short booths to make up the rest of the kitchen-dining room-living room. Chelsea tried to stay out of Jack's way as he set the table, but it was impossible in such close quarters. At the mere touch of a shoulder, the brush of fingers, they both jerked back as if burned. On second thought, this was a terrible idea.

"Why don't you sit down?" Jack said, his voice sounding tight.

She nodded and hurriedly slid into the booth, surprised at her feelings. This Jack was different. More muscular. More solid. More attractive than the younger man she'd fallen in love with ten years ago.

She tried to tell herself that she no longer knew him. But as she watched him move around the tiny kitchen, she realized that was a lie. This man was branded on her. The scent of him. The feel of his skin against hers. The sound of his voice, low and soft in her hair.

She closed her eyes for a moment, the memory too sharp, too painful, the ache too intense. Why had she come here? What had she hoped to accomplish? The answer was obvious. She'd thought that once she told him about the check and the note, he would convince her of his innocence. They would put the past behind them…and take up where they'd left off. How foolishly romantic.

When Sam came back, her hair was brushed out. She handed Chelsea the matches to light the candles, studying her openly. It seemed Chelsea wasn't the only one with questions.

"So when did you meet my dad?" Sam asked, not the least bit shy. She made it sound as if Jack met a lot of women but he'd sneaked this one by her.

"Before you were born, Ms. Busybody." Jack looked as if he could spit nails, but he didn't try to stop her. As if he could. "A lifetime ago."

Chelsea let her gaze rise up to meet his. "Seems like only yesterday," she heard herself say.

Jack made a face. "Doesn't it, though."

"Did you know my mother?" Sam asked.

"No, she didn't," Jack said, answering for Chelsea once again as he put condiments on the table. "Get Chelsea a glass of water with her dinner."

Chelsea closed her eyes again, feeling overwhelmed.

"Is she all right?" Sam asked.

Chelsea opened her eyes to find both Sam and Jack looking down at her. "Fine. Maybe a little tired." She let her gaze rise up to meet Jack's. He knew what was wrong with her. She'd bet her last dime on that.

"Why don't you get Chelsea a glass of water," he said.

"Aren't you going to drink the wine?" Sam cried.

Jack swung his gaze to the bottle of wine, then at Chelsea. "Why not."

Now that Sam had removed her cowboy hat, Chelsea could see how much father and daughter resembled each other. There was no doubt that Jack was Sam's father. How could a mother just dump her baby off and not look back?

She reached for the glass of water Sam had gotten her, but instead Jack pushed a glass of wine into her hand.

"Here, this might be more what you need." He poured himself a glass as well and took a drink, his gaze studying her over the rim of the plastic tumbler.

She took a sip, grateful, her eyes meeting his with a

plea, one she doubted he would grant even if he could. There was an edge to him. A hard, finely honed anger tinged with bitterness. Was this about the check? she wondered. Or about her asking if he was a cattle rustler? It could be either, she realized.

Or he could be guilty as hell, and all that anger and bitterness nothing more than a defense mechanism. Did it really matter?

Yes. She still had to know. Their eyes met and she wondered if he could see what she was thinking.

He raised his tumbler slightly in a mock toast.

She gave him a tremulous smile, the motor home suddenly unbearably hot.

"Tuna casserole, my favorite," Sam said as she slid into the booth opposite Chelsea.

Jack seemed to drag his gaze away. He turned it on the girl, appearing both annoyed and amused. "I thought you hated tuna casserole," he said as he lifted the large, now unwrapped dish to the table.

"I don't know where you got that idea." She gave Chelsea a look that said, "Men!" Then she narrowed her gaze. "So did you have an affair with my dad?"

Chelsea choked on her wine. This kid was way too precocious.

"Samantha!" Jack bellowed.

"I was just asking," Sam said.

"Keep asking and you can go to bed without any supper," he warned.

Sam cocked a brow at him as if the threat amused her.

Jack shook his head, looking tired and vulnerable. His gaze came up to meet Chelsea's and she thought she saw almost a pleading in it, as if her coming here hurt him as much as it did her and he just wanted it to be over. She knew the feeling.

"We should have music," Sam said in a burst of energy, and slid out of the booth.

JACK DROPPED his head down, wanting to tell Sam he gave up. She'd made her point.

A moment later, elevator-type music drifted from Sam's boom box, confirming his suspicions. Terri Lyn had played romantic music at their dinner last night, making Sam roll her eyes whenever he looked at her.

This was definitely payback. Either that or his daughter had been abducted by aliens and a girl from another planet left behind in her place.

Sam shot him a grin as she slid back into the booth. "Nice, huh?"

He drained his wineglass and refilled it with the wine Terri Lyn had so thoughtfully brought to go along with the casserole, the candles now flickering warmly on the table and a CD in Sam's boom box.

His daughter looked expectantly at him and he noticed the not-so-subtle way Sam had sat across from Chelsea in the middle of the booth. It appeared she wanted him to sit next to their guest. He smiled to himself as he refilled Chelsea's glass with wine.

Under other circumstances, he might have found some humor in Sam's scheme to get rid of Terri Lyn.

He glanced at Chelsea, his pulse taking off at a trot at the thought of sitting next to her in the intimate booth. Not a chance, Sam.

"Dad?"

He dragged his gaze away from Chelsea, but not before noticing how she'd changed over the last ten years. She'd matured in ways he had never imagined. She was more rounded. More beautiful, if that was possible.

He felt a stirring within him and cursed the impact she

had on him. Had always had on him. Except now he knew that it could only bring him heartbreak.

"The casserole is getting cold," Sam said pointedly.

As if that would make any difference in the taste, he thought.

The alien Sam was all smiles and almost ladylike. He tried to match her joviality as he slid her over in the booth none too gently. He wasn't about to sit next to Chelsea, no matter how much Sam had hoped to manipulate him.

His daughter's smile faltered a little. His widened.

"So how *did* you meet my dad?" Sam asked again, not to be dissuaded even if one part of her plan hadn't worked.

"We met on her father's ranch," Jack said, his jaw tightening. "I was their ranch hand."

He saw Chelsea's eyes narrow. He reached for her plate. Chelsea wanted to have dinner with them—well, sometimes you got what you deserved, he thought as he slapped a large spoonful of Terri Lyn's casserole down on it, then reached for his daughter's plate.

"Where was the ranch?" Sam asked, her gaze going from Chelsea to him and back again.

"Near San Antonio," Chelsea answered, her cheeks a little flushed.

Jack found himself wondering why she'd really come here—not just to tell him she knew about the check or ask him if he was a cattle rustler. Surely she didn't think there was anything left to say between them?

"Do you know how to cook?" Sam asked Chelsea, as if she'd suddenly taken an interest in cooking.

Chelsea seemed surprised by the question, but no more than Jack himself. What was this, twenty questions?

He gave Sam an extra-large serving of the casserole before handing back her plate. That should keep her quiet.

"Yes," Chelsea said, smiling. "I enjoy cooking."

"What do you cook?" Sam asked, undeterred.

"All sorts of things." Chelsea seemed nervous. She was obviously not used to this sort of interrogation.

Jack groaned inwardly and reached under the table to squeeze Sam's knee in warning. Little good it did.

"Do you have to use a cookbook?" Sam asked.

He'd ground her for a month, he thought. Not that there was much to ground her from on the rodeo circuit. "Why don't we just eat?" he interceded.

"Terri Lyn uses a cookbook," Sam said.

Chelsea obviously didn't know how to answer that one. "I don't always use a cookbook."

He shoved his leg over to give Sam a nudge but his knee brushed Chelsea's under the table instead. The shock was immediate. And intense. He felt as if he'd been goaded with a cattle prod.

"Sorry." He didn't dare look at her, but he felt her stiffen in response and saw her pull her knees over toward the wall.

This was going to be some dinner. Just wait until he got Sam alone. And once Chelsea tasted Terri Lyn's tuna casserole, things were destined to get worse. *"Sam."*

He could tell his daughter wanted to ask a lot more questions, but she bowed her head and whipped quickly through the blessing first.

"Amen. So what do you cook?" she asked the moment her head bobbed up.

Chelsea laughed softly and seemed embarrassed.

"She doesn't have to cook," Jack said, not looking at her. "Her family hires someone to cook for them." He hadn't meant to make it sound so much like a condemnation, but hell, it was true.

"Yes," Chelsea said, ice in her voice. "We do have a

cook, but I can hold my own in the kitchen. I can make vichyssoise, pepper steak, beef bourguignonne.''

''Oh.'' Sam's face fell. ''I like Abigail Harper's macaroni and cheese.''

Chelsea was deflated. She'd been showing off and lost points with Sam. She looked as disappointed as Sam did. And as confused. Chelsea had mistakenly thought Sam would be impressed by the fact that she could cook. What Chelsea didn't know was that Sam was afraid he would fall in love and marry, and she knew he'd never marry anyone who couldn't cook. Chelsea might seem more of a threat than Terri Lyn at this point.

He couldn't understand why Sam was going to so much trouble to get rid of Terri Lyn, anyway.

He caught her eyeing her casserole distastefully, no doubt regretting inviting Chelsea to eat with them.

''How's your dinner, Sam?'' he asked pointedly, taking no little satisfaction in the fact that his daughter had put herself in this predicament and now would have to suffer along with him.

She hurriedly took a bite and pretended it was delicious. No small task considering Sam couldn't abide tuna casserole. And Terri Lyn's was especially bad.

He watched Sam take another bite and smiled to himself. Even if she'd liked tuna casserole, she would have found fault with it just because Terri Lyn had made it. Good thing he wasn't serious about the barrel racer. Not that he had the time or energy for a real relationship. He and Terri Lyn were strictly…consenting adults. Or at least they'd planned to be tonight.

Now he doubted that Terri Lyn would still be talking to him after he'd ruined her little ''romantic'' dinner by feeding it to another woman. The entire camp would be talking about Chelsea. Speculating. His luck had been running bad lately. Obviously, it wasn't getting any better.

Chelsea was the kind of woman who couldn't pass through your life without making ripples, even after a brief encounter. He knew after she left tonight, he'd still be feeling the effects in the weeks and months to come, and he was dreading it.

He didn't like his daughter's devious scheming, either. He would have a good long talk with her about it once Chelsea left. He just hadn't thought of a punishment yet to fit the crime.

"It's very good," Chelsea said politely.

"Mmm," Sam agreed. He watched her choke down another bite, almost feeling sorry for her. Almost.

He took a forkful of the casserole himself and looked up at Chelsea, something he instantly wished he hadn't done. But there was little other place to look, and he had to admit, seeing her there was like waking up to a sunny spring day. He savored it, storing it for the long days ahead when she would be gone from his life again.

Yes, he thought, she'd matured in ways that were hard to define, but the total package was as close to perfection as he could imagine. Five foot seven, slender, graceful and oh so feminine with her long brown hair caught at the back of her sleek neck. A pampered beauty. She couldn't have looked more out of place—drinking wine from a plastic tumbler, sitting in his beat-up old motor home, eating tuna casserole.

"So, do you work?" Sam asked Chelsea between bites.

"Chelsea lives on a ranch," Jack told her. "She's an accountant and keeps track of the cattle. It's not polite to cross-examine dinner guests."

"Sorry," Sam said, and actually looked apologetic.

He reminded himself that this girl with the scrubbed

face, sans cowboy hat, was an alien. Otherwise she'd be rolling her eyes, gagging and complaining.

"It's all right, I don't mind," Chelsea said. He could feel her gaze on him. He didn't dare look at her again. He realized he'd given himself away, knowing too much about her, almost as if he'd kept track of her all these years. Almost as if he cared.

JACK KNEW she was an accountant? That she took care of the financial end of the Wishing Tree Ranch?

She stared at him in surprise. He'd acted as if he'd never glanced back once he left the ranch. Look how quickly he'd met someone and had a child?

"How did you know that?" she asked.

He shrugged, avoiding her gaze. "Someone must have mentioned it."

Yeah, sure. A bubble of pleasure rose before she could slap it back down. Jack had kept track of her! He hadn't gotten over her any more than she'd gotten over him. A cattle rustler-liar-thief wouldn't have done that.

Or, suggested that darned voice that sounded suspiciously like her brother's, Jack had just been waiting for her father to die so he could prey on her again, thinking Cody didn't know about the rustling.

Sam gulped down her dinner and hurriedly excused herself, saying vaguely that she had to see someone about something and wouldn't be gone long. She disappeared before Jack could stop her, slipping out under the table, leaving the two of them alone in the already too small motor home.

Jack looked as if he wanted to run as well. He glanced out the window as if afraid of who might show up next.

She put down her fork. She hadn't had any appetite in the first place and Terri Lyn's casserole certainly hadn't improved it. "Look, Jack, I know I shouldn't have just shown up here like this, but after what Cody told me..."

He nodded, his jaw tensing, then pushed his plate away and got up to clear the table.

"Let me help," she said as he slid out of the booth.

"No!" He gave her an apologetic smile at his curt tone and motioned for her to stay put. "This kitchen is too small for more than one person."

He was right about that. She watched him clear the table, seeing his discomfort in the tensed muscles of his back through the thin white T-shirt. She tried not to notice the way his jeans fit. Or remember the feel of his long legs wrapped around her.

She fanned herself with her napkin, wishing there was more air in the room, wishing she hadn't drunk the wine, wishing there was an easy way to say what she'd come to say. Jack's admission that he hadn't completely forgotten about her gave her courage. That and the wine and the fact that Terri Lyn couldn't cook.

"I'm sure you're wondering about Samantha," he said, his back still to her as he began to wash the dishes.

What was there to wonder about? Jack had found someone else right after leaving the Wishing Tree.

He glanced over his shoulder, then back at his dishes. "What she told you just about covers it. I found Sam on my doorstep nine months after a one-night stand."

"You've raised Sam alone?"

He nodded, still not looking at her. "It wasn't any big deal." He chuckled. "At first I was as lost as a young bull in the ring. But Sam and I have done all right by ourselves. She's taught me a lot."

There hadn't been anyone special in his life besides Samantha? "Then you never married?"

He gave another nervous laugh. "I've been too busy to even date."

"You seem to have found time to attract a casserole maker," she said lightly.

He laughed. "Terri Lyn? We're just friends." He made a noise as if he hadn't meant to say that and instantly regretted it.

She felt her heart inflate like a helium balloon, and without thinking, she opened it to him. "Jack, there's no one serious in my life, either."

He froze but didn't turn around.

She rushed on before she lost her nerve. "I never knew what happened ten years ago. You just up and left. I thought you'd changed your mind about me. Then after my father's heart attack, I found the check he tried to give you."

Still Jack said nothing. Nor did he move, as if he were waiting for a blow.

"I know my father regretted what he did. He tried to tell me in the ambulance on the way to the hospital. He knew how much I—"

"Don't," Jack said, his voice low. "Chelsea, don't."

"But, Jack…" She slid out of the booth and was so close to him that she could feel his body heat. Cautiously, she laid a hand on his back, not surprised this time by the current that raced from her palm to her heart—or his flinch at her touch. "Tell me what happened between us was real. Tell me you weren't rustling our cattle and just stringing me along. Please, Jack."

THE FAMILIAR SOUND of his name on her lips grabbed his heart and squeezed it like a fist. He closed his eyes, her palm radiating warmth that ran like a live wire through him. Heat to heat, reminding him how it had been between the two of them. As if he'd ever forgotten.

"Jack, my father never should have done what he did without giving you a chance to—"

"Chelsea." He turned quickly, breaking the contact between them as he moved. He held her at arm's length, his voice rough with emotions he didn't want to feel. "Listen to me."

She stared at him, her eyes wide, brimming with tears.

He'd almost forgotten how brown her eyes were. How tiny gold flecks shone when she was excited or angry. Or aroused. If only he'd been able to forget the rest. The feel and smell and sound of her. Or the way her father had handed him the check that morning in the corral so many years ago.

"It doesn't matter, don't you see that?" he said. "What happened was for the best. Your father was right. You and I were all wrong for each other. The ranch hand and the rancher's daughter. So he thought I was stealing his cows. He also thought I was trying to steal his daughter, and he wasn't having any of it."

He pushed her away and waved an arm at the confined space he called home, thinking of the Wishing Tree Ranch and its massive rooms and high-timbered ceilings and all the antiques handed down through generations of Jensens.

"There is no way we could ever have made it together," he said, the words beating him like stones. "Look at us, Chelsea. I'm a rodeo cowboy. That, and a ranch hand, is all I've ever been."

"Jack, none of that matters if—"

"It matters to me. And it mattered to your father."

"He was wrong," she whispered. "If only he'd let you explain—"

"Chelsea, why dredge this all up again?" He moved

away, turning his back on her. For years he'd hoped she would come after him. Now he realized just how wrong he'd been—seeing her served no purpose.

"Ryder Jensen did me a favor." The rancher had reminded Jack just who he was. A man not good enough for his daughter. He turned to meet her gaze, something that took every ounce of his will. "He could have had me arrested but he didn't."

Her eyes darkened. She shook her head, a pleading in her gaze that broke his heart. "Tell me the truth."

"Will you leave here and never come back?" he asked.

"Yes." Her voice broke with emotion.

"Then it's true." He turned his back on her, leaning over the counter, the pain worse than being gored by a bull—and he'd been gored enough times to know. He wanted to stop but knew he couldn't. Not if he hoped to finish this once and for all. He should have done this years ago, but he hadn't been strong enough then. He wasn't sure he was now.

"I'm everything your father and brother told you I am. Now get out of here."

CHAPTER FIVE

CHELSEA WINCED as if he'd slapped her. "I don't believe you."

He shook his head, his back to her.

"I know you, Jack. Look me in the eye and tell me you were only after my money, that none of what we shared was real, that you never loved me. Tell me to my face and look me in the eye when you do it."

He turned slowly.

She felt her heart leap to her throat as his gaze came up to meet hers. In his eyes, she saw the answer. Her limbs went weak with relief. "You can't do it, can you?"

"It doesn't make any difference whether or not I was stealing your father's cattle," he said quietly. "I was sleeping with his daughter and I wasn't good enough for her. That was a far greater crime than stealing a few bovines."

"That's not true. If you had stayed, I could have proved how wrong you were about my father and brother."

He let out a laugh. "Chelsea, they'd already convicted me and were ready to slip the noose around my neck."

"If you told my father, I know he would have—"

"He didn't come out to the corral that morning to ask my thoughts on the rustling problem, Chelsea," he snapped. "He came with a check for ten thousand dollars and the threat of the sheriff if I didn't leave the ranch at once."

She felt sick, knowing what that had done to a man like Jack. "If only you had come to me—"

He let out a snort. "You're kidding yourself." He narrowed his gaze. "Did your brother believe you when you told him I didn't rustle the cattle? You did tell him, didn't you?" He must have seen the answer in her face. "That's what I thought. Don't you see? It doesn't matter if I rustled your cattle or not."

"It matters to me," she said defiantly.

He laughed. "Well, you're the only one. Now that you've found out everything you came for—"

"I'm going to prove to my brother that you were innocent," she declared. "I'm going to clear your name."

He shook his head as if he couldn't believe what she'd said and was amused by it. "Even if you could, do you really think it would change anything?"

"Yes. You're trying to sell my brother short. You've already done that with my father and me."

Anger sparked in his dark eyes. "Your family tried to buy me off. They were so desperate to get rid of me that they were willing to pay ten thousand dollars to a man they believed was a cattle thief."

"My father only did that to protect me."

"Exactly. To protect his precious daughter from the likes of me. And you really thought they would ever accept me as more than a hired hand? That's why I left, Chelsea. There wasn't a chance in hell for the two of us but you've never been able to see that."

"Because you were wrong then and you're wrong now. When two people love each other the way we—"

"Don't," he warned, and tried to move away from her, but there wasn't room in the motor home and she was blocking the door.

"I know you still feel something," she said with emotion.

"Even if I did, it wouldn't make any difference." His eyes darkened with anger. "You make it sound as if I left the ranch and you because I wasn't up to the fight. I was just smart enough not to take on a battle I knew I couldn't win. The loss would have been too great."

She opened her mouth, but he didn't give her a chance to respond before he rushed on as if the words had been bottled up for ten years.

"Look at us, Chelsea. You were born to wealth and privilege. Everything has come easy to you. You've never had to prove yourself. You've never had to give up anything or work hard for anything. You've never had to pick yourself up from the dirt because you've never been that low."

His words hit her like stones, stunning her to silence as he rushed on.

"You're soft, spoiled, pampered." He waved a hand through the air. "I've had to prove myself my entire life. Tomorrow after the rodeo I'll drive to another rodeo, then another after that. In my world, I have to keep proving myself over and over but it's on my terms. You came here looking for the truth? The truth is, you wouldn't last a week in my world so don't you dare try to tell me I should have fought to stay in yours. You don't belong here any more than I belonged in your world. Now get out of here and do us both a favor and don't come back."

Closing her eyes, she felt those damned tears, scalding hot behind her lids, as she searched blindly for the door handle. She wanted to tell him how wrong he was. About her. About them. About everything.

But the things he'd said cut too deeply.

"Please go, Chelsea."

She opened her eyes, tears spilling. He was bent over the sink, his arms braced on the counter. It wasn't like her to leave without the last word, but she knew if she didn't get away from Jack, she wouldn't be able to keep from sobbing her heart out.

She found the door handle. The door fell open and she stumbled out into the darkness.

A few campfires lit up the night and voices carried on the breeze. A horse whinnied nearby. She could feel someone watching her, just as she had earlier.

"You're wrong," she managed to say as she closed the door.

IF HE'D BEEN WRONG, she'd have slammed it. And she wouldn't have left without putting up a fight. It wasn't like her not to give him a piece of her mind. Not to argue. He'd almost forgotten what a firebrand she was. Almost.

He ached to call her back, to call back the words, to pull her to him and bury his hands in her hair, to bury himself in her, the only place he'd ever felt at home.

He stood where he was, waiting for the sound of her expensive car engine to turn over, part of him still foolishly hoping she wouldn't go. Damn but he was a fool.

When the door opened, his heart leaped in spite of himself.

"Where's Chelsea?" Sam said, glancing around.

"Gone." He heard the car engine. He turned on the faucet and ran hot water into the sink to do the dishes. He could sense Sam's confusion. The dishes were part of her chores.

"Did you have a fight?" she asked.

"Don't you have some homework to do?"

"No, I already finished it."

"Then why don't you get ready for bed," he said, sounding as tired as he felt.

"Okay."

He could hear the hesitation in her voice, the concern.

"She isn't coming back, is she?" Sam asked.

"No. She's long gone."

Good. Sam didn't say it, but he could hear it in the breath she let out.

"You know, one of these days I might want to get married."

Silence.

"Haven't you ever wanted a mother?" When she didn't answer, he turned to look at her.

She appeared pale, her freckles standing out on her pixie-cute face. "I don't need a mother."

"Some people might argue that."

She shrugged. "You and I get along just fine."

"Yeah," he agreed, reaching out to ruffle her bangs. "Yeah, we do."

Sam seemed relieved as she went back to her bedroom, little more than a bunk and a chest of drawers at the back of the motor home. She closed the accordion door to change into her pjs and he finished up the dishes.

The hard angry knock at the outside door made him jump. He turned as it swung open, still half hoping. Terri Lyn stomped in.

"How was your dinner?"

He held up one soapy hand. "If you'd just let me explain—"

"I already heard," Terri Lyn snapped. "It's all over camp. Who was she?"

"Nobody," he lied.

"She was Dad's old girlfriend," Sam said, appearing in the hallway off the kitchen. "The one he was in love with ten years ago, the one he never got over." She looked to him, already anticipating his reprimand. "Ace told me, so I know it's true."

Ace Winters. Damn. Jack had forgotten that Ace had worked on the Wishing Tree that same summer. Of course, everyone in camp would have been wondering about Chelsea and asking Sam questions—and Ace would have filled them in.

"Your old girlfriend?" Terri Lyn said in that I'm-really-pissed tone that meant there would be hell to pay.

The problem was, he wasn't in the mood and he realized he didn't care enough to pay. "I don't want to talk about it."

Terri Lyn raised a brow.

"Not tonight. Not ever. It really isn't any of your business," Jack said, looking from the barrel racer to his daughter and back. He handed Terri Lyn her clean casserole dish. "I'm sorry about our date, but maybe it's better this way."

"Yeah, maybe it is." She slammed the door on her way out.

He looked at his daughter. She had a satisfied smirk on her face, which she quickly tried to wipe off. "Go to bed," he said. "You've accomplished enough for one day."

She didn't argue, just turned and disappeared, closing her door behind him.

He thought about going out and finding Ace Winters, but he knew that would be a bad idea in the mood he was in. Anyway, he'd see Ace soon enough and tell the bull rider what he thought of him opening his big mouth to Sam. He'd wanted to punch Ace for as long as he'd known him, and his rival would be in the bull riding at tomorrow night's rodeo.

The dishes done, he turned out the light, stripped down and climbed up into the narrow bed over the cab. He didn't have much hope of sleep. The moment he closed his eyes he saw Chelsea's face. Just as he had for ten years. He found himself listening for the sound of her car engine, hoping she'd come back, praying she wouldn't, because no good could come of it. Just heartache. And he'd already had his share.

CHELSEA WOULD HAVE driven away in a cloud of dust if she'd been able to see clearly through her tears.

Unfortunately, she hadn't gotten out of the rodeo grounds gate when she had to stop. She laid her head on the steering wheel and bawled. She was really getting this crying bit down. Her emotions were like a roller coaster. Humiliation. Oh, yes. Anger. Absolutely.

What had she expected?

She'd expected Jack to have tried to convince her of his innocence. She'd expected him to...to... Okay, to have waited for her, damn it. Just as she'd unconsciously waited for him without even realizing it. Instead, he'd jumped right out of the chute and gotten some woman pregnant!

That hurt.

So did all the terrible things he'd said about her, especially the ones that were true.

If she had any sense, she'd get as far away from Jack Shane...Jackson Robinson...as was humanly possible. Seeing him had definitely *not* brought her closure.

She made an attempt to wipe her eyes, telling herself she needed to find Highway 87 and keep her foot on the gas pedal until she reached San Antonio and home. She could go home now and tell Cody that Jack was no rustler.

A jerk. An arrogant SOB. A heartless bastard. But no rustler.

Not that Cody would believe her.

Jack was right about that. But he was dead wrong about her. Spoiled. Soft. Pampered.

Okay, pampered. Maybe a little spoiled. But definitely not soft.

She was crying so hard she didn't hear the tap on her side window. She jerked back in alarm as a shadow figure appeared at the glass.

A man in a cowboy hat and jean jacket tapped at her window again. Probably rodeo security. *Sheesh.*

She hit the power button. The window dropped a few inches. "Yes?" she said, trying to get control of herself.

"Are you all right?" he asked, bending down to look at her. "Chelsea? Chelsea Jensen?"

She blinked in surprise as she recognized him. Lloyd Crandell. She'd seen him only a few weeks ago at her father's funeral. A big man, he was in his sixties with steel-gray hair and a cowboy mustache and crow's feet around eyes as gray as his hair. At one time, he'd been the ranch manager at the Wishing Tree.

"What are you doing here?" she asked. Dumb question. Lloyd raised rodeo stock. His family still ranched in the same area as hers did, only Lloyd had left years ago to follow the rodeo. After being stomped by a bucking bronco, he'd gotten into raising rodeo stock.

"I could ask you the same question," he said, glancing from her stricken, tear-streaked face to the motor home she'd just come racing from. His eyes narrowed. "What has Jack done now?"

Just the mention of Jack's name set the tears falling again.

Lloyd handed her his handkerchief. "You look like

someone who could use some good strong coffee and a shoulder to cry on. Come on. Roberta just put a pot on.''

Maybe it was the fact that he reminded her of her father, whom she missed so desperately, or maybe it was just his familiar face. Whichever, she let him park her car and lead her over to the bus he'd converted into a home away from home.

''Sit down and tell me what in blue blazes has you all worked up,'' he said as he went into the kitchen and poured them both a mug of coffee. ''Sugar? Cream? Brandy?''

She shook her head and worked to get the sobs under control again.

Lloyd's wife Roberta came out then, surprised to see Chelsea. Roberta was an angular, tall ranch woman with short-cropped gray hair and a weathered face. Like Chelsea and Lloyd, she'd grown up on a ranch around San Antonio. Chelsea recalled her dad saying what a sharp businesswoman Roberta was, and that Lloyd owed a lot of his success in the rodeo stock trade to her.

''Chelsea? What in the world…?'' the older woman asked.

Chelsea gave her a weak smile as she took the mug of hot coffee Lloyd handed her, cradling it in her palms, surprised at how much she needed the warmth. The couple sat across from her, both looking concerned.

''It's a long story,'' Chelsea said.

''I got all the time in the world for Ryder's little girl,'' Lloyd said.

That brought on another bout of tears, but eventually she gulped down some of the coffee and spilled out her story, starting with the summer she fell in love with Jack right up to his hurtful words tonight.

Lloyd shook his head. "I'm sure your dad regretted what he did, not giving the boy the benefit of the doubt."

"If only I could get Jack to believe that."

"I think it's a bit more complicated," Lloyd said. "The thing is, that rustling rumor is always going to hang over Jack's head. Your father believed him guilty. So did your brother. That kind of takes care of anything that could have ever happened between the two of you, wouldn't you say?"

Convincing Cody of Jack's innocence would take an act of Congress. Or... She stared at Lloyd as a thought struck her. "What if I could prove Jack was innocent?"

He let out a low whistle. "That's going to be darned hard to do after this many years, and I'm not sure even that will mend the fences between your brother and Jack. You know how bullheaded Cody can be." Lloyd smiled to soften his words. "Just like your daddy."

No kidding. But she'd gotten her share of stubbornness from her father as well.

"Now don't go encouraging her to do something stupid," Roberta said, helping herself to a cookie. "I swear, you're a romantic at heart, Lloyd T. Crandell."

He laughed. "Don't you know it."

Seeing the two older people still so obviously in love almost brought on the tears again. Instead, Chelsea thought about proving Jack's innocence to the world. Actually, just to Cody—and Jack.

"You wouldn't remember who was working on the Wishing Tree that summer, would you?" she asked, getting caught up in the idea.

Lloyd rubbed his stubbled jaw. "Ten years ago?" He turned to Roberta. "That was about the time you and I got into the stock business. I was still working as ranch manager down the road from the Wishing Tree and you were still camp cook…. Wait a minute. That was the summer you had that fire on the north forty,'' he said to Chelsea. ''I remember now. C. J. Crocker hired on as a hand for you dad. I'd forgotten about that.''

She tried to put a face to the name. ''C. J. Crocker.''

''Tall, gangly, with a face like a horse,'' Lloyd said, not unkindly. ''He's a rodeo clown these days—often on the same circuit as Jack. You know someone else who's on the circuit is Ace Winters. Didn't he work for your family?''

Chelsea nodded excitedly. ''I do remember him hiring on just before Jack, now that you mention it.'' She hadn't had eyes for anyone but Jack. If she remembered correctly, Ace had quit not long after Jack left—and not on the best of terms.

''Ace is a crackerjack bull rider,'' Lloyd was saying. ''Almost as good as Jack, although Ace would definitely argue the point.''

''Between Ace and C.J., one of them might remember who else was on the ranch that summer,'' she said, more to herself than Lloyd. Her father always hired about a half-dozen men for the season.

''Lloyd, don't go getting her hopes up,'' Roberta warned. ''Ten years is a long time and there's a good chance none of them knew anything about any rustling.''

''She has a point,'' Lloyd agreed. ''But from what you've told us, Ray Dale couldn't have been working alone. He'd have had to have help to get a bunch of cattle into Box Canyon.''

Her hopes soared. ''Someone has to know.''

''I hate to be the one to throw the cold water on this,'' Roberta said, ''but if you're right, one of the cowhands was a rustler. I doubt he's going to just confess. Nor would he take kindly to you asking a lot of questions.''

Lloyd smiled sheepishly at his wife. "She's right. I don't know what I was thinking. You start asking questions about cattle rustling and you could raise some hackles."

"Or get yourself hurt," Roberta said.

"Don't worry." She put down her mug and got to her feet. "I'm my father's daughter."

Lloyd laughed as he stood. "That you are. Ya know, Jack's been quizzing me for years about you. With my folks living just down the road from your ranch, he was always wanting to know how you were doing and what you'd been up to. He wasn't the least bit surprised when you graduated with honors in accounting."

Chelsea felt her heart lift like a rocket. So that was how Jack had known about her. She smiled and thanked them for the coffee—and the shoulders to cry on.

"Maybe our paths will cross again," Lloyd said.

Maybe.

As she left the Crandells' bus, she glanced in the direction of Jack's dark motor home, his words echoing in her ears. *You wouldn't last a week in my world.*

CHAPTER SIX

IT STILL HURT. The things Jack had said. But now she had a plan. Something she could do. And she felt considerably better.

"I need to know who worked on the ranch that summer," she said the moment Cody picked up the phone at the ranch.

"Hello, sis. I'm fine, thanks for asking." She could hear him grumbling under his breath. "So where are you?"

"Lubbock. I found Jack."

Cody made a disgusted sound.

"I also found Ace Winters and C. J. Crocker," she said.

"I didn't know they were missing."

Cute. She waited him out.

"So was the reunion as touching as you thought it would be?" he finally asked.

Why did Cody have to be like this? Because they were brother and sister, she reminded herself. Sibling rivalry and all that.

"It was much more than even I had anticipated," she said honestly. She could tell Cody was dying to ask her if Jack had confessed all.

"So when will you be home? Do you want me to come get you?"

She closed her eyes to fight her irritation. Cody was so

sure that Jack was guilty on all counts. That Jack had broken her heart. Again. Well, at least Cody was right about that. "Jack wasn't rustling our cattle."

"Didn't we already have this conversation?" her brother asked. "What did you *think* he'd say, Chels?" He let out an impatient sigh.

"I'm staying on for a few days," she told him. "Maybe a week."

Cody swore.

"Humor me on this."

"I've been doing that my whole life."

"Well," she tried to joke, "no reason to stop now. So who did Dad hire that summer other than Jack, C. J. Crocker, Ray Dale Farnsworth and Ace Winters?"

"I don't remember and I don't care. Cripes, Chels, it was ten years ago. What could it possibly matter now?" He swore again. "You aren't thinking what I think you're thinking?"

"Oh, shoot, I've got to go. If you come up with any names, call me on my cell phone." She hung up before the coming lecture, turned off her cell phone temporarily and found herself a motel not far from the rodeo grounds.

The problem with being alone in a strange motel room in a strange city was that it gave a person too much time to think. She turned on the TV but quickly turned it off again, too antsy to follow even a sitcom plot tonight.

Unfortunately, she couldn't forget one word Jack had said to her earlier. But damned if she was going to cry again. He didn't want her in his life. Okay. But she still had to find out who'd been rustling cattle that summer with Ray Dale Farnsworth.

Whether Jack cared or not, and she now suspected he just might, given what Lloyd had told her, she planned to clear his name. She couldn't go home until she could prove that Jack had nothing to do with the rustling. At least she would have the satisfaction of proving Cody wrong.

She didn't get to sleep until the wee hours of the morning, finally waking up late from a bad dream involving Jack and Terri Lyn and...a bull? She shook her head, feeling like a black cloud was tracking her.

In the light of day, her big plan from the night before seemed anything but feasible. Finding the men who'd worked the ranch that summer shouldn't be so hard, but how was she going to get the truth out of them?

She showered, ordered an early lunch and called Dylan. As much as she feared what else he might have found out about Jack, she preferred to hear it from Dylan rather than anyone else. Dylan was out of the office so she left a message that she would call him later. She kept her cell phone on just in case Cody might relent and call.

It dawned on Chelsea that she had access to the names of the cowhands her father had hired ten summers ago through payroll at the ranch. She found a computer store in the phonebook, called and reserved a computer.

For the next few hours, she linked up with her home computer and went through the files. The older files were harder to find since they'd been before her time, when her father had just started to computerize the ranch.

But she finally found the names and wrote them down. Ace Winters. Jack Shane a.k.a. Jackson Robinson. C. J. Crocker. Tucker McCray. Ray Dale Farnsworth. Lance Prescott.

She already knew where to find C.J., Ace and Jack. Ray Dale, of course, was dead, which only left Lance and Tucker.

DYLAN DROVE to the prison. What he planned to do was a gamble, but unlike mobster J. B. Crowe, his resources were limited. Even from prison, Crowe would be keeping tabs on Sebastian's activities.

Dylan was waiting in the long narrow room when J. B. Crowe was let in. Crowe wasn't a big man, just five foot ten, but everything about him was intimidating, even in prison garb. Crowe lifted a brow when he saw Dylan sitting behind the glass barrier.

For over a year Dylan had worked undercover to try to bring down the mobster. They weren't strangers. They were enemies. Dylan despised the man and would have liked to see Crowe go to prison for a lot more than the black market baby ring he'd been running at the time of his arrest.

Dylan picked up the phone on his side of the glass and waited for Crowe to do the same.

"You like prison, Crowe?" Dylan asked. "You sure don't dress as nice as you used to."

"Did you just come here to talk about fashion?" Crowe asked.

"No, I came here to gloat. One of your former associates has offered the feds enough evidence on you that you'll never see daylight again."

The mobster didn't even blink. "Even if that were true, why would you bother to come here to tell me?"

"Because I wanted to see your face when I told you that Sebastian Cooper is turning state's evidence and taking you and your organization down," Dylan said, playing his trump card and hoping the hell it worked.

"Sebastian Cooper?" Crowe said. "I don't know anyone by that name. I'm afraid your visit was for nothing."

Dylan shrugged. "My mistake. Sorry to have wasted your time, but then, time is about all you have, right,

Crowe?'' He signaled to the guard and left the mob leader in the bare room, still holding the phone.

Outside the prison, Dylan waited anxiously for the call from his snitch inside. All those years as a cop were finally paying off. The call came not ten minutes later.

''Crowe just contacted someone on the outside. He's sending out word to keep tabs on a guy named Sebastian Cooper.''

Dylan smiled grimly. He'd just set a pack of rabid dogs after his once best friend.

FROM THE NONDESCRIPT van he'd rented, Sebastian Cooper watched Dylan drive away from the prison and swore. He could think of only one reason Dylan would visit J. B. Crowe. He slammed his fist down on the steering wheel. His friend had just screwed him. As if things weren't bad enough.

''What now, boss?'' the bozo in the van's passenger seat asked.

Sebastian watched Dylan disappear in his rearview mirror, then studied his own reflection. His dark good looks had always gotten him what he wanted, the jet-black hair, the ebony eyes, the hard, lean jawline. His looks had gotten him Julie.

Julie. Damn her soul.

He reminded himself that it was his brains that had gotten him through Texas A and M with a business degree, hooked him up with a troubleshooting consulting firm and finally gotten him his own business, Cooper Consulting, Inc.

And it was his brains that he needed to use now.

He knew that he should never have gotten involved with the mob. He had J. B. Crowe to blame for that. J.B. was still running the mob from behind bars through his captain Luke Silva. While Silva was no match for Sebastian, Crowe still had an incredible amount of power. And everyone knew it was just a matter of time before he was out on good behavior and back on the streets, so to speak.

Sebastian didn't want that day to ever come. If he could get rid of Crowe permanently, he could take over the organization in this part of Texas and the Southwest. Killing Crowe was out of the question. That would just invite retaliation.

But if Crowe were to spend the rest of his life in prison... Well, that was another story.

Sebastian had been smart. He'd protected himself by collecting evidence against the mob and putting it on microfilm. If that evidence were to end up in the hands of the feds—anonymously, of course—Crowe would never see the light of day again. Sebastian had been extra careful to cover his own tracks so he wouldn't be implicated along with the mobster.

But he had made one mistake. Trusting his damned wife, Julie.

He had to find her and get the locket she wore around her neck, the locket with the microfilm inside. Julie didn't have a clue what she had in her possession. That she held his entire future in that locket. Julie's own future didn't look as bright.

When she'd first disappeared, he'd thought she might really be dead. But his old friend Dylan had found her— Sebastian was sure of that now. Julie had become a liability, an expendable one. Only when Sebastian tracked her down and she was out of the picture would he be safe.

WHILE SHE STILL had the computer, Chelsea did some checking and found that Ace Winters would be bull riding at the Lubbock rodeo tonight and C. J. Crocker was one of the clowns, just as Lloyd had thought. She printed out a copy of both schedules, and Jackson Robinson's while she was at it. When she compared them, she was surprised to see that both Ace and Jack were riding in the same rodeos. Wasn't that odd?

She compared C. J. Crocker's schedule and noted that he would be at most of the same rodeos as well. She called Lloyd.

"It's not that strange, really," he said when she told him. "Those are the top-paying rodeos and these are the top guys in their fields. Jack and Ace are trying to make enough to qualify for the Big Dance."

"The Big Dance?" she asked.

"Sorry. The National Finals Rodeo in Las Vegas in December. The top fifty cowboys who've earned the most money on the circuit get to ride for the big bucks and buckles in Vegas."

"Oh." She realized she didn't know diddly about professional rodeo. Or Jack's life, for that matter. But while on the computer she did find out that he'd won seven world championships at the National Finals.

"I hope you've given some more thought to what we talked about last night," Lloyd said. "Roberta's right. Might be best to just let sleeping dogs lie, you know?"

She knew. But damned if she could do it.

Back at the rodeo grounds, she asked where she could find Ace Winters, but was told he'd already ridden. No one seemed to know whether or not he'd left for the next rodeo yet. As for C. J. Crocker, one of the cowboys pointed to a small trailer at the edge of the camp.

She glanced around. She knew it was just a matter of time before she ran into Jack. Just as she knew he wasn't going to like seeing her again any more than he had last night.

As she made her way to C. J.'s trailer, she had that eerie feeling once again that someone was watching her.

She glanced around but didn't see anyone paying her undo attention. Everyone seemed to be busy getting ready for the upcoming rodeo. Or packing for the next.

She tapped lightly at C. J. Crocker's trailer door.

"Come in," he called.

She opened the door to find him sitting in front of a mirror, applying his makeup. His long, thin face was already covered in white and he was drawing an exaggerated bright-red mouth when she stepped in.

He didn't seem to recognize her. And now that she was here, she didn't know where to start. As was her character, she jumped in with both feet.

"I'm Chelsea Jensen and I need to ask you some questions."

He nodded and continued putting on his face. "Now isn't the best time for an interview, Ms. Jones."

"Jensen, and I'm not a reporter. I'm the daughter of Ryder Jensen. The Wishing Tree Ranch. Outside of San Antonio."

He stopped applying his makeup for a moment.

"You worked for the ranch about ten years ago," she said, waiting for some recognition in his happy-clown face.

"This isn't about some tax thing, is it?" he asked.

"No." She looked around the cramped trailer. "Would you mind if I sat down?" Her legs were shaking.

He glanced at his watch.

"It will only take a minute and you can keep getting ready. I don't mind."

He shrugged. He appeared to have filled out some, but was still tall and slim, and God help him, his face was definitely horsey, just as Lloyd had said. He finished the big red mouth and began to draw large black circles around each eye. It reminded Chelsea of her first attempts at makeup.

The only other seat was the couch against the wall behind him. She sat down, watching him in the mirror, and tried to think of some diplomatic way to launch into cattle rustling. She already had the man worried about taxes.

"That summer, there was a fire, you might recall."

He didn't act as if he'd heard her.

"And later in the season Ray Dale Farnsworth was killed. Bucked off his horse in Box Canyon."

C.J. filled in the black around his eyes and began to draw two tears under one eye, taking what she thought was undo care for a man who'd be spending a great deal of his night in a barrel.

"Let me be honest with you," she said. "Ray Dale was rustling our cattle. I'm trying to find out who he was working with. The statute of limitations on such a crime has long since run out," she rushed on. "I have no intention of taking any action. I just need to know who it was. I was hoping you might have some idea and could help me." She finally took a breath. "The six of you were all living in the same bunkhouse that summer so I thought…"

C.J. stopped working on one large tear to meet her gaze in the mirror. In stark contrast to his smiling clown face, his brownish-green eyes were as hard and cold as marbles. Chelsea actually felt a little afraid.

"I don't know anything about anything, especially Ray Dale and rustling," C.J. said, drawing out each word. "I hope I've made myself clear."

Perfectly. Chelsea got to her feet, then hesitated, not wanting to give up this easily. "Anything you tell me would be kept in the strictest confidence." His deep-freeze glare followed her as she moved to the door. "If you should change your mind…" She put her card on the small shelf by the door with both the ranch number and her cell phone on it, then ventured one last glance in the mirror at him.

His expression said he wouldn't be changing his mind anytime soon.

She reined in a shudder. After today, she'd never feel the same way about clowns. She bolted from the trailer.

"I thought you left?"

Damn. Chelsea recognized the voice at once. She turned slowly to find Terri Lyn Kessler, barrel racer and bad cook, scowling at her.

"I hate to miss a rodeo when I'm in town," Chelsea quipped. She was still shaking from her encounter with C. J. Crocker and not up to a battle.

Terri Lyn was all decked out in her rodeo cowgirl outfit, big hair, glittery gold western duds and almost as much makeup as C.J. the clown. She was holding the reins of a horse and looking very angry. Not that Chelsea could blame her. Under the same circumstances, she would have been a little miffed herself.

The announcer's voice echoed across the grounds, calling for all riders to check in. Relieved that the rodeo was about to start and Terri Lyn had better things to do than light into her, Chelsea made her retreat with a quick, "Break a leg."

She could feel Terri Lyn's gaze boring into her back like a knife as she made her way up to the stands and sat down at the end of one of the long rows of almost-full wooden bleachers. Her legs felt like rubber and her heart was pounding.

Settle down. It wasn't as though C.J. threatened you. Not exactly. Or Terri Lyn, for that matter.

But C.J. had scared her. And Terri Lyn had wanted to. She was safe now, though, sitting among the rodeo crowd. Her heart rate calmed. But Lloyd and Roberta were right. This could be more dangerous than she thought.

C. J. Crocker's response still bothered her. She just didn't know what to make of it.

Did he know something? He'd certainly acted as if he did. Was he covering for someone?

The rodeo started with a group of cowgirls riding in with the U.S. and Texas flags and a variety of business banners. Chelsea bought a program from a cowgirl dressed in red, white and blue and thumbed through it, disappointed to find that Ace Winters wasn't listed. But Jack was. He was riding a bull named Free Wheelin'.

When she looked up, she saw Jack over on the rail fence with some other cowboys. Just the sight of him kicked up her recovering pulse rate. Damn, she hated her body's reaction to him, especially knowing the way he felt about her. What a waste of lust. And love.

"I thought you left."

Is that all anyone could think to say to her? Chelsea looked up to see Jack's daughter standing over. Sam had on a western hat and shirt, jeans and boots. The hat was pulled low over her face, her braid tucked up inside. Nothing about her resembled a girl. But with that face and those long legs, Chelsea predicted Sam was going to be a real beauty one day.

"I decided to stay for the rodeo," she told Sam.

The girl eyed her suspiciously from beneath the brim of her hat. "Does Dad know you're here?"

Chelsea glanced toward the fence. Terri Lyn had horned in on the group of cowboys and hung on the rail next to Jack as if she belonged there. "Not that I know of." Chelsea slid over a little to give Sam room to sit down. "Want to join me?"

Sam looked anything but delighted at the prospect, but reluctantly, she sat down.

"I thought Ace Winters was riding today," Chelsea said.

"He probably rode slack and skipped the perf." She must have seen Chelsea's confused look. With obvious patience, Sam explained, "There are more bull riders than there is time during the rodeo, so some ride early so they can get to the next rodeo."

"What's the point of riding if there isn't anyone to see you ride?" she had to ask.

Sam rolled her eyes. "The idea is to get the best score, win the purse and get on to the next rodeo. That's how you make it to the National Finals."

Oh.

The afternoon kicked off with saddle bronc riding.

"That was a good ride," Chelsea said after the first cowboy finished, trying to make conversation with Jack's daughter.

"He dropped a leg and didn't spur," Sam said, looking at her. "Don't you know anything about rodeo?"

"My brother used to ride saddle broncs." Not that Chelsea had paid much attention, except when Cody was thrown. She enjoyed that part because then he wasn't quite so smug.

The ground crew set up for the next event: barrel racing. Chelsea watched Sam out of the corner of her eye during Terri Lyn's ride. The girl didn't like the barrel racer and Chelsea wondered if there was more to it than jealousy over Terri Lyn's interest in her father.

"She rides well," Chelsea commented.

Sam let out a snort. "Shows what you know. She should have cut in tighter on that second barrel."

On a hunch, Chelsea asked, "Do you ride?"

"Sure. Some of the cowboys let me ride their horses when Dad's there to watch. He's afraid I'll get hurt if I do anything more than trot around the arena." She stopped as if she'd said too much. "Do you ride?" Her tone indicated she highly doubted it.

"I'll have you know I've been riding alone since I was three."

"Three?" Sam cried. "Your dad let you ride at *three?*"

"That's when he bought me my first horse, but I'd been riding from the time I could sit," Chelsea said in her defense.

Sam looked dutifully impressed. She stewed on that thought for a while. "You ever barrel race?"

"No," Chelsea had to admit.

"Barrel racing is for *girls*," Sam said.

"What's wrong with being a girl?" Chelsea had to ask.

"Nothing. As long as you aren't a *sissy* girl."

"Oh. I guess I didn't understand the distinction."

Chelsea offered to buy them something to eat if Sam would get it. The girl returned a few minutes later with two Cokes, popcorn and a hot dog.

Sam handed Chelsea a Coke and the popcorn. "Has the bull riding started yet?" she asked as she devoured the hot dog, which was smothered in ketchup, mustard and pickle relish.

"Just about." Chelsea had spotted Jack over by the chutes.

"Dad got a bad bull," Sam said, sounding glum.

"A bad bull?" Chelsea knew enough about rodeos to realize that bull riding was the most dangerous event, and she doubted having a "bad bull" was a good thing.

She felt her heart rate jump up a notch as she watched Jack climb to the top of the chute. Did this bull have a reputation for hurting riders? Or had it never been ridden yet?

She still couldn't see the bull in the chute but she could hear him in there banging around. There seemed to be some problem. Her anxiety level rose as she watched Jack hover over the chute—and the bull.

"Our first rider is Jackson Robinson, all-around top bull rider for eight years before his accident."

Accident? Chelsea shot a look at Sam.

"This Texan from Amarillo took a nasty spill last year and got himself gored and out of the running," the announcer was saying. "But this year he's back and on his way to reclaiming his title."

"Your dad got hurt last year?" she asked, her voice a little too high.

"Almost died. Devil Twist put him into the fence, then stomped and gored him." Sam made it sound like a badge of honor. "But Dad says he's too tough for a bull to keep him down."

Yeah, right. Chelsea stared at Jack, wondering what in the hell he was doing riding bulls.

"We seem to have a little problem with this bull," the announcer said as the animal banged around in the chute. "Free Wheelin' is just not willing to cooperate it seems."

A clown—not C.J.—was doing silly things in the middle of the arena with a golf club and a giant ball. Nervously, Chelsea glanced over at Samantha. The girl didn't seem worried, just unhappy, and wasn't even looking in the direction of her father or the clown.

Chelsea followed Sam's gaze and saw what had drawn the girl's attention. Terri Lyn Kessler had moved to a section of fence away from the bull chutes to watch. She hung on the fence, her gaze intent on Jack.

Chelsea smiled to herself. Terri Lyn was going to have a terrible time getting close to Jack if Sam had her way.

"Dad should have just turned out on this one," Sam said, her attention returning to the cowboys trying to get the bull to calm down enough so Jack could ride him.

"Turned out?" Chelsea asked.

"Not showed up."

"Can he do that?"

"Sure. He can do whatever he wants. It's his career."

It was obvious Sam was repeating something she'd heard Jack say. His career. Chelsea turned again to watch Jack lower himself to the bull's back. Jack considered this a *career*?

She was just beginning to realize how little she knew about pro rodeo. She certainly couldn't understand why Jack had chosen to ride bulls. Maybe she hadn't known him as well as she'd thought.

She could see the bull slamming around in the chute, snorting and kicking at the wooden slats as Jack moved to straddle the bull. As she watched, he slid a gloved hand into what looked like a leather noose tied to the bull's girth.

Her heart nearly stopped. "He's not tying himself on, is he?" she cried as she watched him work one gloved hand into whatever was tied around the bull, while another cowboy on the fence leaned over the chute to pull the rope tight.

"He has one hand tied by a rope to the midsection of the bull," Sam said, not bothering to look at her. "The rope is held tight by Dad's grip."

Jack raised his other gloved hand and gave a nod. The gate swung open and he and the bad bull burst out.

"He has to keep his other hand up at head level or he can be disqualified," Sam said. "And he gets more points for spurring the bull."

The bull began to spin in a tight circle.

"Not good," Sam said, raising Chelsea's anxiety level. "He's too far inside the spin. He's heading for the well."

The bull was still whirling, Jack still spurring him on. "What happens if he falls into the well?" she asked on a breath.

"The bull keeps spinning. The rider can be crushed by

its hooves. That's what happened to Brent Thurman on Red Wolf. Crushed his skull.''

Chelsea winced, then jumped at the sound of a horn. The ride was over, but Jack seemed unable to get off the bull. She found herself with her hands over her mouth, watching in horror as the bull continued to buck.

Two riders on horseback positioned themselves along each side of the bull. One of them reached over to jerk on the rope that still had Jack tied to Free Wheelin'. At what seemed like the very last moment, Jack jerked free, grabbed hold of one of the riders and swung from the bull to the ground.

"That wasn't much of a ride," Sam said, rising to her feet. "He'll be mad."

Not much of a ride? Chelsea staggered to her feet, her heart still pounding.

"Seventy. That's seven-oh for Jackson Robinson on Free Wheelin'," the announcer said over the loudspeaker. "Disappointing ride for this cowboy, but let's give him a big hand."

"He isn't going to like that," Sam said as she led the way from the grandstands. "He's had a streak of bad luck. He even wore his lucky shirt today but it can't help when you draw a bad bull."

Chelsea was still trying to take it all in. "What happens now?"

Sam stopped abruptly, turned and squinted up at her. "We drive to the next rodeo."

"Oh. Where is the next rodeo?"

"Dallas. Dad rides again tomorrow."

Dallas was at least a day's drive. "He plans to drive there before he rides?"

Sam was giving her that disbelieving look again. "We'll drive all night tonight."

"Isn't there a closer rodeo?" Chelsea asked.

"Not with the purses Dad needs to make National Finals." Sam studied her for a moment, then turned and headed for the chutes.

Chelsea stood watching her go, not sure what to do next. Already, she was proving Jack right. She knew nothing about his world. Worse, she didn't understand why Jack was doing this. Riding wild bulls. Risking life and limb when he had a young daughter who needed him. What was wrong with this man? What was wrong with her for thinking they had anything in common anymore?

Out of the corner of her eye, she caught sight of him. He came out of the chute area, dusty, obviously disappointed but not defeated. No, not Jack. She watched him walk toward Sam, his head down, and felt a yank at her heart so strong it made her hurt inside.

His head came up as he saw his daughter, a smile lifting his lips. He pulled Sam to him, and the two talked for a moment before he swung her up and onto his shoulders, Sam giggling like the nine-year-old she really was.

Chelsea tried to swallow the lump in her throat. Their closeness reminded her of her relationship with her own father.

As she turned, she came face-to-face with Ace Winters. "I heard you've been looking for me."

CHAPTER SEVEN

"I THOUGHT YOU LEFT," she said, trying to mask her surprise.

"Obviously not." Ace Winters had blond boyish good looks that obviously got him what he wanted. He flashed a smile at Chelsea as if women came looking for him every day of the week.

But Chelsea didn't like him any more than she had ten years ago. She wasn't sure what it was about Ace that put her off. It wasn't just his arrogance. Lord knew, Jack had more than his share. But there was something slimy about Ace, and she didn't trust him.

Unfortunately, she needed something from him.

"I wanted to ask you a few questions," she said.

"Sure, but you'll have to ask while we walk. My plane is waiting and I've already filed my flight plan and can't change it." He must have seen her surprise. "I bought my own plane and try to fly to all the rodeos. Saves a lot of wear and tear on my body." He gave her a broad smile. "I can get to where I'm going and relax a little before my next ride. Sure beats driving like in the old days...."

She nodded and trotted along beside him, trying hard to figure out a way to broach the subject with more finesse than she had with Crocker.

"I wanted to talk to you about the summer you worked on the Wishing Tree."

"Great," he said, looking around. "Terri Lyn was supposed to give me a ride to the airport. Damn that girl. I don't see her anywhere around.''

She was probably with Jack. ''I can give you a ride,'' Chelsea suggested.

''You don't mind?'' he asked, sounding not in the least surprised.

''Not at all. My car's right over here.'' She motioned to the baby-blue Mercedes.

''Oh, sweet,'' Ace said as he climbed in the passenger side. ''This is one fine car.'' He ran his hands over the leather interior and eyed her as if she was suddenly more interesting.

''Anyway, you remember that summer you worked for my family on the ranch?''

''Your family? You're going to have to refresh my memory,'' he said as he gave her the directions to the airport, then lay back to enjoy the ride.

''The Jensens. The Wishing Tree Ranch.''

''How many years ago was that, anyway?''

''Ten.''

He let out a low whistle. ''Well, you certainly have grown up,'' he said, shooting her an assessing glance out of the corner of his eye. ''Sorry to hear about your dad. That must be tough.''

''Yes. About that summer…''

''How's your brother Cody? He still riding any?''

''He's fine. He gave up rodeoing after college.''

''Too bad,'' Ace said. ''Rodeoing is like a religion to me.''

Chelsea had to restrain from rolling her eyes. ''That summer was the one we had that fire in the north forty, you probably remember,'' she said, trying to refresh his memory.

He frowned. ''Can't say I do. You're sure that's the year I worked your ranch?''

"Positive. Jack was there and C. J. Crocker."

"Sorry," he said as he told her to turn onto a small airstrip not far from the rodeo grounds. "You say Jack worked there? Jackson Robinson?"

"He used to go by Shane. Jack Shane." Was Ace putting her on or did he really not remember?

He had her park next to his Cessna 185 and checked his watch as he opened his door to get out.

"It was the summer Ray Dale Farnsworth was killed," she blurted, afraid he'd have the same reaction C.J. had.

"Ray Dale. I do remember," Ace said suddenly. "He was a stocky kid, looked more like a prizefighter than a cowboy. Always picking fights and drinking too much."

Finally. "Well, what I—"

"Hell, I remember this one night when Ray Dale and Jack got into it," Ace said, cutting her off. "I do remember Jack working for your family that summer, now that I think about it. Oh, hell, yes."

"Jack and Ray Dale got into a fight?" she asked, scrambling after him as he exited the car and headed for his plane.

"Chelsea, honey, I'm sorry, but I got to get going. I'd love to reminisce about the old days but I've got to get to Dallas and— Wait a minute, what are your plans? Why don't you come with me and we can talk? I can have someone bring your car."

She blinked at him. He wasn't serious? "You mean fly to Dallas now?"

"Sure, you're not afraid to fly, are you?"

"No, but—"

"Come on, then. It will be fun to have some company. We can talk all you want. Grab your bag and let's go." He climbed up onto the wing and slid into the plane, motioning for her to get moving.

She stood staring at him for a moment. Damn him. He

could take a few minutes and answer her questions, unless he was just putting her off. Thinking she wouldn't do it.

Flying to Dallas with Ace Winters was the last thing she wanted to do, but she would have a few hours to get answers and Ace wouldn't have any way to get away from her.

But then, she wouldn't have any way to get away from him. It was a price she'd have to pay.

AFTER ALL THE YEARS Jack had spent looking for Chelsea's face in the rodeo crowds, today was the one day he hadn't expected to see it.

He thought Chelsea would be back in San Antonio by now. The last place she'd be was here—and with Ace Winters. The two of them walking toward Chelsea's car.

"She didn't leave," Sam said as Jack froze in midstep.

"I can see that. Did she say what she was doing back here?" he asked Sam.

"Said she just wanted to see the rodeo, but she doesn't know *anything* about it."

He swore under his breath as he watched Chelsea and Ace drive away. What was she still doing here? Let alone taking off with Ace. She wasn't just here for the rodeo. He'd bet money on that.

"Dad," Sam asked. "Can I go see Becky Harper until we have to leave?"

Jack swung his daughter down from his shoulders and stood her in front of him. "Aren't you grounded?"

"No, you never got around to grounding me," she admitted. "But you don't need to. I learned my lesson," she rushed on, her face a mask of innocence, her voice sugary sweet. "I'm not going to interfere in your personal life ever again."

Yeah, right. Until the next time.

He knew he should stick to his guns and punish her,

but he also knew he was too hard on Sam sometimes, expecting too much of her. Life on the circuit was difficult for all of them, especially her. He should cut her more slack.

He also wanted to be alone for a while so he could fuss and cuss. "All right. But we pull out in forty-five minutes. Set your watch and be back by then."

"I promise," Sam said, all smiles. She gave him a kiss on his cheek and a quick hug.

He held her tight for a moment, marveling at this child of his and wondering what he'd have done without her. Then he watched as she took off at a dead run toward the Harpers' trailer.

Hard to imagine that when he'd found her on his doorstep, he'd thought having a baby was the worst thing that could happen to him. At the time, it had seemed that way.

But the moment he'd looked at her face, he felt as if he'd been sucker punched. He was hooked, and somehow he and Sam had gotten this far.

Now Chelsea had turned up to remind him of the past, the mistakes he'd made and everything he could never have.

He turned and stalked over to the motor home, telling himself he had to get moving. He still had to drive to Dallas tonight. But he knew nothing was going to help his bad mood.

He'd felt like hell all day. After a sleepless, troubled night, he'd woken up tired, grouchy and definitely down. He'd spent his day doing chores and helping Sam with her homework, leaving enough time to go to the zoo before he had to ride. Sam loved zoos and he tried to take her whenever the opportunity arose.

Terri Lyn had come by this morning to apologize for last night and try to make up. He liked her and didn't want there to be any animosity between them, but he wanted to cool it for a while. And it didn't take a rocket scientist to figure out why. Chelsea. She'd always spoiled him for other women.

"It's that…woman," Terri Lyn had said.

"No, it's me. I'm not ready for a relationship."

"A *relationship?*" Terri Lyn had laughed. "Darlin', I'm just looking to have a little fun. You do remember fun, don't you, Jack?"

Sam had interrupted them, thank goodness, and Terri Lyn had left with a wink and a grin.

Just when he'd thought the day couldn't get any worse, he'd drawn a bull that he knew wouldn't give him the score he needed—and it hadn't. Then, to add to his misery, he'd seen Chelsea—with Ace.

He knew what was bothering him. He regretted what he'd said to Chelsea and mentally kicked himself for saying it. At the time, he'd thought he was doing them both a favor.

They were just too different. She was too rich, and he was too poor and too proud. But it was deeper than that. She could never accept life on his terms. And there was no part in her life for him. Her future was at the Wishing Tree Ranch, a place he would never be welcomed again. And he sure as hell couldn't see her settling for less.

They had no future together. Never had.

Last night he thought she'd hightail it back to San Antonio and the ranch.

Instead, she hadn't left, and now was on her way somewhere with Ace. Of all people. Jack swore as he disconnected the sewer hose and went to work on the jacks and blocks under the motor home. Wasn't it bad enough that Ace had gotten a better score than he had riding slack today?

The two of them had been neck and neck heading to

the finals. And now… Well, all Jack could do was hope for a good ride in Dallas. Once he got there.

Chelsea and Ace. Damn.

At this rate, he would never make the National Finals, and now he had to drive all night to Dallas for his next rodeo.

As he finished loading up for the trip, he told himself if Chelsea wanted to hang out with Ace, it was her choice and none of his business.

But he couldn't help worrying about her. Chelsea was no match for a man like Ace Winters.

THE FLIGHT with Ace was blessedly short and definitely not sweet.

"Rustling?" he had asked. "I don't know why you think I'd know anything about it. As if Ray Dale had been smart enough to pull off rustling cattle. No, I think you've got your facts wrong. You should ask your…friend Jack why he was so mad at Ray Dale that time."

"You think they were fighting about rustling?"

Ace shrugged. "All I know is that Jack was furious. I thought he was going to kill Ray Dale. But the next day, I heard Jack apologize and they seemed fine again. In fact, they were thick as thieves after that. And Jack is smart enough to be a damned good rustler."

Nothing like a backhanded compliment. But she couldn't discount the bunkhouse fight. If there really had been a fight, it might mean that Jack had known about the rustling, or at least suspected something. Then why hadn't he come to her?

She tried a different approach. "When I talked to C. J. Crocker—"

"You talked to Crocker?" Ace appeared surprised by that. "What did he say?"

"Not much." How about nothing at all? "But he made it sound as if Jack wasn't involved." A small fib.

Ace shot her a look. "You can't believe anything Crocker tells you. He's a clown, for hell's sake." Ace laughed and changed the subject, but he seemed edgy after that.

For the remainder of the flight, Chelsea only half listened to Ace's stories of his daring bull rides and his climb to success.

Lloyd and Roberta were right. Finding out who'd been rustling that summer seemed an impossible task. But she still had a couple more cowboys to talk to if Dylan could find them. *Someone* knew the truth.

The moment they landed, Chelsea called for a rental car, then dialed Dylan's number. He answered on the second ring.

"It's Chelsea," she said, watching Ace unload his gear from the plane into another cowboy's pickup.

"Where are you?" Dylan asked, sounding worried.

"In Dallas. In a phone booth beside a small airstrip."

"So you're headed home?"

She watched Ace and his buddy drive away. Ace was leaning back, his hat pulled low, but his gaze held hers until the pickup disappeared around the corner of the building. She shivered, although it must have been 110 degrees in the booth. "Not exactly. Did you find either Tucker or Lance?"

"Tucker McCray owns a small ranch outside of Oklahoma City," Dylan said, sounding hesitant about telling her.

Oklahoma City? Wasn't it on the rodeo schedule she'd printed up? She pulled it out of her purse. Ace and Jack would be riding there in a few days. And C. J. Crocker was one of the bull riding clowns.

"Chelsea?"

"Sorry, what did you say?"

"Lance Prescott is not far from where you are now. You sure you want to continue this?"

It did feel like a fool's errand. Especially after all the things Jack had said to her last night. But she feared some of them were true and she wasn't about to let this go now. "Where can I find Lance?"

"He works at a carnival called Extravaganza, and it's in Fort Worth right now," Dylan said. "He operates one of the rides. Chelsea, listen. Be careful. This guy has done time for assault."

"Thanks for warning me."

"I put together some information on all of your cow-hands that summer, some of which might convince you to drop this," Dylan said. "Is there someplace I could fax it to you?"

She knew of a hotel in town where she'd stayed during a business conference and gave him the name and number from the phone book hanging in the booth.

She hated to ask. "Anything more on Jack?"

"Not yet. I'm still digging."

Relieved, she hung up. Dylan wasn't going to find anything suspicious about Jack. She knew it.

She looked at her watch as her rental car arrived. Too late to go to the carnival. All she could do was drive to the hotel, get something to eat and see what Dylan had faxed her.

It was at least a seven-hour drive from Lubbock to Dallas. That meant she wouldn't get her Mercedes until morning. Jack wouldn't be getting in until after midnight.

As antsy as she was, she would have to wait until morning to ask him about the fight with Ray Dale. Maybe she'd try to talk to C. J. Crocker again. One thing was clear, she'd be traveling with the rodeo at least as far as Oklahoma City. Wasn't Jack going to love that. The thought gave her the only satisfaction she'd had all day.

CHAPTER EIGHT

JACK WAS SITTING beside the motor home in his lawn chair, drinking a cup of coffee in the warm sun and hoping his luck was going to change.

But when Chelsea drove up in her fancy sports car, got out and headed toward him with a look in her eye he definitely didn't like, he knew neither his luck nor his mood was about to improve soon.

"I want to take you up on your offer," she said, haughty as you please. It appeared at least one of them had gotten her beauty sleep last night.

His offer? He rubbed one aching temple as he tried to remember anything she might have taken as an "offer."

"One week in your world."

He stared at her. She had to be kidding. "That wasn't an offer, Chelsea. That—"

"—was a challenge," she corrected. "A challenge to a woman who's never been challenged, who's soft and spoiled and pampered beyond hope."

He winced. Damn but he regretted those words. "Look, about what I said, I'm sorry."

She put her hands on her hips and cocked her head at him.

"I was completely out of line," he went on, hoping that would be the end of it.

"So you admit you were wrong about me lasting a week on the rodeo circuit?" she asked.

He narrowed his gaze, alerted by the edge to her voice, and no doubt hesitated just a little too long.

"That's what I thought," she said, giving him a smile that chilled him to the bone. "Let's make it a wager."

"Now wait a minute—"

"Not money, since I have too much," she said sarcastically. "I know! If I make a week on the circuit, then you have to admit you were wrong about me—and us." She raised a hand to silence him. "If I don't make the entire week, then I'll admit everything you said about me was dead on and you'll never see me again. Okay?"

"Hell, no."

She raised a brow as if surprised he wouldn't go along with a deal like that. "You slandered me and now you owe me the right to prove you wrong," she said, that damned determination of hers burning in her eyes. "Unless you intend to go back on your word."

He'd die first and he figured she knew it. But why would she want to spend a week on the circuit? Certainly not just to prove him wrong. Could Lloyd be right?

"Lloyd told me that you're trying to find out who was rustling with Ray Dale ten years ago," he said. "Have you lost your mind?"

She didn't look happy about Lloyd telling him. "I intend to clear your name whether you like it or not. I do what I say I'm going to." Unlike him, her tone implied.

"You and I know I didn't rustle your cattle. Isn't that good enough?"

"No, it's not," she said. "Don't tell me you aren't still angry about being unjustly accused."

"Well, I'm not."

"Too bad. I'm angry for you."

He pushed back his hat and looked at her. Man, had he forgotten what a hellcat she could be once she set her mind to something. "This is all about convincing your brother, isn't it?"

"No," she answered. "It's about you and me. We never got the chance we deserved. Maybe it's not too late."

He definitely didn't want to go there. "It wouldn't work."

She shrugged. "You were right about a lot of things you said about me the other night."

"I'm sorry I said any of those things."

"No," she said. "I've never really had to go after what I wanted, never had to prove myself or get down in the dirt and fight. Maybe it's high time."

He pulled off his hat and raked his fingers through his hair. "You pick the damnedest times to put up a fight. Did it ever cross your mind that this...quest of yours might be dangerous?"

Her gaze was hot enough to burn him. "Very dangerous."

He could see she wasn't referring to finding the rustler. "I think you're headed for one big disappointment—or worse."

Out of the corner of his eye, he saw Ace Winters headed in their direction. Jack swore under his breath. As if he didn't have enough trouble.

"Do we have a deal or not?" Chelsea asked. "Because one way or the other, I'm going to follow the circuit this week."

"A week on the circuit isn't going to prove anything," he said, trying to keep his voice down so Ace didn't hear.

"It will prove that you were wrong. At least about one thing." She smiled. "Maybe more."

He definitely didn't like the gleam in her eyes.

"And who knows, I could get lucky and find my rustler," she said.

"Mornin'," Ace greeted them. "I see you got your car delivered all right," he said to Chelsea. "Anytime you want to fly with me..." Ace gave her a suggestive grin. "Will you be staying at the hotel again tonight? I thought maybe we could have dinner."

"Excuse me," Jack said pointedly to Ace. "We were in the middle of a conversation here."

Ace pretended to be offended. "Little testy this morning, aren't you? Worried about that bull you've drawn?" He grinned. "You should be. See you at the rodeo." He tipped his hat to Chelsea. "Let me know about dinner, darlin'," he said, and sauntered off chuckling.

Jack swore under his breath again and turned his scowl on Chelsea. "If you think following the circuit means flying around with Ace Winters and staying in fancy hotels and eating at pricey restaurants, well, you're sadly mistaken. It's living in a tiny motor home, driving all night between rodeos, eating hot dogs at gas stations while the fuel tank is filling—"

"I accept."

"What?" He stared at her, realizing belatedly that he'd just backed himself into a corner. There was only one way out. To admit he was wrong about everything. Better to admit that than even contemplate a week with her around.

"Never mind. I was wrong about everything."

"I know, but someday you're going to admit it—and mean it," she said with a laugh. "I'm still spending the week on the circuit, Jack. And I'm still going to find out who was working with Ray Dale. And I'm still going to make up my mind whether there ever was anything between you and me—or still is. I guess I'll be flying, and

staying at fancy hotels and eating pricey food, though."
She turned as if going after Ace.

Jack couldn't imagine anything worse than having
Chelsea traveling with him for a week in the motor
home—except her traveling with Ace Winters and looking
for a rustler on her own. Damn. What choice did he have?

"You'd have to leave your car and your money and
rough it with Sam and me in the motor home for the entire
week," he said, stopping her in her tracks.

She turned slowly and smiled. "No problem."

He doubted that. "Understand, the only reason I'm doing this is because I'm worried about you getting yourself
into trouble and I feel responsible since it involves me."

"Of course," she said with a big smile. "What other
reason could there be?"

He already wished he'd kept his mouth shut. Again.
But she was trying to clear *his* name. And someone
needed to protect her from herself. Besides, it was only
for a week, probably less once Chelsea realized what rodeo life was like.

"When do you plan to tell Sam?" she asked, eyeing
him as if he might try to use his daughter to get out of
this.

"Tell me what?"

He turned at the sound of Sam's voice and grimaced.
She wasn't going to like this. He didn't like it, either; but
if he'd done things differently ten years ago, none of this
would be happening now.

"Hi, sweetheart," he said, reaching out to pull her to
him. He gave her a smile, his hand on her shoulder.

His daughter looked suspicious. "Tell me what?"

Jack braced himself. "Chelsea thinks she'd like to learn
more about the rodeo life. We have kind of a bet going
that she won't last a week on the circuit."

Sam said nothing, just stood eyeing him, then Chelsea, waiting for the rest.

"Chelsea's going to travel with us in the motor home for a while," Jack said, and waited for Sam to erupt.

"All three of us?" Sam asked in surprise.

He nodded.

"How long is a while?"

"A week."

"Where would she sleep?" she asked, eyes narrowed.

"Well," he said, a little flustered. "We'll be driving all night between rodeos. But she can make up the dinette during the day and nap there."

"What would she do?"

"Well..." He hadn't given it any thought since he'd only just come up with this outrageous plan. "I guess she'd help drive, cook, clean the motor home and—" he tried to think of as many vile things as he could that Chelsea would hate doing "—and she'd do the laundry and shop for groceries."

Sam swung her gaze to Chelsea. "You want to do all that stuff?" she asked, sounding disbelieving.

Chelsea nodded, a steely determination in the set of her jaw. The woman didn't have a clue what she'd gotten herself into.

Sam studied her for a long moment. "Okay."

Jack stared at his daughter, waiting for her to say more. When she didn't, he said, "That's it?"

Sam shrugged. "You're going to do it anyway, right? So, it's okay with me."

Chelsea looked more than relieved. Jack stared at Sam, wondering when the aliens would return his real daughter.

"Can I go play with Becky until lunch?" she asked, as if the whole subject bored her.

"Sure, I guess.... Be back by noon. On the dot."

With a nod, Sam left. He watched her meet up with Becky at the side of the Harpers' trailer, watched them put their heads together in hurried conversation, then look back toward him and Chelsea and the motor home. In no time, this would be all over the camp. What had he been thinking?

He glanced at Chelsea. She seemed a little pale to him, as if maybe she was just starting to realize what she'd gotten herself into. She didn't know the half of it.

"You're sure about this? It's not too late to change your mind and go home."

"Absolutely," she said, lifting her perfect little chin into the air.

He swore under his breath. "Fine. You heard the deal. You cook, clean, do laundry and help drive. I give the orders. You screw up and you're out of here." With luck, she'd be too busy to look for rustlers.

Her gaze held his. "I guess we have a deal." She held out her hand, her look daring him to seal the bargain.

He enveloped her hand in his own rough and callused one, his grip strong, unlike the grip he had on his sanity at just the thought of a week with this woman. He pretended not to notice the chemistry that flared between them. He could take this if she could.

She smiled as he released her hand, then turned on her heels and headed for her car.

Cursing himself, he watched her go. Why was she doing this? The woman had nothing to prove. Why put them both through this? To show him she wasn't that spoiled little rich girl they both knew her to be? To find a rustler? Surely she was too smart to think she could convince him they still had a chance.

CHAPTER NINE

A WEEK IN Jack's world. Chelsea looked at the tiny motor home, still in shock. While she'd planned to follow the rodeo at least as far as Oklahoma city so she could talk to Tucker McCray, she'd never dreamed Jack would actually suggest she travel with him and Sam.

"Get just what you need to bring," Jack told her. "We don't have much space so travel light." His tone said he didn't believe she could travel light any more than she could make a week on the circuit.

Oh, how she wanted to prove him wrong. And on so many counts.

But the reality of it petrified her. How could she stand being that close to Jack for an entire week? She would be putting everything on the line. Especially her feelings.

She could humiliate herself in so many ways. She might discover she wasn't the woman she thought she was. Worse, she might find that Jack wasn't the man she believed him to be. That he was a rustler with a knack for lying. That he didn't still love her. Had never loved her. If she wasn't careful, she could get her heart broken all over again and it wasn't in great shape to begin with.

As she fished out her cell phone and called about having her car put in storage, she saw Terri Lyn sashay by. Oh yes, and there was Terri Lyn, the cute and capable barrel racer who not only lived in Jack's world but excelled there. And who had designs on Jack.

Chelsea took a deep breath. *You asked for this.*

But not in a million years had she thought Jack would take her up on the deal. She glanced back toward the motor home and Jack. He stood watching her, his expression saying he expected her to jump in her car and hightail it back to the Wishing Tree. Fat chance.

She pulled her overnight bag from the trunk and started toward the motor home. Suddenly, it seemed as if everyone in the small encampment stopped what they were doing to stare, as if everyone knew she didn't belong here.

"Here, I'll take that," Jack said, pulling the bag from her shoulder, seeming almost embarrassed by the attention they were getting.

"What will you tell them?" she asked.

"Nothing. It's none of their business."

As she trailed after him, she felt like an outsider, wondering if she could ever fit in with these people. It was the first time she'd ever worried about fitting in. It made her feel strangely vulnerable and more than a little afraid. She had to admit that so far, she'd led a protected life.

As she reached the motor home behind Jack, she turned, aware of being watched with more than just curiosity. Terri Lyn stood next to her pickup camper, her expression venomous. Yes, if Chelsea wanted Jack, it appeared she'd have to fight for him. But she'd already won the first round, right?

She dragged her gaze away from Terri Lyn to Jack's broad shoulders retreating into his home. For a moment, she almost called him back with her bag.

But stubbornness propelled her forward. She followed Jack inside, closing the door firmly behind the onlookers. She'd tough out this week if it killed her.

"I hope you can fit all of your things in here," Jack said as he swung open the closet door.

She stepped down the hall into the dim cool darkness, brushing against him as she tried to look past him to the closet.

He swore under his breath. From frustration? Or the jolt of electricity that arced between them? She wished she knew. Frowning, he motioned her into the bathroom so he could get past her. "You get the top drawer."

She stepped into the small cubicle while he cleaned out the closet drawer. When he'd finished, she moved back into the narrow hallway, brushing against him again.

This time he froze, and glared at her. "You're going to be the death of me." Without another word, he turned and left, slamming the motor home door behind him.

Chelsea smiled. At least now she knew he was on the receiving end of that chemistry as well as the giving end.

JACK AVOIDED all the speculative glances that followed him as he stalked down the row of campers. Pulling his hat down low, he moved quickly, discouraging conversation.

He could see Terri Lyn's camper ahead. Might as well get this over with, he told himself. But as he neared the rig, he saw that Terri Lyn wasn't anywhere around. He stopped, jerked his hat from his head and wiped the arm of his shirtsleeve across his forehead, stringing together a few cuss words under his breath.

How had he gotten himself into this? He knew only too well. Him and his big mouth.

"Taking in boarders, are you?"

He turned to see his friend Rowdy Harper sitting in the shade of his awning. In the trees behind the trailer, Jack could hear Sam and Becky playing.

"You look like a man who could use a drink," Rowdy said, holding up his coffee cup.

Jack shook his head but walked over to sit down in the shade.

"Wanna tell me about it?" Rowdy asked.

Jack grunted. He didn't want his friend knowing what a damned fool he'd been.

"Or I can wait for the story circulating through the camp, the one Ace is telling," Rowdy said with a smile.

With a curse, Jack started at the beginning, the day he drove up the long, tree-lined road to the Wishing Tree Ranch and saw Chelsea for the first time. He ended with the deal he'd just made with her. It was the first time he'd ever told anyone the whole story.

Rowdy listened without saying a word, just nodding occasionally. "Wow," he said when Jack finished. "That's quite the story. And now she's going to be traveling with you for a week?"

"It's going to be hell."

"Or something like that," Rowdy said with a laugh.

"What she doesn't get is that finding this rustler won't change things between her and me. There is no chance for us."

"None at all," Rowdy agreed. "Even if you loved this woman."

Jack caught the mocking tone and got to his feet. "Love has nothing to do with it."

"Of course not." Rowdy laughed. "I swear, Jack, sometimes you're a bigger fool than even me."

"I don't know why I bother talking to you," Jack snapped. "You're no help at all."

Rowdy was still chuckling when Jack saw Terri Lyn return to her camper. Without a word of explanation, he headed in her direction.

"Good luck," Rowdy called after him, laughter in his voice.

Nice that he could amuse his friend, Jack thought.

Terri Lyn didn't take the news of his traveling companion well. She slammed into her camper, leaving him standing in the dust. But he figured he owed her at least the truth, even if their relationship hadn't progressed past a few kisses and çasseroles.

The last thing he wanted to do was go back to the motor home, but it was too early to head to the arena. As he passed the Harpers' trailer, he noted that Rowdy had gone inside, but his wife Abigail was rounding up Sam and Becky.

"Jack!" Abigail called to him.

Abigail supported Rowdy's career as a rodeo announcer by home-schooling her eight-year-old daughter Becky while they were on the road during the rodeo season. She also helped Jack with Sam's schoolwork when their schedules coincided. Jack had always admired her commitment because life on the road was hard on families. They'd made their marriage last and Rowdy had never seemed happier.

"I wanted to ask you and Chelsea for lunch," Abigail said, surprising him.

He glanced at Sam. Lunch was obviously not her doing but it was clear she or Rowdy had told Abigail about Chelsea. He wondered how much more she knew? "That's really nice of you, but—"

"If she's going to be traveling with you this week, I'd like to meet her," Abigail said.

He knew that wasn't why she was inviting the two of them for lunch. She wanted to help Chelsea's induction into their rodeo family. If Abigail Harper accepted Chelsea, the rest would, too. Eventually.

"Thank you," he said, touched by her thoughtfulness.

"Good. Say twelve-thirty?"

He thought he should explain his relationship with Chelsea so Abigail didn't misunderstand. "About this situation—"

Abigail waved him off. "I trust you're doing what you need to do. I think we'll eat out here in the shade." She turned and headed back into her trailer, stopping at the door to smile over her shoulder at him. "I hope you like pigs in a blanket. That's what the girls wanted."

CHELSEA LIKED Abigail Harper immediately. The woman, not much older than her, was warm and friendly and went out of her way to make Chelsea feel at home.

They were joined for lunch by Abigail's husband Rowdy. He was a nice-looking man, slimmer than Jack, with dark hair and a wonderful sense of humor. Chelsea recognized his voice at once as the announcer she'd heard last night in Lubbock.

A light Texas breeze stirred the leaves of the nearby trees, and Chelsea listened to the three adults chat about rodeo life as the girls whispered to themselves, looking up only when Rowdy teased one of them.

It was obvious that Sam adored this family, and Chelsea could see how thankful Jack must be to have the Harpers on the circuit.

"So you're going to spend some time on the road with us," Abigail said to Chelsea.

"Yes, I'm looking forward to it."

Jack kept his eyes on his lunch.

"It can be exhausting," Abigail said, glancing fondly at her husband, "but there's no other place I want to be."

Chelsea could feel Sam's gaze on her through most of lunch. The girl had been watching her and Jack from under the brim of her hat.

She still couldn't help but wonder why Sam wasn't

more upset about her tagging along for the week. All she could figure was that Sam had an agenda of her own— just like she had the first night with the casserole. Perhaps she should be worried, Chelsea thought.

Sam and Becky excused themselves and took off to play in the trees again. Rowdy said he had to get back to the rodeo office. Chelsea could tell Jack was worried about leaving her alone with Abigail, but he obviously had things he also needed to do, so he and Rowdy left together.

"It's wonderful that Sam has Becky," Chelsea said as she helped pick up the lunch dishes. "I would imagine all this traveling could get lonely for a child."

"It is nice they have each other," Abigail agreed. "I worry about what Becky will do without her friend when Jack leaves the circuit."

"Jack plans to leave?" Chelsea asked in surprise as she followed the woman into the homey trailer.

"All bull riders have to at some point," she said, looking as if she'd spoken out of turn.

Chelsea watched Abigail fill the sink with hot soapy water. "Jack was my first love." She almost added *only love.*

Abigail looked up. "You don't have to tell me."

"I'd like to. I really need to talk to someone who might understand. I can see how much you care about Jack and Sam."

Abigail nodded. "Jack is a good man."

"Yes, he is." Chelsea picked up the dish towel and began to dry the dishes as Abigail put them on the drainer. "There was a misunderstanding the summer he worked on my family's ranch. Jack was terribly hurt. Before that the two of us were planning to spend our lives together. I'm here hoping to rectify that misunderstanding. We were young, but—'' She glanced out the window to the chutes, where Jack was standing with the other cowboys. ''But it was the kind of love you don't ever forget.''

When she looked back, Abigail was smiling.

''The problem is my family has money,'' Chelsea said.

''That doesn't sound like much of a problem.''

''It is to Jack. I'm hoping it's something we can get past, but I'm not sure how he feels and...'' She stopped and smiled at her hostess. ''I'm sorry, I didn't mean to—''

''If you love him, don't give up on him,'' Abigail said, reaching over to squeeze Chelsea's hand. ''Men seldom know what they really need.''

Chelsea finished helping with the dishes, feeling as if she had at least one supporter in the camp, then went to find Jack.

''I need to run a couple of errands and see about getting my car put in storage while I'm gone,'' she told him, not daring to admit where she really had to go—to see one of her possible suspects, Lance Prescott.

''We leave right after the rodeo,'' he warned.

''I'll be back in time to see you ride.''

It seemed to surprise him that she would want to see him ride.

She found the carnival in Fort Worth where Lance Prescott was working, and after asking directions, walked through the swarm of people to a ride called Hell on Wheels. The air reeked of corn dogs and cotton candy, reminding her of the rodeo. Children cried and argued with their parents, while vendors badgered customers to try their wares and patrons shrieked over the clamor of the whirling rides.

Lance Prescott was right where she was told he would be, sitting by the gate to a caged bumper-car ride, looking bored and cranky. He was of average size, with muscular arms and shoulders like the fighter he was purported to be. He looked a little less bored as she approached. Chelsea couldn't remember the man at all from that summer ten years ago.

But last night she'd read everything Dylan had been able to dig up on him. Lance had had several run-ins with the law and served some time for assault. He'd drifted from job to job and seemed to have trouble staying with one more than a year. Alcohol and possibly drugs had contributed to his problems and, no doubt, his two divorces. Dylan had noted that the man should be considered dangerous. All in all, he seemed like a perfect rustling suspect.

"Lance Prescott?"

Suspicion instantly flared in his eyes. "Who's asking?" He checked his watch, then glanced toward the half-dozen bumper cars banging around inside the caged area.

"My name's Chelsea Jensen." The name didn't seem to ring any bells. "I'm from the Wishing Tree Ranch outside of San Antonio." Was it her imagination or did his gaze narrow? "I'm trying to find out about something that happened ten years ago, the summer you worked there."

This time there was no doubt about it, his gaze closed down. He stood and flipped a switch. A bell clanged, and all the bumper cars stopped, frozen in motion. Lance turned his back on her and went inside the gate to unbuckle some of the younger kids behind the wheels.

She waited, more determined than ever after her talk with Abigail. If she and Jack had a chance at a future, she needed Cody on her side. And there was only one way to make that happen—to prove once and for all that Jack was no thief.

She watched Lance take tickets from another half-dozen kids, get them buckled into cars, then come back to flip the switch. The bell rang again and the cars began to move.

"I really could use your help," she said over the racket. "I'm trying to find out who was working with Ray Dale that summer, rustling cattle."

He didn't look at her.

"I don't want to cause anyone any trouble. I just need to know for personal reasons."

"Even asking is causing trouble," Lance said, watching the kids ram into each other.

A thought struck her. "I could make it worth your while." She pulled a fifty out of her purse. "Anything you tell me would be kept in the strictest of confidence."

Nervously, he glanced at the fifty, then at the carnival crowd. "Talking about Ray Dale could get a person hurt. Maybe even killed. It would take a lot more money than that."

Get a person killed? "I'm sure you're exaggerating about the danger—" He met her gaze. Like C. J. Crocker, he appeared scared, and Lance Prescott didn't look like the kind of guy who scared easily.

"Why would talking about Ray Dale be dangerous?" she asked quietly.

Lance shook his head as if he was done talking.

"I might consider...offering a reward," she said, the idea and the amount just popping into her head. "Say...ten thousand dollars?"

He jerked back as if she'd slapped him. "Dead men have no need for cash. Ray Dale made the mistake of talking to the wrong people. That's one mistake I don't intend to make." He hit the switch. The bell rang, the cars stopped. Lance didn't look back as he went to unbuckle the kids.

Stunned, she watched him glance around as if he feared he'd already been seen talking to her. Murder? Was that what he meant? Had Ray Dale been murdered for talking to the wrong people?

She scanned the crowd just as Lance had, wondering if the person he feared was here. But she didn't see anyone watching her.

As she left she felt a shiver. There was no statute of limitations on murder.

While she made arrangements to have the car stored, she called Dylan.

"I have to ask you something," she said when he answered. "Is there any chance that Ray Dale could have been murdered?"

"Murdered? Where did you hear this?" Dylan asked.

"Lance Prescott."

"Did this exchange involve money?" Dylan asked suspiciously.

"He wouldn't take a dime. In fact, like C. J. Crocker, he seemed...scared, said even talking about Ray Dale could get him hurt or killed. He implied that Ray Dale was killed because he talked to the wrong people. He wouldn't tell me any more. What does 'the wrong people' mean to you?"

"Law enforcement," Dylan said.

"That's how I took it. But why would a rustler be talking to the cops?"

"Not cops. Brand inspectors," he said. "Don't do any more investigating on your own until I get back to you. Instead of a rustler, you might be looking for a killer."

She shuddered at the thought.

"Are you at home?"

"No, I'm traveling with Jack on the circuit. It's a long story. You can reach me on my cell phone, though."

"Chelsea? Be careful. You don't know who you can trust, and three of the six men who worked for your father that summer are following the circuit with you. Another one's in the same town. And we can't be sure that Tucker McCray won't hear you've been asking questions and show up as well."

Especially since she'd just offered a ten-thousand-dollar reward for information.

CHAPTER TEN

THERE WAS NO SIGN of Jack when Chelsea returned, but Sam came barreling out of the motor home with her friend Becky.

"Hi," Chelsea said. "Want to help me put away the groceries?" She hoped she could get to know Sam during this week, maybe bond with the girl.

"What did you buy?" Sam asked, peeking into the bags.

"Lots of good stuff. Since I'm supposed to cook and we have to leave right after your dad rides, I thought I'd make a mushroom-and-asparagus quiche for dinner. How does that sound?"

Sam nearly gagged. "Quiche? Is that the icky stuff that looks like a pie?"

"Well, I could make something else I guess...."

"Do you know how to make enchiladas?" Sam asked.

"Enchiladas?" She could run get the ingredients and make them before Jack rode if she hurried. "Sure. Would you like that?"

"Great. I'll be at Becky's." The girl was gone before Chelsea could ask what kind of enchiladas.

After a quick return trip to the store, Chelsea made a batch of cheese enchiladas and put them in the oven so they'd be ready. Still no Jack. She'd almost think he was avoiding her.

She realized she hadn't had a chance to talk to him

about the fight he'd supposedly had with Ray Dale. Given what Lance had told her, she was all the more anxious to hear his side of it.

She glanced at her watch. If she hurried, she would have time for a shower before Jack's ride.

The door banged open and Chelsea turned, hoping it would be him.

"Dad wants to see you," Sam said. "He's over by the chutes. He said to hurry." With that, Sam took off running. Chelsea could hear Becky giggling behind the motor home as Sam went to join her.

Suspiciously, Chelsea glanced out the window. Sure enough, there was Jack standing with Terri. Neither looked the least bit interested in talking to her.

The barrel racer turned suddenly, as if she sensed Chelsea might be watching, then leaned closer to Jack and whispered something in his ear that made them both laugh.

Chelsea let out a mild expletive and dropped the curtain back into place. Just because she was traveling with Jack didn't mean he wouldn't still be seeing the barrel racer.

Heartsick, she told herself what she needed was a shower. A very cold shower. Maybe it would bring her to her senses. What was she doing here anyway? What was the point? Jack didn't care if she cleared his name. Actually, he'd prefer she forget the whole thing.

"Chelsea?"

"Sam!" she said, her hand dropping over her heart to keep it from leaping out of her chest. "You startled me!"

"I thought you were going to go talk to Dad."

"Nope, you're going to have to do your own dirty work," she told the girl as she pulled off her boots and dropped them beside the chair. "I'm going to take a shower." She could see the disappointment on Sam's face, but Chelsea hadn't finagled her way into this week in order to help break up Jack's little affair. Right now she couldn't remember *why* she was here, or exactly what she'd hoped to accomplish.

But at least now she had a pretty good idea why Sam hadn't thrown a fit about her coming with them. It appeared Sam was hoping to pit Chelsea against Terri Lyn.

At least she and Sam had *something* in common, Chelsea thought. Neither wanted to see Jack around the barrel racer. Of course, Sam didn't seem to want her father interested in any woman, something Chelsea knew she should keep in mind.

She quickly padded barefoot into the small bathroom before Sam could argue. Once she'd closed herself into the tiny compartment, she realized there wasn't room to turnaround, let alone undress.

"It helps if you close this door," she heard Sam say from the hall. When she looked out, Sam had shut the folding door that separated the back bunk and miniature bath from the rest of the motor home.

Quickly she stripped down, left her clothing in the hallway, and stepped into the shower. It was claustrophobic at best, and the tepid water quickly turned cold. Be careful what you wish for, Chelsea thought as she hurriedly rinsed in the freezing water.

But the shower did manage to cool her off, and she found herself all the more determined to stick out the week against all odds.

Her hair wet, no makeup on, and still buttoning up her shirt, she opened the folding door expecting to see Sam. Instead, Jack stood in the middle of the room.

"Is something wrong?" she asked in surprise.

He opened his mouth as if to answer, then closed it again as he stared at her.

She looked down self-consciously to make sure she'd buttoned up her shirt. Nothing exciting going on there. "The enchiladas are cooking."

"When did you think we were going to eat them?" he asked.

She stared at him. "After your ride."

"After my ride, we're heading for Kansas City. Didn't Sam tell you we would eat on the road? I told her to tell you not to make anything for dinner."

So Sam had set her up. Great. "We don't have to eat the enchiladas." She reached over to turn off the oven.

"No, since you went to the trouble of making them, we'll eat them," he said, sounding put out. "We'll just get a later start." With that, he turned on his heel and left.

She was definitely having an effect on Jack, Chelsea realized, but was it really the one she wanted?

She fought the urge to kick something. And to strangle Sam.

As she started to close the door behind Jack, she spotted C. J. Crocker in what appeared to be an intense conversation by his trailer. The clown seemed to be arguing with someone just out of her view.

Still barefoot, Chelsea stepped outside and tiptoed to the back of the motor home, where she could see who C. J. Crocker was arguing with. Ace Winters. As she was watching, Ace grabbed C.J. by the neck of his costume and shoved him up against the trailer.

Rowdy Harper's voice came over the loudspeaker in the rodeo arena to announce that the bull riding was coming up. Ace let go of C.J. and stalked toward the ring. For a long moment the rodeo clown stood there, leaning against his trailer, then headed for the arena behind him.

Chelsea rushed back inside to get her boots on. What

had that been about? Rustling ten years ago? Murder? More than likely, it had nothing to do with Ray Dale Farnsworth. Still, she couldn't help but wonder as she found her boots. She had to hurry, since Jack would be riding first.

Even with the oven on low to keep the enchiladas warm, it was unbearably hot in the motor home. She took her socks and boots outside and sat down on the step, thinking about Ace and Crocker.

A scream rose in Chelsea's throat as she thrust her foot partway into her second boot. Something cold and crawly was moving beneath the ball of her foot. "Ohhh!"

She snatched the boot from her foot, sending it cartwheeling across the grass, where it came to rest on its side. A large, ugly dark-brown thing crawled slowly out of the boot.

Chelsea swallowed back the scream as the toad hopped away into the cool shadows at the edge of the trees. From those same shadows she heard muffled girl giggles.

Picking up a boot, she shook it out and pulled it on. It had only been a toad. A childish prank. She shook her head at her own foolishness. Sam was just having a little fun at her expense. She'd win the girl over, just as she hoped to win Jack over. Shoot, she had a whole week.

She glanced at the stand of trees, but saw no sign of the girls, so she headed toward the grandstands.

A glob of wet mud struck her just below the shoulder and stuck to her clean shirt and skin. She stopped walking and turned slowly, catching sight of her attackers. Sam and Becky peered around a large tree at the edge of a shallow ditch, dressed in only shorts and T-shirts. Their eyes widened in alarm as if they hadn't expected to actually hit her with the mud.

Chelsea reached down and pulled off one boot and then

the other as she advanced on the girls. They scrambled to get away, but the muddy bank was too slick and Chelsea too fast.

"Now you've had it!" Chelsea cried as she leaped into the muddy ditch after them.

The girls squealed as Chelsea grabbed for them, all three of them going down in the mud. Chelsea managed to get to her knees and found herself eye to eye with Sam.

"I didn't mean to hit you," Sam cried.

Both girls appeared shocked to see Chelsea down in the mud with them, and a little concerned about what she would do to them.

"Too bad," Chelsea said, "because now you're in for it." With one finger, she smeared mud down Sam's cheek. Then she looked over at Becky and drizzled mud down her arm. At their shocked expressions, Chelsea began to laugh, and suddenly they were all slinging mud and laughing hysterically.

"What the—"

"Dad!" Chelsea heard Sam say, and saw the girl's eyes widen in concern. She turned to find Jack standing over them, a shocked expression on his face.

"We were just—" Chelsea tried to get to her feet, but the mud was slick and she went down again.

"I don't think I want to know." He shook his head and left, but Chelsea could have sworn she saw him fighting a grin.

The three sat in the mud in silence for a few moments, then they looked at each other and burst out laughing.

Outside the motor home Chelsea hosed the girls off and sent Sam to get a shower so they wouldn't miss her dad's ride. She took Becky home herself.

"A mud fight?" Abigail asked.

"It was really fun," Becky said. "You should have been there."

Abigail laughed. "I miss all the fun."

When Sam was through, Chelsea jumped into the cold shower just long enough to get the rest of the mud off. Once she'd hurriedly dressed, she and Sam raced over to the grandstands in time to see Jack ride.

Tonight he drew a bull called Blue Blazes, got an eighty-five and seemed pleased as he stood up and dusted off his hat. Looking up to see them in the stands with their wet hair and shiny faces, he smiled, a smile that warmed Chelsea more than the Texas sunshine.

She hurried back to the motor home and quickly set the table outside because the weather was so nice. By the time he and Sam came walking up, she had everything ready.

"Maybe it was your lucky shirt," Sam was saying to her dad.

"Something sure smells good," Jack commented, surprising her with a smile. "You saw the ride?"

Chelsea nodded enthusiastically.

"My luck seems to be changing," he said, his gaze locking with hers.

Chelsea felt herself slowly melt inside.

"Go wash up, Sam," Jack told his daughter, never taking his eyes from Chelsea's.

"But I just had a shower," she protested. Then, grumbling to herself, she did as she was told.

"Can I help you with anything?" Jack asked Chelsea.

She shook her head, glowing in the warmth of his good mood.

"We're going to eat outside?" Sam asked when she returned. "Where are those candles we had?"

"We don't need candles," Jack replied almost distractedly as he dragged his gaze away from Chelsea's.

"But what about the ones—"

"Sam," he interrupted, obviously not wanting to discuss what had happened to the candles. Had Terri Lyn come back to use them at some point?

Chelsea had been flying high, airborne by Jack's warm look alone. But the thought of Terri Lyn grounded her with a thud.

"SAM? Why don't you sit over here?" Jack motioned to the bench of the wooden picnic table provided by the rodeo grounds. "And by the way, didn't I ask you to tell Chelsea not to go to the trouble of making dinner tonight because we'd be leaving right after I rode?"

Sam's gaze shifted to Chelsea. It was clear she expected Chelsea to snitch on her.

"She told me, it just slipped my mind," Chelsea said quickly.

The girl shot her a look of disbelief.

"Are you ready for enchiladas?" Chelsea asked, hoping Sam would like them. "I've been told I make a killer version." She smiled at Sam and was surprised when the girl dropped her gaze. "They're cheese," she added.

Sam only grunted.

So much for the progress Chelsea had hoped she'd made.

Jack put the enchiladas in the center of the table. "Sam?"

Sam mumbled the blessing. Chelsea saw Jack frown at his daughter, but Sam didn't seem to notice. He held out his daughter's plate and Chelsea slid on one fat enchilada, then put two on Jack's plate. She took one herself but didn't pick up her fork, waiting to see their reactions.

Sam stared down at hers for a long moment, then

scooped up a small piece. She studied her fork, looking almost as if she were going to cry, then took a bite.

With a squeal Sam lunged for her water glass. Gripping it with both hands, she brought it to her mouth and gulped wildly.

Chelsea shot a look at Jack. His eyes were also wide and his face red as he too grabbed for his water glass.

"These *are* killer enchiladas!" he cried.

Chelsea hurriedly took a bite of hers and felt as if her mouth were on fire.

Tears filled her eyes, only partly from the too spicy dish. She had so hoped Sam and Jack would love her cooking. But the enchiladas were so hot they weren't even edible. How could that have happened when she'd been so careful to make them mild?

"Oh, Sam, Jack, I—" She shook her head, too disappointed to even speak. Reaching for the casserole dish, she rose from the table.

"They're not that hot," Sam cried, and started to take another bite, obviously not wanting to hurt Chelsea's feelings.

Chelsea was touched but stopped her. "I think there's some leftover chicken in the fridge. I'll get that."

"I'll tell you what," Jack said, standing up. "We need to get going. Why don't we just grab something down the road?"

All she could do was nod, take their plates and the rest of the enchiladas, and rush inside.

What had happened? Her family and friends had always raved over her enchiladas. She glanced down at the offending dish. It appeared there was a different colored sauce on top from the one she'd made. How could she have not noticed? She touched her finger to it and put it to her tongue. The sauce was so hot she almost cried out loud.

Someone had sabotaged her meal. But when? She hadn't left the enchiladas except for that short period when she was in the shower.

Opening the cabinet door, she pulled out the trash. At the bottom of the bin was a bottle of hot sauce with a little devil on it and the warning, Hotter than Hades.

She stared at the bottle, pretty sure she knew which little devil had killed her killer enchiladas.

"Hey." She heard Jack open the door and come in behind her.

Hurriedly, she closed the cabinet door on the incriminating evidence. With her back to him, she started washing up the dishes so they could be on their way. She'd already delayed them enough.

"I'm almost ready," she said, not turning around. Then she felt his large hands on her shoulders, easing her around to face him.

"Hey," he said again. "There's no reason to be upset. They're just enchiladas."

A heck of a lot *he* knew.

"I wanted to make something that I thought you and Sam would like," she explained.

"Oh, Chelsea." He smiled sympathetically at her. "If you'd asked, I could have told you that Sam doesn't like enchiladas." The little darling. "But I thought they were great." She started to argue the fact. "Maybe they were a little hot."

She let out a laugh at that.

"Next time you make them—" He stopped as if he realized there might be a next time.

She felt tears coming and hated him seeing her like this

even more than she hated all the crying she'd been doing lately.

"Hey, it's okay, really." Awkwardly, he pulled her to him, his arms coming around to comfort her.

It had been so long since she'd been in his arms. For a moment, she didn't realize the warmth and comfort had changed to something else. Something hotter than her killer enchiladas.

Jack must have felt the change, too. He drew back as if he'd been burned. "Think you can be ready in fifteen minutes?" His voice sounded a little hoarse.

She nodded and met his gaze. They stood for a moment, the chemistry between them throwing off sparks.

Clearing his throat, he edged toward the door. "Great. Fifteen minutes." And he was gone.

For a moment she just stood there, trying to get her heart rate back down to normal, then hurriedly got ready to leave. She couldn't help smiling through her tears as she recalled the feeling of being in his arms again. Maybe all was not lost.

But when Chelsea turned, she saw Sam and knew by the look on her face that she had seen Jack hug her. The little girl was not pleased.

"Why didn't you tell him?" Sam challenged. She sounded close to tears herself.

"About you purposely having me make a dinner you don't like, knowing it would upset your father? Or about the creature you put in my boot? Or about the mud you threw at me? Or about what you did to my enchiladas?" Chelsea asked quietly.

Sam dropped her gaze to the floor. "It was a toad."

Chelsea reached out to lift Sam's chin up so she could see her freckled face beneath the brim of the hat. "Sam, I can see that you're afraid some woman will change things between you and your dad. I understand that. But no one is going to come between the two of you. He will always love you in a way he could never love anyone else.'' Chelsea thought of her relationship with her own father. ''I promise you that.''

Tears welled in the girl's eyes. ''I'm sorry.''

''Ready to roll?'' Jack called to them as he opened the door and slid into the driver's seat.

Chelsea handed Sam a tissue. ''Ready!''

SEBASTIAN REACHED for the Rolodex sitting on the corner of his wife's too-clean desktop. He'd always hated how organized Julie was. Until now.

Methodically he flipped through the names, addresses and phone numbers she had meticulously printed on each card. Julie had sources all over the Southwest that she used for her newspaper columns, and beside each name was a reference. Ralph Harris, geologist, earthquake specialist, Austin, Texas. Frank Barnhart, child care services, Oklahoma City, Oklahoma.

He didn't know what he was looking for exactly. Someone Julie might run to. After all, she'd been pregnant. She would need help, maybe a doctor. He found a variety of listings from infertility specialists to neurologists. But where would she have gotten the money to pay for medical services?

He went through the names again, there were so many, but none set any bells ringing. And then he knew he'd found it.

Hattie Devereaux—midwife.

Oh yeah. That would appeal to Julie. But there was no phone number, no address—just Louisiana. How the hell would he find this Hattie Devereaux? Julie's columns. Of course.

Sebastian smiled to himself as he turned out the desk lamp. He'd all but found her.

CHAPTER ELEVEN

"HOW FAR IS IT to Kansas City?" Chelsea asked from her post in the motor home's passenger seat.

Sam was seated at the dinette, buckled in with an array of books spread out on the table. Something to do with an earlier punishment.

Jack tossed Chelsea a map. "About five hundred miles. We average about fifty miles an hour in this rig. Math is your thing, right?"

It was a no brainer. "Ten hours."

"Plus stops for gas. We should get in about eight in the morning. Maybe a little earlier depending on traffic."

Gad. Chelsea opened the map, telling herself she'd known this wasn't going to be easy. But she was with Jack.

She studied the map for a moment, watched for road signs and figured out they were on Interstate 35 headed north. In the middle of Kansas, they could catch Interstate 70 and head east to Kansas City. Got it. She refolded the map and wondered if she should mention to him that she'd never driven a motor home.

Probably not, considering he was in a pretty good mood and she definitely didn't want to spoil it. That was one of the reasons she decided not to ask him just now about his fight with Ray Dale ten years ago. She also didn't want to bring it up in front of Sam.

"You can get some sleep if you want," Jack said when the lights of Dallas disappeared behind them.

He hadn't ordered her to sleep. In fact, he hadn't ordered her to do anything for quite a few hours now. She wondered what had changed. Something. She could feel it, a softness in him toward her. And all because of some ruined enchiladas?

She tried to remember the last time she'd driven all night. No wonder Ace had bought a plane.

"I picked us up some dinner at that last gas station," Jack said. "Help yourself."

She lifted the bag from the floor between the seats, almost afraid to look inside.

"You're not a vegetarian, are you?" he asked, as if suddenly worried.

"I live on a beef ranch," she said. "Remember?"

She'd meant it to be funny, but from the face he made, it was obvious he didn't appreciate the humor.

Inside the bag, she found a box containing roast chicken, Caesar salad and biscuits with butter and honey.

Sam eyed the food, then her father. "Roast chicken?" she asked, reading the side of the box. "Where is the fried chicken and potato salad?"

Jack looked embarrassed. "I was just trying to get something a little different."

Neither Sam nor Chelsea believed that. He'd tried to get something he thought Chelsea would like. She was so touched she decided to try to sleep after she ate, just to please him. Sam was not pleased, though.

"How's the homework coming?" Jack asked her once dinner was over. Unlike Chelsea, he didn't seem to have any trouble driving and eating, even though the lumbering box of a vehicle rocked wildly at the slightest bump in the road. "Sam?"

Chelsea glanced back to see the girl make a face at her father, one she obviously knew he couldn't see. She did, however, open one of the books on the table and take out her pencil and a sheet of paper from inside. "I'm doing it," she grumbled.

"Isn't school out?" Chelsea asked.

"Not for another few weeks, but she hasn't been in school since February," Jack said. "She can't very well attend school with us on the road so I'm home-schooling her. Abigail is helping me."

Home-schooling? She would never have imagined Jack in such a role.

She felt sorry for Sam though. School was about more than just studies. "It's good she has Becky." But it was clear that Becky wasn't always at the same rodeos as Sam, and they had little time together when they were.

"There's always kids around the fairgrounds when the rodeo comes to town," he said. "And she has plenty of friends among the cowboys."

Chelsea could feel his gaze on her. She hadn't meant to sound disapproving. She watched the blacktop disappear under the short hood of the motor home and tried to think of something to say to reassure him. But a child needed stability. A home. Friends.

No matter how hard she tried, she couldn't imagine Sam's life. Or Jack's, for that matter. Being on the road for months on end had such a rootless feel to it. The ranch had always been her home, her foundation, her strength. The Wishing Tree was an integral part of who she was. She knew Jack had had an unhappy childhood and was obviously doing the best he could for his daughter, but how could he know how important a stable home was for a child when he'd never had one?

"Bathroom, snack break," he announced a couple of hours later as he pulled into a gas station.

Sam asked for an ice-cream sandwich, nothing else. She seemed to be pouting.

Chelsea couldn't wait to stretch her legs. She climbed out, surprised how stiff and sore she was from sitting for so long. She headed for the ladies' rest room, then got a bottled water, an iced latte for later, some sunflower seeds and an ice-cream sandwich for Sam. When she looked around for Jack, he was nowhere to be seen. She felt a flicker of alarm. Would he just leave her if she wasn't ready in time?

Hurriedly she paid for her purchases and rushed outside. He was sitting behind the wheel, looking anything but happy. "You're to be ready when I'm through gassing up," he snapped.

"Sorry." She started to hand Sam the ice-cream sandwich but saw that Jack had already gotten her one. She offered the ice cream to Jack, who declined it, so she ate it herself rather than let it melt. The tiny freezer in the motor home was packed.

The night air coming in the window as they drove felt cool, the music on the radio familiar and soft. She finished her ice cream, licked her fingers and snuggled into the seat, not in the least bit sleepy. "Tell me about bull riding."

He shot her a look. "There isn't anything to tell."

Chelsea wasn't going to let him get off that easy. "What's it like?"

He looked over at her again, his gaze softening a little. "It's...frightening, exciting...challenging."

"How did you get started?" she asked, turning in the seat to watch his face in the dim glow of the dash lights.

He shrugged. "You don't really want to hear this."

"I do."

He drove in silence for a few minutes. "Some things just pull at you."

How well she knew.

"I'd tried my hand at a few rodeo events before you met me. Bull riding is learned mostly by observation and instinct." He seemed to watch the dotted white line on the dark pavement for a moment. "There is an interaction between animal and rider. Similar to a dance."

"Like ballet."

He laughed. "More like a waltz. In spite of the bucks and jumps, it actually resembles three-quarter time."

She smiled over at him, surprised. "You make it sound almost…romantic."

"It's anything but that. Some people say rodeo is part physical ability and part poetic interpretation." He scoffed at that. "It's actually just a lot of balance. And a test of endurance."

Behind them, Sam put away her books and turned out the light before coming up front to give her father a kiss good-night.

"Buckle in," he said.

"I will." She ignored Chelsea as she retreated to the back of the motor home and her bed.

"What do you think about when you're on the bull?" Chelsea asked, not wanting him to quit talking. She loved the sound of his voice and the intimacy of the cab in the dark night.

"There are a thousand things going through your head," he said after a few moments. "Your only hold is your grip on the rope. For eight seconds you rely on your sense of timing, anticipation and balance." He chuckled. "Mostly, it's just adrenaline flow. Then the ride is over and all you're concerned with is getting away from the bull and out of the ring.''

She said nothing, remembering him trying to get away from the bull the first time she saw him ride.

"I know you don't understand why I'm doing this," he said quietly. "Sometimes I don't, either. It's grueling, both physically and mentally. Being on the road for months on end, riding day after day. I'm always tired and sore, always looking for the bull that will put me in the money.''

"Then why do you do it?'' she had to ask.

"For me it's more than a sport. It's a means of making a living and accomplishing something with my life. It's also something I'm good at.''

She remembered what Dylan had sent her on Jack and what she'd found on the computer about his pro rodeo bull riding. Only 120 cowboys qualified for the National Finals Rodeo every year out of almost six thousand competitors. Jack had been eight times over the last ten years. Of those 120 competitors, only seven were awarded world titles at the end of the event. Jack had won seven out of the ten years for bull riding.

"I heard about your world championships," she said. "It seems you're very good at what you do." Which would make it all the harder for him to quit.

"You don't sound very happy about that fact," he noted. She could hear the disappointment in his voice.

"I'm very proud of you," she said honestly. "It just scares me, Jack. I don't want to see you hurt.''

"There are risks to any challenge, Chelsea.''

"Yes," she agreed, reminding herself of the risk she was running right now. "But how do you know when to stop?''

"Depends on what you want.''

"What do you want, Jack?"

He stared at the road ahead, and even in the dim lights from the dash, she sensed his expression alter.

For a moment the only sound was the hum of the tires on the pavement. "I remember when you wanted a ranch of your own," Chelsea said when he still hadn't answered.

"Some dreams don't change," he replied without looking at her.

"Jack—"

"You should get some sleep." His words were clipped and cold. "You're going to have to drive soon." He reached over and turned up the radio, putting an end to further conversation.

She leaned back in her seat and turned her face toward the night. What had upset him? Had it been bringing up the past? Or bringing up his dream for a ranch? She closed her eyes, unable to let go of that slim thread of hope. Jack still wanted a ranch and she just happened to have one.

"YOU LIKE HER, don't you?" Sam said, suddenly appearing at Jack's right shoulder.

He looked back from his driving. "Hey, why aren't you asleep?" he whispered so as not to wake Chelsea.

"I had to go to the bathroom." She folded down the seat he'd made for her when she was smaller and sat down between him and the sleeping Chelsea.

"Get yourself buckled up, young lady," he ordered.

"You do like her, don't you?" Sam persisted as she snapped her seat belt in place.

"Who?" he asked, pretending stupidity.

"Chelsea," she said in a whisper, then gave him a "duh" look.

He glanced over at Chelsea, listened for a moment to

her steady breathing. "Sure, I like her," he said, his eyes on the road.

"Do you think she's pretty?"

"What's with these questions?"

"Do you think she's pretty?"

"Sure. Not as pretty as you, though," he said with a grin, hoping to change the subject.

She swatted his arm. "We're not talking about me."

"I like talking about you," he said.

Her look assured him she wasn't going to be dissuaded.

"Would you want to marry her?" Sam asked.

"Hold on," Jack said. "Nobody's talking about marriage here."

"You said you might want to get married someday."

"Well, yeah, but—"

"Didn't you want to marry her a long time ago?" Sam asked. "Ace said—"

"I really wish you wouldn't listen to Ace." In fact, he didn't like his daughter having any contact at all with the cowboy, but that would be difficult since rodeo was just one large family.

"Were you going to marry her?" Sam asked.

Jack looked again at Chelsea. Her head rested against the back of the seat, her long dark hair like a soft cloud around her peaceful face. Chelsea Jensen wasn't pretty, she was beautiful. He felt that jolt, like a lightning strike. "Yeah, I was going to marry her."

"What happened?" Sam asked.

He didn't want to get into this. Especially with Sam. But he owed her some explanation since Chelsea was traveling with them. "We were too young. Her dad and older brother didn't think we were ready for marriage." All true. Just not the whole story.

Fortunately, that seemed to satisfy Sam, at least temporarily.

"Is that why she came here? To tell you she wasn't too young anymore?"

He laughed but found himself studying his daughter. She'd always been bright, way ahead in maturity compared with most kids her age. But sometimes, she blew him away with the questions she asked. He'd had to tell her about the birds and bees when she was six. Six!

But he'd always tried to be honest with her. He wished he could be right now. "You'd better get some sleep." He could tell she wanted to fight him on it and ask a lot more questions he didn't have answers for. "Bed. Now. We can talk about this some other time."

Sam gave in. She kissed him on the cheek. "Good night, Daddy."

She hadn't called him Daddy for a while. He'd missed it. He didn't want her growing up too fast. But just this morning, he'd caught Sam looking in the mirror, assessing herself as if suddenly aware that one day she would be a woman. That scared him.

"Look, if you don't like having Chelsea along—"

"No, it's fine."

Fine? He knew his daughter. Things were either amazingly cool or they were just too awful for words. There was no in between. There was definitely no "fine." What had happened to his little tomboy cowgirl?

He thought he knew the answer to that one. Several times today, he'd caught her staring at Chelsea, studying her, head cocked, the way she might inspect a bug she'd found.

"Good night, sweetheart," he said.

Sam trotted back to her bed without an argument or

any attempt to trick him into letting her stay up later. This was definitely not his child.

After Sam left, he glanced over at Chelsea again. For miles, he'd tried hard not to look at her, pretending nothing had changed. Just him and Sam and the motor home, driving to the familiar sound of country-and-western on the radio and the hum of the tires on the pavement.

Not that he hadn't been aware of Chelsea every second. Her every breath. Her every movement. Every sound she made. Trying to ignore her had nearly worn him out.

When he couldn't stand it any longer, he'd glanced over at her, only to find her sound asleep. There was a dab of chocolate ice cream at the corner of her mouth, and she appeared to be smiling in her sleep. He smiled in spite of himself and wondered how much more of this he could take.

CHELSEA HAD AWAKENED miles back but kept her eyelids closed, blatantly eavesdropping on Jack and Sam's conversation. What conversation there was.

Jack had succeeded in avoiding most of Sam's questions, questions Chelsea would have loved to have heard the answers to. Was it hard on him, having her this close? She only hoped it was half as hard on him as it was on her. Just being this near to Jack and not being able to get him to open up to her, let alone touch her, was torture.

As the motor home slowed, she opened her eyes and feigned waking up. It was still dark out. Jack pulled into a rest stop.

"Your turn to drive," he said to her. "You *have* driven a motor home or something comparable, right?"

"It can't be any harder than a truck. I have driven those, you might recall."

He groaned. "How many years has it been?"

He had her there. She hadn't driven a truck since she used to hang around Jack, helping him haul hay. But it was probably a lot like riding a bike.

She waved off an answer to his question, got out and stretched, then trotted over to the ladies' room. After using the facilities, she splashed cold water on her face, completely ruining her makeup. She dried her face with the stiff paper towels, telling herself that staying awake was more important than looking good. As if Jack was going to notice anyway.

She went back out and climbed into the driver's seat of the motor home.

Jack was already in the passenger seat, looking disapproving because she'd taken so long. He seemed to study her as she got her latte where she could reach it and her sunflower seeds. The ice would have melted and diluted the coffee, but she could use the caffeine jolt. The combination of seeds and coffee had worked in college, and she figured this wasn't that much different from studying all night.

She started the engine, found first gear and eased off the clutch. The engine died.

She shot him a look and smiled. He just shook his head, dropped his hat over his face and crossed his arms as he leaned back to go to sleep.

Just like riding a bike, she thought as she tried again. She restarted the motor home and got it moving. Finding the other gears was a little trickier. Several times Jack peeked out from under the hat, his gaze saying a hundred times over how out of her realm she was.

She drove through the night, careful to make sure she stayed on the highway to Kansas City. Jack woke to help her fill the fuel tanks whenever she stopped, then went right back to sleep.

She listened to talk radio, sang along with several country-and-western stations and ate sunflower seeds. She thought about the other rustler. She thought about Ray Dale and who would want to kill him. Maybe in Kansas City, she would try to talk to Crocker about the argument she'd seen between him and Ace.

Even though Dylan had told her to let him handle it, she was here. She'd just make sure there were plenty of people close by when she talked to Crocker.

The more she dug, the greater the mystery grew, and she'd come no closer to proving Jack's innocence.

As day broke, she saw the tall buildings sprouting out of the Kansas horizon and finally admitted just how tired she was. Her shoulders ached from manhandling the motor home and her head throbbed after staring down the white line of the highway for miles and miles of nothing but open country.

Proving herself to Jack wasn't going to be easy. Maybe impossible. His life was hard and his days long. She couldn't imagine what the last ten years had been like for him, doing this all alone. On the road, traveling from rodeo to rodeo, raising a daughter by himself. She was impressed—and at the same time horrified he would choose such a life for himself and Sam.

As the sun came up, she glanced at him, wondering what it would take to get him and Sam back to the Wishing Tree Ranch.

AS IF ON CUE, Jack woke with the sun. He opened his eyes, looked over at her and then out the windshield at the city. "So you made it." He sounded vaguely impressed.

Chelsea was too tired to comment, her eyes sand-filled and dry as Texas dust.

"Pull over. I'll drive."

She wasn't about to argue. And yet she felt pretty proud of herself for not only mastering the motor home, but getting them this far. All in a day's work for Jack.

Pulling over, she stopped and switched seats. All she wanted to do was curl up and sleep. But Jack, it seemed, had other plans for her. He drove up to an all-night, coin-operated laundry and glanced over at her.

"This is where you get out," he announced as he parked the motor home then climbed into the back to retrieve a huge overstuffed canvas bag that she assumed contained dirty clothes.

"I have to go check in at the rodeo and see what time my ride is," he told her. His gaze dropped to her chest, and she felt her breasts tightening in response. Until he said, "You might want to throw that shirt in the wash."

Glancing down, she saw she'd gotten salad dressing all over the front. How attractive.

He grinned. "Haven't eaten in a lot of motor homes?"

Sam stirred. "I want to stay with Chelsea," came the murmur from the bunk bed in back.

Jack seemed surprised. "Then you'd better get up." Sam quickly pulled on clean clothing, washed her face and brushed her teeth as Jack waited none too patiently.

Chelsea watched, blurry-eyed, as Sam handed her father a hairbrush, then knelt in front of him at the dinette while he took out her braid and brushed her long, reddish-brown hair. Jack began to braid the little girl's hair with an expertise that blew Chelsea away and oddly brought a lump to her throat.

"All done," he said when he'd finished, bending down to plant a kiss on Sam's cheek.

She smiled up at him. "Thanks." Then, as if on impulse, she threw her arms around his neck.

It obviously surprised—and pleased—Jack. He shot Chelsea a questioning look over Sam's shoulder.

Chelsea shrugged. Sam was a mystery to her. But she had to look away as she felt her eyes water.

Sam got the laundry soap and a handful of quarters from a cabinet. "Ready?" she asked.

Chelsea nodded.

"I'll be back in a couple of hours," Jack told her. "You should be able to get some coffee and juice from one of the machines. We'll grab some breakfast when I get back."

"No problem," Chelsea said as she dragged the heavy bag out the side door of the motor home. She glanced around for a coffee shop. None. Vending-machine coffee. Great.

She halted on the sidewalk to wait for Sam, who had stopped to get some last-minute instructions from her father.

When Sam joined her, the two of them watched Jack drive away.

"Dad said I'll have to show you how to wash clothes," Sam said, sounding amazed.

"I've washed clothes before," Chelsea said a little defensively.

Sam cocked her head, a gesture Chelsea had seen Jack do dozens of times. "In a laundry where you have to use quarters?"

Chelsea glanced at the dusty windows and sniffed the scent of fabric softener wafting out the front door on a current of hot air. "No," she admitted.

Sam smiled. "Don't worry, it's not hard." She strutted off ahead of Chelsea, her braid swinging. Chelsea followed the girl into the surprisingly busy laundry, feeling as out of her realm as she had felt at the rodeo grounds.

Once inside, she was instantly grateful for Sam's help and expertise. The little girl quickly sorted the clothes, filled three machines, popped quarters into the slots and shoved them home. Chelsea added the soap.

Several attendants bustled around the machines, stuffing large amounts of wet wash into dryers and folding huge stacks of clothing. Some patrons milled around, watching the clock, obviously anxious to finish their laundry and get off to their jobs. Others sat reading the dog-eared magazines as if they had all day.

Chelsea got a cup of coffee from the machine and almost gagged at the taste. But caffeine was caffeine. She purchased a juice for Sam and stood leaning against a rocking washer next to the girl.

"Why don't we go see if we can find a café?" she suggested. "We could get some real coffee and maybe a cinnamon roll or some fruit for you."

Sam shook her head and hopped up onto the washing machine. "Can't leave the clothes."

She looked over at the girl to see if she was serious. "You really don't believe that someone would steal them?" Chelsea whispered in disbelief as she remembered the work clothes she'd seen Sam put into the washers.

Sam nodded. "Real cowboy clothes, they will. Betty Jean lost all of her Wranglers."

"Who is Betty Jean?" Chelsea asked, and instantly wished she hadn't.

"A barrel racer," Sam said. "One of the ones who liked my dad." She shot Chelsea a knowing look. "She doesn't come around anymore."

"Let me guess, toads in the boots?" Chelsea asked.

"And other stuff," Sam admitted.

Chelsea had to laugh, then asked seriously, "Haven't you ever wanted a mother?"

Sam shrugged and changed the subject.

"Do you have your own horse?"

"Yes. Her name's Scout."

Sam seemed surprised. "What's she like?"

Chelsea described the bay mare, realizing how important the horse was to her. She missed her rides. She'd always had a horse. She and her first horse, Gertie, had been inseparable.

"Gertie? You named a horse Gertie?" Sam exclaimed, and made a dopey face.

"I was only three," Chelsea said in her defense. "What would you name your horse?"

Sam didn't have to think about it. "Sam's Star," she confided, swinging her slim legs as the washer under her clanked and groaned and shook. "Dad and I have a star that he named for me. We always look for it wherever we are. He says someday when I'm grown and gone, we can find the star, no matter where we are, and still be together." She shot Chelsea a challenging look.

"I think that's beautiful," she said. "I hope you get your Sam's Star one day."

Sam nodded. "We can't have a horse now. But Dad is going to get me one someday. When we get a place of our own."

Chelsea's heart ached for this little girl whose dream was a horse named Sam's Star and a home without wheels. "When is he planning on getting a place?" she asked, remembering the way Jack had clammed up last night on the subject.

Sam shrugged. "When he has enough money. He has to make the NFR first," she said, as if she'd spoken the same words a hundred times. Like a mantra.

Chelsea downed the rest of her coffee. Everything hinged on making it to the NFR? She wondered what happened if Jack didn't make Vegas this year. Would he ever quit rodeoing and buy a place and horse for his daughter? Or would there always be another NFR he had to make? Another rodeo bull he had to ride? Until one day, he just couldn't ride anymore. Or got himself killed.

"He's been to the National Finals Rodeo eight times, world champion seven," Sam said with obvious pride.

Chelsea pretended surprise. "Has your father always ridden bulls?"

Sam nodded. "Except for last year when he got hurt and couldn't ride."

At the thought, Chelsea felt her heart lurch.

The moment the washing machine stopped, Sam slid off and wrangled them a dryer. Chelsea loaded all of the clothes in, then dug fifty cents out of her pocket for another cup of coffee. "You want another juice?"

Sam shook her head.

The second cup tasted even more bitter than the first. When she'd finished it, Chelsea went to perch near the dryer with Sam. She felt hot and sticky and wished for a shower and a fresh change of clothing. Even better would be a flat space to lie down where she could get some sleep.

She realized that this time back home, she'd still be in bed. She *was* soft, spoiled and pampered.

"So you've always lived in the motor home?" she asked, trying to stay awake.

"One time Dad took me to my grandma's. I heard them talking about me staying there, but Dad said I wasn't havin' none of that. He said I raised holy heck, but he couldn't leave me behind anyway." She looked at Chelsea. "He says he couldn't ride if I wasn't there."

Chelsea smiled at the love in Samantha's voice for her

father. Her heart squeezed with envy. "Sounds like you're lucky to have each other."

"That's what Dad says."

If Sam was trying to convince her that she and Jack didn't need Chelsea in their lives, she was doing a great job of it.

They found a corner of one of the tables to fold the clothing on. Chelsea watched the girl neatly fold a pair of her jeans and put them in the bottom of the bag. Sam didn't seem to have anything but jeans and western shirts, most of them quite worn. Glancing through the pile of clothing, Chelsea saw no girl clothes, nothing frilly, nothing feminine. Even Sam's underwear was more practical than pretty.

She thought of the old motor home, the food budget, the girl's clothing. Was Jack hard up for money? The thought made her hurt, especially considering how much money she herself had. If only Jack would let her help. She quickly squelched the thought. She knew him better than that.

Chelsea picked up one of Jack's shirts to fold. The fabric felt warm and soft, and without thinking, she brought it to her face and breathed in the aroma. It smelled clean but still held just enough of Jack's masculine scent to make her ache. She could imagine the cloth stretched across his broad shoulders. Closing her eyes, she hugged the shirt to her the way she wanted to hug the man.

When she opened her eyes, she saw Sam watching her, an odd expression on her face, and hurriedly folded the shirt and put it into the bag.

When they'd finished, there was still no sign of Jack. Chelsea spotted a western clothing store across the street and, carrying the bag full of clean clothes, talked Sam into going with her.

"You can stand lookout at the window and let me know when your father comes."

Sam obviously had no interest in shopping for clothing for herself but agreed Chelsea needed to buy something.

"Terri Lyn Kessler says you dress like a buckle bunny," Sam told her.

"A buckle bunny?" As if she cared what Terri Lyn thought.

"It's one of those silly girls who hang around rodeos trying to get cowboys," Sam said.

"I know what a buckle bunny is," Chelsea snapped. It seemed Sam thought Terri Lyn was right.

Chelsea started to explain that she'd only brought good jeans because she didn't know she'd be living at the rodeo in a motor home and doing chores. "I definitely don't want to be a buckle bunny." Although in truth, that was kind of what she felt like right now. "You'd better help me get something appropriate to wear."

Once in the store, Chelsea let Sam make the selections while she browsed. She was looking at a pair of dress jeans, trying to stay awake, when Sam returned.

"Those jeans are for *girls*," Sam said when she saw the designer brand Chelsea had been admiring.

"I am a *girl*," Chelsea pointed out indignantly. And was about to add, "So are you," but bit her tongue. She went back into the dressing room and put on the inexpensive boot-cut jeans Sam had picked out and the utilitarian cotton western-cut shirts. The boots Sam had chosen were just as plain as the rest of the clothing.

When she came out again, Sam rewarded her with a smile of approval. "You just need to do something with your hair."

"My hair?" Chelsea glanced in the mirror. Her hair

looked just fine, thank you. It was pulled up off her neck in a chignon that she thought flattered her.

Sam handed her a western hat. Chelsea looked from the hat to her hair, then began to pull out the pins with an inward groan. She was letting a nine-year-old tomboy dress her.

Her long hair fell around her shoulders. She took the hat from Sam and put it on.

Sam stepped up to adjust the brim, then smiled broadly. "You look...good," the girl conceded, studying her.

"Thank you."

"Dad likes long hair," Sam said, and went to the window to look for her father.

Chelsea raised a brow. Was Sam shifting gears here? Or was the girl setting her up again?

"There's Dad," Sam said. "Wait until he sees you!"

CHAPTER TWELVE

JACK DID a double take. First at Chelsea. Then at his daughter. Sam was grinning from ear to ear, that smug little alien grin he'd caught on her face a lot since Chelsea had come back into his life. It made him extremely nervous, as if having Chelsea around wasn't nerve-racking enough.

As for Chelsea… He stared at her, surprised how good she looked in regular clothes. He could almost pretend she wasn't filthy rich. Almost. Just like he could almost pretend that the way the jeans hugged her bottom, the shirt accentuated her slim waist and her full breasts didn't affect him.

"Her hair looks nice, huh?" Sam said as she passed him with that grin.

Yeah, her hair looked nice, so nice he remembered the feel of it running through his fingers, the way it fired in the sunlight, the way it fell around her bare shoulders.

"I liked it better up," he said with a frown as Chelsea passed him.

"Good," she said, flipping her hair back over one shoulder as she swung the laundry bag, hitting him in the stomach. "I'll wear it down then."

Sam giggled and smiled at Chelsea.

Taking a deep breath, he hefted the bag of clean clothes and followed the two to the motor home, more worried than ever that this had been a really bad idea. The last thing he wanted was these two females finding any common ground.

"Dad, can we go to that pancake house, the one we always go to?" Sam begged. "Please. I want to show Chelsea. They have pancakes that look like horses. Well, they're supposed to look like horses and some of them do. Huh, Dad?"

"I doubt Chelsea likes pancakes," he said. In fact, with that figure of hers, he'd bet she couldn't remember the last time she'd even eaten a pancake.

"I *love* pancakes." She shot him a smile. "Especially ones shaped like horses."

"We need to talk," Jack said to her as Sam raced on ahead of them. "About Sam."

Chelsea lifted a brow. "Sam seems fine to me. She's a happy kid."

All Jack could do was grit his teeth.

Sam called for them to hurry, saying she was starved. It seemed to Jack she was always starved lately, no doubt heading into another growth spurt.

"We'll discuss this later," he said.

At the pancake house, he watched his daughter and had to admit she did seem happy. That's what worried him. He'd stake his next ride that she was up to something.

They ate pancakes that at least Sam thought looked like horses. Sam told corny jokes she'd picked up from rodeo clowns and Chelsea laughed with her. Their laughter was contagious and Jack found himself joining in.

He couldn't remember a breakfast where he'd had more fun. His daughter was glowing and he noticed she'd taken off her hat without being asked. Of course her entire behavior was cause for concern.

Chelsea felt pretty good as Jack drove them to the rodeo grounds. She'd driven a motor home, conquered coin-operated laundry—with Sam's help—and seemed to have made a little progress with both Jack and Sam.

But she could tell Jack was worried and she had a pretty good idea what it was about. Sam's change of heart concerned her, too, and she didn't want the little girl to get her hopes up. One of them having a broken heart was quite enough, and if it had to happen, Chelsea would rather it be her.

She had a solution for that problem, of course. She just wasn't sure it was one Jack was going to like—or even Sam, at this point.

As soon as Jack got the motor home parked along a small creek in a stand of cottonwoods, Becky came running over, with Abigail behind her. Like Sam, Becky was a tomboy, one with blond hair and blue eyes. But unlike Sam, it was obvious that Becky enjoyed being a girl.

"Can Sam come swimming with us?" Becky asked Jack.

Chelsea could see him hesitating.

"Oh, Dad, please," Sam pleaded. "I never get to go swimming."

He smiled. "All right, if it's okay with Mrs. Harper."

Abigail nodded. "I thought it would be good for the girls. We'll make a day of it, if that's all right with you." It was obvious to Chelsea, at least, that Abigail was trying to give her and Jack time alone.

After the three left, Chelsea noticed Jack rubbing his shoulder. She followed him inside the motor home and watched him dig a bottle of liniment from his bag, realizing from his drawn face that he was in pain.

"Here, let me do that." Without waiting for a response, she took the liniment from him. "Take off your shirt."

He hesitated, but only for a moment, making her realize he must be in a great deal of pain to give in so easily.

She warmed the oil in her hands as she watched him un-snap his shirt and slide it from his broad shoulders.

"Sit," she ordered.

"We need to talk about Sam."

"First things first. Sit."

He complied, taking a seat on the floor with his back to her. She dropped to her knees behind him and, leaning forward, gently touched his shoulder.

He winced.

"Oh, Jack, I'm sorry. Did I hurt you?"

"No, my shoulder's just sore from my ride yesterday."

She touched him again, putting both oiled hands to his back and gently moving across the muscled expanse. Circling slowly, she felt his skin begin to warm, then grow hot as she rubbed the ointment in.

He let out a small "Ahhh." It was the sound of pleasure rather than pain, so she continued massaging the tight muscles, kneading his shoulders with her fingers. He leaned back into her, into the pressure.

As she slowly worked his back and shoulders, Chelsea felt herself becoming hypnotized by the feel of his skin beneath her palms and the hardness of his muscles. Yet she couldn't help but be aware of the familiar tingle the intimate contact was producing in her, a sensation she associated only with Jack.

Suddenly he turned and grabbed her wrist, lowering her hand to his chest. Slowly her hand circled over the powerful pectoral muscles, seeming to move of its own accord. Her gaze locked with his and a flash of molten need shot to her core as her palm brushed his hardened nipple.

He shuddered and grasped her wrist again. "That's enough," he rasped.

"Jack—"

"No." He released her wrist and stood up, backing

toward the door. "This can't happen, Chelsea. I don't know what I was thinking."

She wanted to beg him not to go, beg him to stop fighting her. Instead, she concentrated on putting the lid back on the liniment, her face flushed with the heat of desire as she stumbled to her feet. She turned her back to him, not wanting him to see how disappointed she was, how badly she'd wanted him to make love to her.

Behind her, she could hear him putting his shirt back on. The soft snap of each closure.

He seemed to hesitate. She knew that if he touched her—

"I'll see you later." The door opened, then closed behind him.

Only then did Chelsea let out the breath she'd been holding.

JACK MENTALLY kicked himself all the way to the arena. First he berated himself for opening up to her last night, but it had felt the way it had all those years ago when he was at the ranch and Chelsea would listen to him ramble on about his dreams. But he was even more upset about what almost happened a few minutes ago. What the hell had he been thinking? He still ached from it, the unfulfilled desire making him physically hurt, and he knew she did, too. Damn.

The last thing he could do was make love to her. That would make everything so much worse when they parted again. And they would part. Chelsea would tire of this soon and move on. They might have the right chemistry when they were together, but there was no future for them. Yet when he thought of the desire he'd seen in her eyes, it took all his willpower not to go back. Hadn't he known it would be hell having Chelsea this close?

"Jack?"

He grimaced as he turned around to face Terri Lyn.

She'd been standing at the edge of the grandstand it seemed, but he'd been so busy beating himself up, he'd failed to notice her.

"Terri Lyn." She was the last person he wanted to see right now.

"I've been looking for you," she said as she stepped close. "I've been thinking about the two of us getting together for some of that...fun we talked about." She traced a finger lazily down his arm.

He caught her hand to end her touch, a touch so different from Chelsea's it was more like pain than pleasure. "I'm sorry, but I don't think so."

She pulled her hand back, frowning at him. "So it's like that, is it?"

He wasn't sure what it was like. He just knew there was only one woman he wanted to make love to and that was Chelsea.

"You're a fool, Jack. You don't stand a chance with that rich bitch."

Didn't he know it.

As he watched Terri Lyn storm off, he realized what he needed was a walk. A long one. He took off down the road, not sure how to get Chelsea out of his system, but desperately needing to try.

AFTER A COLD SHOWER, Chelsea considered a nap—anything to keep from remembering how close she and Jack had come to making love. She ached inside and knew sleep would not come easily.

As she glanced out the window, she saw C. J. Crocker pull into camp with his pickup and trailer. She needed to do something to put the past behind her and Jack and get him to believe they had a second chance.

This would be the perfect opportunity to talk to C.J. about the argument he'd had with Ace. Very few of the other riders had come in yet so the camp was almost empty, but there were enough people around that she felt safe.

"Hello," she said brightly as she came up behind him, hoping this would go better than the last time.

C.J. had gotten out of his pickup and was working on leveling up his trailer. He jumped at the sound of her voice and looked anything but happy to see her.

"Sorry," she said. "I just—" Oh, hell. "I saw you and Ace yesterday arguing by your trailer."

C.J. looked at her as if she'd caught him in his underwear. "Why do you keep sticking your nose in where it doesn't belong? I already told you I don't know anything," he snapped, glancing around and acting almost as paranoid as Lance Prescott had.

"I don't believe you," she said bluntly. "I think you know who murdered Ray Dale and that's why—"

"What!" C.J. looked as if he might jump out of his skin.

"Isn't that what you and Ace were arguing about last night?"

"Oh, God," C.J. said. "Murdered."

Chelsea was quite certain this was the first time he'd heard anyone suggest Ray Dale had been murdered. She'd seen C.J. fill in for the regular clown and he was no actor. But he knew something. "You know who the other rustler was, don't you?"

He didn't seem to be paying attention, but glanced furtively toward the arena, then behind him, a look of panic in his eyes. Just then a pickup truck came rattling into the camp.

"Tell me who the other rustler was and I won't bother you again," she said, feeling his need to run.

"Meet me in thirty minutes by the creek where it pools in the rocks." The pickup truck went by in a cloud of dust, followed by Terri Lyn's rig. Ace wouldn't be far behind. "Please go! Now!"

She left by way of the creek and trees so she wouldn't be seen. C.J. had looked more than scared, giving credence to Lance's assertion that Ray Dale had been murdered.

Back at the motor home, she was hoping Jack had changed his mind and returned. No such luck.

When her cell phone rang, it was Dylan. "I just got off the phone with the former brand inspector, a man named Tom Burton," he said, sounding upset. "There was a rustling ring operating in the county that summer. When I told him about the rustling on the Wishing Tree, he was furious that your father had never reported it. This was no small-time rustling operation. Burton thought they were close to busting it until—"

"Until Ray Dale got killed." She had to sit down.

"You guessed it. Burton caught Ray Dale rustling on another ranch and made a deal with him. To avoid prosecution, Ray Dale was going to help bring down the ring leader. The way the ring worked was that an inside man on each ranch recruited one of the other ranch hands. Ray Dale was recruited. Are you sitting down?"

She was now.

"Ray Dale said he was recruited by Ace Winters, but Burton couldn't get any evidence against Ace after Ray Dale was killed. As far as Burton could tell, the ring ceased operations after that. Burton says he's always suspected that Ray Dale's death was no accident, but had no proof.''

"You think the ring leader somehow got wind that Ray Dale was part of a sting operation?'' she asked.

"Must have,'' Dylan said. "The sting was to take place the night after Ray Dale was killed.''

"Cody didn't see Ace that night,'' she noted.

"The thing is, how reliable was Ray Dale?'' Dylan said. "He might have lied about who recruited him, knowing Burton was only after the ring leader.''

"Where does C. J. Crocker fit in?'' She recounted the argument she'd witnessed between Ace and C.J. the night before. "It looked as if Ace was threatening him.'' Then she told him about her conversation with the bull riding clown. "I'm meeting C.J. in a few minutes by the creek.''

"Bad idea, Chelsea,'' Dylan said, sounding like her brother. "Stay clear of Ace—and C.J. Let me handle this from here on out. I've put out feelers with my sources in the police department to find out who might have been marketing rustled cattle ten years ago. It's a long shot. I have some other business I have to tend to, but in a few days I can catch up with the circuit—''

"It can't wait a few days. C.J.'s scared—of Ace, I think. He wants to tell me something. In a few days, he could change his mind. Lance Prescott was scared, too, and believe me, he didn't look like a man who frightens easily. I'm wondering how many of them knew about the rustling or were maybe involved? Jack suspected Ray Dale. That's why he was out there that night when Cody saw him.''

"You're still sure Jack wasn't involved?'' Dylan asked.
"Positive.''

"Chelsea, I feel like you're in the middle of a rattle-snake den and any one of them could strike without warning. Cody and I are concerned about your welfare and with good reason.''

"Cody?'' she asked in surprise.

"I didn't tell him anything about the case, but from what you've told him and the fact that he knows you, he's worried. He's talking about coming after you.''

Oh, brother. "Thanks for the warning. I appreciate your concern but I'm being careful. I'll call you when I know something.''

She hung up and called Cody. "Hi, big brother,'' she said cheerfully.

"Where are you?'' he demanded.

She could tell he was on his cell phone and probably out in some pasture from the sounds of it. "Kansas City, Missouri. I just got through eating pancakes lathered in butter and blueberry syrup.''

"Now I know you're in trouble,'' Cody said.

She laughed, determined to keep things light. The last thing she needed was her brother coming up here. "Did I mention the pancakes were in the shape of horses?''

"Ashley called.'' Ashley Garrett, Dylan's little sister. "You haven't forgotten her wedding, have you?''

"Of course not. Saturday afternoon in San Antonio.''

"You aren't still chasing rustlers, are you?''

"After all the pancakes I ate?'' She laughed. "Don't worry. I'm having the time of my life.''

WHEN SHE REACHED the pool behind the camp, C.J. wasn't there yet. The new spring leaves rustled softly in the breeze, and as she stood in the cool shade, she was tempted to take off her boots and wade in the water. From her vantage point, she could see when C.J. arrived, so she sat down to wait.

Forty-five minutes later, she'd removed her boots and

had her feet dangling in the cool water. No C.J. The clown had stood her up.

She dried her feet in the sun, put on her socks and boots and headed back toward the motor home, feeling tired and even more frustrated.

Of course Jack was nowhere around. She wandered over by the long row of vendors, the smell of corn dogs already permeating the air, to see if she could find him. Out of the corner of her eye she caught a movement and turned, shocked to see Lance Prescott disappearing around the end of the grandstands.

It had been Lance, hadn't it? What was he doing here in Kansas City? She rushed after the retreating figure, determined to find out.

But when she cleared the corner of the grandstands, he was gone. She told herself she must have been mistaken. As frightened as he'd been of being seen with her, he certainly wouldn't come here.

She walked back to the motor home, again considering taking that nap, but instead she opted to put away the laundry. She'd have plenty of time for a nap before Jack rode.

THE WALK WAS just what Jack had needed. As he neared the rodeo office, he saw Lloyd Crandell. Their paths had crossed often over the years and they'd become friends. Lloyd had been managing a ranch Jack worked on around San Antonio and was the one who'd told him about the cowhand opening at the Wishing Tree. Since Lloyd knew Chelsea and her family, Jack had a way of finding out about her without any worry that his questions would go further than the two of them.

"I see Chelsea's still here," Lloyd said. "Still looking for rustlers?"

Jack scowled. "Stubborn damned woman."

Lloyd laughed. "She does tend to go after what she wants," he said meaningfully.

Fortunately Roberta came out of the bus then and joined them.

"We were just talking about Chelsea," Lloyd said.

"She making any progress?" Roberta asked.

Jack knew she meant with finding the rustler—not seducing him. "Not that I know of."

"I can't imagine how she will, not after this much time," Roberta said.

"I wish to hell she'd drop this," Jack muttered.

"I don't think that's what she's really doing here anyway, do you?" Lloyd winked.

Roberta laughed and told Lloyd she was going into town to shop in the small Jeep they pulled behind the bus.

After leaving the Crandells, Jack went over to the rodeo office and checked in, then headed for the motor home, realizing he couldn't avoid Chelsea any longer. The reason he'd let her come along was to try to protect her. He wasn't doing a very good job, considering he spent most of his time trying to avoid her.

And he really needed to talk to her about Sam.

As he came around the corner, he saw Ace. The bull rider seemed to be waiting for him. How perfect.

"So you're riding Devil Twist tonight." Ace made a scared face. "Sure hope what happened last year doesn't happen again."

Jack didn't need this. He stepped past Ace.

"I wish I knew who was rustling cattle that summer we worked together on the Wishing Tree," Ace said. "I could sure use that reward money."

Jack stopped in his tracks and turned slowly.

"Oh?" Ace said. "Didn't Chelsea tell you about the

ten-thousand-dollar reward she's offering? I thought you knew, since she's...*traveling* with you.''

Ten thousand? Now there was a familiar number. Jack swore under his breath.

''If I were you I'd keep a closer eye on her, though,'' Ace said, echoing Jack's earlier concerns. ''Especially with her asking all those questions about rustlers. That's a lot of money. Who knows who'll try to collect, or what that person will say. Might even name you as the rustler.'' Ace walked off, obviously accomplishing what he'd intended.

Jack spotted Terri Lyn waiting for Ace by the trailer. He'd heard the two were ''seeing'' each other. He wondered if Terri Lyn knew what she was getting herself into. But he only wondered for a moment. He had other things to occupy his mind as he marched toward the motor home. A ten-thousand-dollar reward? What was Chelsea thinking? She'd just upped the ante and put herself in even greater danger. Damn.

He reached for the door an instant before he heard her scream.

CHAPTER THIRTEEN

As Jack rushed into the motor home, Chelsea screamed again and stumbled toward him.

He caught her in his arms. "What is it?"

She buried her face in his chest, shaking so hard she could barely speak. "In the drawer."

He set her aside and moved down the little hallway.

"Be careful," she cried after him.

The light in the back was dim but he could still make out the coiled shape inside the drawer.

Stepping back to open the broom closet door, he withdrew the broom and, using the stick end, cautiously picked up the rattlesnake.

It proved to be dead. He swore under his breath. A rodeo prank. He'd seen it pulled on enough rookie cowboys.

"It's all right," he said to Chelsea. "It's dead." But it wasn't all right. He knew what this must have done to her. "Step back and I'll get rid of it."

She moved to stand by the driver's seat and turned her face away as he took the snake out and tossed its lifeless body into the trash. Who the hell had done this?

"It's gone," he said when he returned, knowing that every time she opened that drawer she'd expect to see it again.

She turned to look at him, tears in her eyes.

He reached for her and she flew into his arms again.

Holding her, he swore he'd find out who had done this and teach them a lesson they wouldn't soon forget.

"I'm sorry, I know I overreacted," Chelsea said after a moment, stepping back to brush at her tears. "I usually never cry...."

He remembered his reaction as a rookie cowboy when he'd reached into his gear bag and felt a snake the first time. "Trust me, your reaction was a hell of a lot milder than most people's would have been."

"I just have this thing about snakes." She shivered.

"I remember. Do you have any idea who did this?" he asked.

She shook her head.

"When Sam gets back—"

"You don't think Sam has anything to do with *this* prank," Chelsea cried.

"*This* prank?" he asked, narrowing his eyes at her. "This isn't the first, is it?" Her expression gave her away. "How long has this been going on?" he demanded, angry with her for not telling him, scared for reasons of his own.

"They started the first day but—"

"And you didn't bother to tell me?"

"They seemed so harmless. The ruined enchiladas, the toad in my boot..."

"You should have told me, Chelsea."

"I thought I could handle it myself," she said.

He swore softly. "Just like this crazy rustling investigation of yours." He didn't know what possessed him. Maybe it was the shock of hearing her scream, or the fact he was still aching from her touch earlier. Whatever it was, he suddenly needed her with an intensity he'd never felt before.

Dragging her into his arms, he crushed his mouth against hers, claiming her for his own. She gave a quick intake of breath and her body stiffened in surprise, then melted into his.

Her mouth was just as he remembered it. Soft, lush and inviting. The desire it evoked in him was as blinding as brilliant sunshine—and just as familiar. A part of his mind tried to remind him of all the reasons the last thing he should be doing was kissing Chelsea Jensen. But nothing mattered except the feel of her in his arms. It had been too long.

CHELSEA LOST HERSELF in his kiss, her body molded to his, returning his heat with her own. As her lips parted to allow him in, she realized she'd been waiting ten years for a kiss to rattle her to her roots. Hadn't she known Jack was the only who could do it?

He let out a little sigh against her mouth, and his gaze met hers. Any questions she had were answered right there in glowing neon.

Drawing his lips back to hers, she deepened the kiss, her blood surging through her and her heart...oh, her heart. That's why at first she thought the pounding was inside her chest.

"What the hell?" Jack exclaimed, pulling back his lips, then his body.

Someone was beating on the door.

Chelsea moaned. Not now.

Jack's eyes reflected her own regret as he moved to open the door.

Rowdy Harper stood below the step. One look at his face and she knew something had happened. Something bad. Sam! Oh, God, not Sam!

"There's been an accident in one of the bull corrals," Rowdy said without preamble. "It's Crocker. They've rushed him to the hospital. He's in critical condition."

"What was Crocker doing in a corral with the bulls?"

"No one knows." Rowdy shrugged. "I just thought you'd want to know. His family is having him flown to the emergency center in San Antonio. He might not make it. Sorry if I…interrupted anything." He tipped his hat and left.

Jack closed the door. "C.J. saved my life on more than one occasion. What in the hell would he have been doing in the corral with the bulls?" He turned and saw her expression. "What is it?"

"I was supposed to meet him earlier down by the creek, but he didn't show."

Jack looked at her as if she'd lost her mind.

"He was ready to talk to me about the rustling operation that summer. He was scared, really scared."

When Jack seemed skeptical, she rushed to explain.

"It looks like there was more than just rustling going on that summer." She hesitated. "I think Ray Dale might have been murdered."

She told him about her conversation with Crocker and the argument she'd seen between him and Ace. She recounted her talk with Lance Prescott and what Dylan had said about the brand inspector's sting operation. The last thing she mentioned was her certainty that she'd seen Lance earlier.

"Who's Dylan?"

"Dylan Garrett. He's a private investigator for Finders Keepers."

"Dylan. That friend of your brother's."

There was bitterness in Jack's tone.

He moved to close the drawer where she'd found the snake earlier, but stopped before he closed it all the way and reached down to pull something out.

She watched him unfold a piece of white paper, which he slowly handed to her.

The words of the note had been cut from a magazine: *Next time it will be a live snake.* How original, she thought.

Jack was looking at her, his face hard with anger. "This isn't Sam's doing."

"I know." She wished he'd just kiss her again. That was the only thing that had felt right in this crazy world.

"Ace just told me you're offering ten thousand dollars for information. *Ten thousand?*"

"It seemed an appropriate amount at the time."

"Dylan used to be a cop, right? You *are* letting him handle this from here on out?"

"Yes." She was becoming a believer after the snake and the note.

"Damn, Chelsea." He shook his head. "This is all my fault. If I'd made your father listen to me ten years ago... I let my pride and anger keep me from telling him about Ray Dale."

"Ace told me he witnessed a fight between you and Ray Dale one day in the bunkhouse," she said.

Jack frowned. It was obvious he didn't like Ace nor the fact she'd talked to him. "Ray Dale was trouble waiting to happen. We got into it."

"Ace said you apologized later."

"Ace sure had a lot to say about me," Jack noted. "Yeah, I apologized to Ray Dale. Then a couple of nights later I followed him when he left the bunkhouse in the middle of the night."

"The night he was killed in Box Canyon. Does anyone beside my brother know you were there?"

He looked up as he realized what she was getting at. "I didn't see or hear anyone else, not with the thunderstorm that night. Once I saw the cattle Ray Dale had rounded up, I headed back, planning to tell your father the next morning. I don't know if anyone saw me besides Cody.''

''What about when you got back to the bunkhouse? Was everyone accounted for except Ray Dale?''

''I don't know. I crept in and went to bed without turning on a light.'' He met her gaze. ''From now until you return to your ranch, I don't want you out of my sight. I want you in the stands where I can see you whenever I ride, and no more investigating. Agreed?''

She nodded. She could live with that. All except for the part where she returned to the ranch.

''I have to get ready to ride,'' he said.

She nodded. ''I'll be in the stands where you can see me.''

As CHELSEA SAT DOWN in the grandstands, a clown joked around as the two pickup men tried to catch the bull from the last ride.

''That bull reminds me of my wife,'' the clown said. ''You know what the difference is?''

''No, what?'' the announcer asked, playing along.

''About thirty pounds!'' the clown replied.

The crowd laughed.

''They feed that bull and he'll catch up to her, though,'' the clown quipped.

Chelsea thought of the jokes Sam had told at breakfast and the way the three of them had laughed together. She couldn't bear the thought that she might be leaving here without them. But she had to admit, this week could definitely turn out to be a heartbreaker just as Jack had warned her.

Seeing the clown made her think of C. J. Crocker. What had happened after he'd arranged to meet her?

She was surprised when Roberta Crandell came and sat by her. Roberta's husband Lloyd was down by the arena, working with the stock he'd brought for the rodeo, and Rowdy was in the announcer's box, his voice a comforting sound over the loudspeakers.

"Wasn't that just awful about C. J. Crocker?" Roberta said.

Chelsea nodded.

"Rodeos are dangerous places," the older woman went on. "But that's part of the thrill for the crowd. They come here because they know someone could get hurt."

"You make them sound so bloodthirsty," Chelsea said.

"They are, honey," Roberta told her. "That's why we raise rodeo stock. We want to give them a show for their money. And that's why men like Jack ride bulls."

"It isn't just to get chicks?" Chelsea said, trying to lighten the mood. But she felt a chill, afraid C.J.'s fall into the bull pen wasn't an accident, and they might have a killer among them.

"Next up in chute number three is a bull that has made a reputation for himself," Rowdy said over the loudspeaker. "And so has the cowboy riding him. Here come Devil Twist and Jackson Robinson of Texas."

Jack was perched on the edge of the chute. Devil Twist slammed around inside while Jack teetered over him, obviously waiting for the bull to settle down.

"This bull has been ridden the full count by nary a few cowboys," Rowdy was saying. "This is one contrary bull. But this is also one contrary rider. These two have met before. Last year this bull took Jackson out of the running and landed him in the hospital for three months."

Chelsea gasped. This was the bull that had stomped and gored Jack last year?

"But tonight folks, Jack's going to get back on that two thousand pounds of twisting, turning, bucking bull. I think we've got a grudge match going between this here tough cowboy and this blamed ornery bull."

Chelsea stared in shock and disbelief at the bull snorting and kicking behind the metal bars of the chute. Was Jack completely crazy? Why would he get back on a bull that had almost killed him? Especially after what had just happened to C.J.

What if Ray Dale's killer was knocking off the cowhands one by one, and Jack was next?

Her pulse pounded so loudly she could barely hear the announcer. She tried to find breath as Jack lowered himself to the bull's back. No! Her rational mind argued that a killer would have no way of controlling the bull or Jack. But how had Jack gotten this awful bull? Could the killer have manipulated the draw?

Jack raised his free hand and gave the gatekeeper a nod. The gate opened and Devil Twist lunged out with Jack on his back.

The bull twisted fiercely one way, then the other, bucking and spinning, then charging headlong toward the fence. Jack hung on, thrown this way and that. The fence was coming up. Wasn't that what Sam had told her? The bull had put him into the fence, then stomped and gored him?

It appeared Devil Twist intended a repeat performance.

Chelsea found herself on her feet with the rest of the crowd. At first people were hooting and hollering, then the crowd fell deathly silent as the bull made a swipe at the fence. A loud, "Oh!" rumbled from the crowd.

The crowd let out another cry, this one more frightening, and Chelsea squeezed her eyes shut, praying Jack wouldn't be hurt. What was she doing here? What was Jack doing here? Thank God, Sam wasn't here to witness this. Had she witnessed the last time he was almost killed? How could Jack do this to his daughter?

The buzzer sounded. The audience was screaming now. Chelsea opened her eyes, terrified of what she'd see.

Jack was on the ground. The clowns were scrambling to get between him and the bull. The arena was in a state of pandemonium as the bull ran at Jack, horns lowered for the attack.

At the very last moment, one of the clowns jumped between Jack and the bull, distracting the bovine just long enough for Jack to be pulled clear.

Then he was on his feet, waving his hat in the air to the cheering crowd. She watched him climb the fence as the bull made another lunge at him, her heart in her throat. Anger mixed with her fear in lethal proportions.

"That was some ride," Rowdy was saying, sounding as scared as she felt. "That one will go down in the books. And it's good for a...ninety-five!"

The audience went wild with applause. She stared down at Jack's smiling face as a bunch of rodeo cowboys swarmed around him to congratulate him. What was wrong with these people?

"Did you see that?" a cowboy sitting in the stands commented. "I've never seen a bull do that before."

She didn't know what the bull had done, nor how Jack had survived it. She couldn't have cared less. She rushed from the grandstand as the rodeo crowd swarmed around him as if he were a hero. When he spotted her, he pointed to the motor home and headed in that direction himself, breaking free of his friends.

She caught up with him just before he reached it. Grabbing his arm, she swung him around to face her.

"Chelsea, did you see—"

The smack she gave him made him jerk back in shock.

CHAPTER FOURTEEN

"WHAT THE HELL is wrong with you?" Jack demanded.

"That's exactly what I want to know. Have you lost your mind, getting back on a bull that almost killed you? Did you ever think about Sam or me or—" Angry sobs choked off the rest of her words.

Jack pulled her into his arms. She struggled at first, then let him hold her. "It's okay, baby," he whispered. "It's okay."

But it wasn't okay and they both knew it.

Without another word, Jack led her to the motor home. He could see she was scared and mad. "This is why it would never work between you and me," he said quietly once they were inside.

She looked up at him, tears still in her eyes. "It doesn't have to be like this."

He shook his head. "I ride bulls. It's what I do." That she cared this much made him ache inside. But her anger and fear only emphasized the problem between them.

"You rode a bull that almost killed you last year! What kind of sense is that?"

"I ride whatever bull I draw. Maybe you don't understand what we're doing here."

"No, I don't! Risking your life? And for what?"

"A ninety-five and the National Finals Rodeo and a shot at another world championship," he said, annoyed with her for not realizing how important this was to him.

"For a good score? A title? Money?"

Her derisive dismissal of money struck another blow. He wouldn't always be a bull rider, but he would always be poorer than Chelsea Jensen.

Anger rose deep within him. "Yes, money, Chelsea. Some people have to make it. It isn't just given to them."

"You could have been killed," she said more quietly. "At least with *my* job I don't have to risk my life every day."

"A lot of jobs are dangerous. This one is mine." It hurt that she'd belittled his accomplishments. "If you knew me, you'd know how much this means to me. It's more than a good score, Chelsea. More than titles. Even more than money. That's something you obviously won't be able to understand. Not in one week, one year, one lifetime."

"What about the people who love you? What about them?"

"I'm trying to give Sam a good life," he said, hurt that she didn't seem to acknowledge that. "She likes you, Chelsea, but I don't want her thinking there's a chance for you and me because obviously there isn't."

"Of course not. Because of your *pride*. You love me, Jack, I know it. I feel it." She slammed her hand down over her heart. "But you couldn't possibly be with a woman who has more money than you do. Even if it is the best thing for you and your daughter."

"I know what's best for my daughter," he snapped.

"Really? Do you know how badly she wants a home that doesn't have wheels on it? A horse of her own? To go to school with other children?"

"Someday she'll have all of that..." He waved a hand through the air. He didn't have to explain himself to her.

"What about now? She isn't a baby anymore, Jack. She needs a woman in her life. A mother.''

His gaze narrowed. "She didn't before you came along.'' Was Sam getting her hopes up that Chelsea could be her mother?

"This isn't about my rodeoing or about Sam having a house and you know it,'' he said, angry with her, and even more angry with himself. "It's about you thinking you can get me back to the Wishing Tree. It isn't going to happen, Chelsea. If that's what you thought, then you've been wasting your time.''

What had he been thinking, letting Chelsea tag along with him on this quest of hers? All it had done was given Sam false expectations and put Chelsea in physical danger.

He'd thought he could protect her until she tired of her search, but the truth was, she'd be safer back at her ranch with her brother and all their hired help around to watch her.

Sam would be disappointed. As much as he hadn't wanted or expected it to happen, she had gotten attached to Chelsea. His daughter would get over it, though, and so would he. "I think it's time for you to go home. I'm going to see if Sam's back, then I'm going to turn out of my ride in Oklahoma City and take you home.''

TAKE HER HOME? Chelsea wanted to tell him that she was perfectly capable of taking herself home. But who said she'd be going home just because she wouldn't be traveling with Jack? Hadn't she started out determined to find who had been rustling cattle with Ray Dale? Now she realized that rustler might also be a murderer. None of this had gone as she'd planned.

But Jack was right about one thing. She was wasting

her time with him. She would never understand him any more than he would ever get over the fact that she had money. And he'd made it clear he would never come back to the Wishing Tree.

She was just winding up to tell Jack what she thought of him taking her home, when her cell phone rang. "Don't move," she told him. "I have to get this." She could see it was from Dylan—and urgent.

"I just got a call from the sheriff in Kingfisher County outside of Oklahoma City," Dylan said without preamble. "Tucker McCray's body was found crushed under his tractor. It appears he was working on it and it fell off the jack."

She felt a chill and hugged herself. Another accident. She told him about Crocker.

"Chelsea, it looks as if someone is covering his tracks," Dylan said. "I'm going to keep working on this, but until this person is caught, there could be more…accidents. I can't stress enough how dangerous this is."

Dangerous for anyone who might know about the rustling? Or the murder?

She looked up at Jack, her heart taking off. Had someone seen him at Box Canyon that night? Did that someone think he knew more than he did?

"Don't worry," she assured Dylan. "Thank you for letting me know." She hung up and looked at Jack. "Tucker McCray's been killed in a tractor accident. I was planning to talk to him when we got to Oklahoma City."

Jack let out an oath. "That's why you were so determined to stay on the circuit. You knew I would be riding in Oklahoma City in a few days and you saw a way to kill two birds with one stone. First Ray Dale, then Crocker and now Tucker McCray. That cuts it, Chelsea. You're going home where you'll be safe.''

Before she could protest, he turned on his boot heel and walked away. She was getting damned tired of him giving her his backside and no opportunity for the last word.

She hugged herself against the chill he'd left behind, the taste of him still on her lips.

He still loved her.

The thought gave her little consolation. She'd failed. Jack and Sam weren't coming back to the Wishing Tree with her and there wasn't any kind of life for her on the rodeo circuit, even if Jack had offered.

Between them stood her money, her family and above all her ranch. The Wishing Tree was her home. Her history. The ranch was an extension of her. How could she deny that part of herself? For Jack, it represented broken dreams, shame and humiliation.

Jack was right. He'd been right about everything, especially that she didn't belong here. And now she might have put him in danger. She went to pack. It was time to go home.

JACK WALKED through the camp, his hat pulled low against the building wind, his heart aching. He'd known he wouldn't be able to keep away from her. Just as he'd known this week would only end up hurting them both. And now he feared it had hurt Sam as well, and put Chelsea in danger.

He shouldn't have kissed her. That had been a mistake. He shook his head, angry with himself. Angry with her. She'd wanted the truth. Well, now she had it. But no good would come of it. And he had only himself to blame.

He neared the Harpers' trailer and heard his daughter's

laughter, a sound that invariably made him smile in spite of himself.

As he came around the corner of the trailer, he found Sam and Becky on the step. Abigail was handing them a plate of cookies out the door.

"Dad, please don't make me leave," Sam cried the moment she saw him. "Look, we have the tent all set up and blankets and a flashlight and food—"

"Please, Mr. Robinson, please," Becky begged, locking her arm with Sam's.

"Oh, let her stay, Jack," Abigail chimed in. "The girls hardly ever get to see each other. They've worked so hard getting that old tent set up."

Jack looked at the lopsided tent already leaning in the breeze and the two girls standing in front of it. "What about the storm?" A thunderstorm was predicted, and from the looks of the sky, it wasn't far off.

"If the tent leaks or we get scared, Mrs. Harper said we can come inside and sleep," Sam assured him.

Sam had her "Say yes, you're the best daddy in the whole world" look on her face—the one that never failed to turn him to putty.

"Okay," he agreed. She threw her arms around his neck, something she seldom did anymore. He was struck with the realization that she was growing up too fast—and that he didn't want her to.

"Tell Chelsea to come see our tent," Sam said.

"Chelsea has to go back to the ranch," he said. "Something's come up and she's needed there."

The disappointment in his daughter's eyes almost killed him.

"But she has to stay all week or lose the bet," Sam cried. "You had a fight, didn't you?" she accused, tears welling in her eyes.

"Sam, if you come home with me we can talk about this."

She shook her head angrily and ran to Abigail. The woman took Sam in her arms and looked over the girl's shoulder at Jack, her gaze concerned and, it seemed to him, disappointed, too. "Give her some time," Abigail whispered. "I'll talk to her."

He nodded, but the last thing he wanted to do was leave his daughter. The only reason he did was because he could see that Sam needed a woman's comfort, something he hadn't wanted to admit.

The rodeo was over. Everyone had gone home except for the few cowboys who wouldn't be leaving until tomorrow. Smoke drifted up from a couple of campfires, and laughter carried on the breeze.

He headed toward the grandstands, not knowing where else to go. He wasn't about to go back to the motor home until Chelsea was packed and ready to leave. He sat down and realized he'd gone to the very spot Chelsea had sat and watched him ride. He felt bad about scaring her, but why couldn't she understand what rodeo meant to him? It had saved him after he left the Wishing Tree.

Was she right, though? Was it just stubborn pride? Could he marry a woman who had more money than he did?

He was grumbling to himself when he heard someone approaching. Looking up, he watched as Rowdy Harper came over and sat down beside him.

THE TAP ON the door surprised her. Chelsea stopped packing and went to answer it, knowing it wouldn't be Jack. Abigail Harper stood on the step. The woman's smile widened a little. "Jack asked me to stop by. He wants you to meet him in the barn. The big old one at the edge of the grounds.'' She shrugged as if it were a mystery to her.

''Thank you.'' Chelsea couldn't help but frown. This was so unlike Jack. Why would he ask Abigail to come tell her instead of doing it himself?

''He said to tell you to wear your blue dress and he'd meet you in thirty minutes.'' Wear her blue dress? She didn't even think Jack had noticed her blue dress hanging in the closet. It wasn't as though she'd had a chance to wear it. But to the barn?

''Really?'' she said.

Abigail smiled and crossed her fingers.

It took Chelsea a moment. Had Jack changed his mind?

It seemed unbelievable. Not Jackson Robinson. But who was she to question it? Excited and hopeful she rushed into the bathroom to get ready. Maybe, just maybe...

THE AIR WAS RICH with summer smells as she walked to the barn. In the distance, she thought she heard thunder, but it could have just been her heart. As she neared the barn, she saw a light coming through the cracks in the door.

Cautiously, she pushed open the door. A tiny table had been set in a corner of the barn and the wooden floor swept clean. The table was covered with a tablecloth and set for two with plates, silverware and wineglasses. A candle glowed at the center.

Chelsea smiled. Maybe, just maybe...

She didn't see Jack anywhere, but near the table she spotted a large picnic basket and caught the aroma of something mouthwatering. When she lifted the lid, she discovered lasagna and warm bread with herbed butter. A bottle of wine cooled in a bucket of ice beside the table. "Oh, Jack."

"Oh, Jack, indeed," said a familiar male voice behind her. He stood just inside the barn door at the edge of the candlelight, dressed up but frowning. "Quite the setup."

"I should say." She smiled but noticed he didn't return the smile. "You don't think I did this?"

He raised a brow. "Well, it certainly wasn't my doing. Rowdy told me—"

"Abigail told me—" She tried to hide her disappointment.

Suddenly the soft sound of a slow country-and-western song drifted down from the loft along with a few pieces of straw.

"Sam," they said in unison. Jack shook his head and Chelsea smiled, thinking how much she was going to miss Sam. Several hushed whispers sounded from above.

"They went to an awful lot of trouble," Chelsea said quietly.

Jack nodded. "I just don't want Sam getting the wrong idea."

"By tomorrow, she might change her mind about us getting together," Chelsea said.

He nodded, almost looking hopeful. "It does smell awfully good, though. Abigail is a great cook and obviously she and Rowdy are in on this."

"Yes." Sam, their little matchmaker. And Abigail. She'd more than accepted Chelsea from the start and had done her best to keep Sam busy to give Chelsea time with Jack—for all the good it had done.

"There's wine," Chelsea said.

"Seems they've thought of everything." He walked over to the bucket and pulled out the bottle. "I suppose one glass wouldn't hurt." He filled their glasses and handed her one. She started to take a sip.

"Toast!" came a small voice from the loft, followed by the rustle of straw.

Chelsea met Jack's gaze. He shook his head and smiled in spite of himself. "Kids," he said. "What should we toast?"

Chelsea could think of all kinds of things. "To Sam," she said, and clinked her glass with his before taking a drink.

Another slow song came on, one Chelsea had told Sam that she really liked. She was touched that the girl remembered.

"Dance!" came the whisper from the loft.

She met Jack's eyes. He looked as if he might rebel, but instead put down his glass and tipped his hat to her. "May I?"

Putting down her glass, she took his hand and let him pull her close. The music seemed to flow like a gentle breeze through the barn. Outside the wind had picked up, but in here it was warm and dry. Familiar ranch smells mingled with the scent of Jack's aftershave just as they had ten years ago.

The candlelight flickered across the high ceiling as they danced. Being back in Jack's arms felt so right. Did she dare hope? She rested her head against his shoulder, reveling in the strong feel of his arm around her.

He drew her even closer, his breath warm on her temple. When she looked up, her breath caught at the expression in his eyes.

"Do you realize I've loved you since I was seventeen?" she whispered.

"Chels—"

"There's never been anyone but you."

She saw his throat contract. "Oh, Chelsea," he said, and closed his eyes.

"I know you still love me," she whispered.

He opened his eyes, looking as if he no longer had the strength to lie. "And I've regretted it every day for the last ten years."

"That's not true," she whispered, smiling up at him.

"You made me believe that I could have you and everything I ever dreamed of with you," he said.

"And you can. We just need to find some common ground."

"Common ground for you, Chelsea, means me giving up my life to be a part of yours. You want me and Sam at the Wishing Tree."

She didn't deny it. She couldn't.

"Even if your brother..." He waved a hand through the air. "You want too much."

"I only want you, Jack," she said softly, holding his gaze.

"We'd better eat," he whispered, his voice husky.

She swallowed and nodded, but neither of them quit dancing—or let go of each other. The song came to an end.

Jack grinned just before he dipped her dramatically.

Giggles erupted from the loft, the sound so delightful Chelsea and Jack both laughed. He was still smiling as he served the dinner and refilled their wineglasses.

"This was a wonderful idea," she said. "And very sweet of Sam."

"Yes. But it doesn't solve the problem, does it?"

"No, that would take a compromise," she agreed.

He lifted a brow. "That sounds dangerous."

She raised her wineglass to him. "I thought you lived for danger."

He actually smiled at that.

"No matter what tomorrow brings, can't we just have tonight?"

"I'll drink to that," he said, touching his glass lightly to hers.

While they ate, they talked of safe subjects: Texas, summer, their love of thunderstorms.

The lasagna and bread were wonderful. So was the music that drifted from the loft. They danced after dinner, holding each other, moving together as if they always had.

It broke her heart to think that tonight might be their last night together. But if it was, she had only one wish. And that was to spend it in Jack's arms.

The song ended and she looked up at him, love in her eyes.

Jack stopped dancing, Chelsea still in his arms, his gaze meeting hers. The look in her eyes engulfed him, drowning him in memories, in dreams, in promises never kept. She pushed herself up to kiss him, and when he felt her mouth on his, the soft sweet breath, he drew her to him. He couldn't keep lying to himself. He loved this woman. But the price of loving Chelsea Jensen had always been high.

The sound of clapping brought him up from the kiss like a swimmer surfacing from a deep dive. He'd almost forgotten the girls.

He pulled back to look at Chelsea. Desire made her eyes gleam in the candlelight, and in the distance lightning zigzagged across the sky, lighting up the old barn. Thunder rumbled overhead. The air suddenly smelled of rain as the storm moved in.

"Come on, girls," he heard Abigail say. "Time to get into the tent." The girls scrambled down from the loft, giggling as they raced to the door. They gave a little wave as they headed outside. Then Abigail peeked around a corner of the barn. How much more of an audience did they have? Jack wondered wryly. "Rowdy and I'll clean this up," she said. "The two of you should get to someplace dry. It's going to pour any moment."

Rowdy appeared beside his wife. "You do have enough sense to get out of the rain, don't you, Jack?"

He smiled at his friend. "Thanks, you two."

"Thank Sam, it was her idea," Abigail said. "This means a lot to her, Jack."

He nodded, realizing how much it meant to him. He took Chelsea's hand. "Come on."

They raced toward the motor home as huge wet drops of rain began to fall. By the time they reached it, they were soaked and laughing.

Inside he found soft music playing and candles set out. "The matchmaker has been everywhere tonight," he said, lighting the slim tapers. He felt a surge of emotion at just the thought of what his daughter had done to get him together with Chelsea.

Thunder boomed and the rain began to fall in deafening sheets.

Chelsea was still laughing, her hair wet, raindrops on her lashes, the blue dress clinging to her skin. She'd never looked more beautiful.

Impulsively, he cupped her face in his hands and gazed down into her eyes. The desire he saw there almost buckled his knees.

She nodded as if she'd seen the question in his gaze, and he promised himself that this was just a beginning for them. They would find a way. They had to.

Then he kissed her, slowly, feeling her shiver. "You should get out of those wet clothes," he whispered against her temple.

"Oh, yes."

How many nights had he dreamed of this? "Oh, Chelsea," Jack breathed into her hair, afraid this was a dream and he would soon wake up. "I don't think I ever stopped loving you for even a minute. But when I saw you and Sam and Becky in that mud hole, covered from head to foot in mud, I fell in love with you all over again." He laughed softly. "I was wrong about you in so many ways. Can you ever forgive me?"

SHE LEANED UP to kiss him, just a brush of her lips on his. His muscles tightened and she caught her breath as he pulled her to him, his kiss anything but light.

"I love you, Chelsea," he whispered against her mouth.

How many years had she waited to hear those words? Her body seemed to melt against his, her knees like water.

He gazed down at her again, as if he couldn't believe his eyes. But then she barely believed it herself—that they were here together and he was saying he loved her.

Slowly, he reached out to push back her hair, the tips of his fingers brushing her cheek, a soft feather of a caress. She saw him draw in breath as she took his hand and held it against her cheek, her lips dropping to the tender inside of his wrist to kiss the warm bare skin.

He let out a soft groan as his thumb moved to her lips, the rough pad stirring a need deep within her as it brushed across them. Then her lips parted, and her tongue flicked across his skin.

"Chelsea." It came out a whispered plea. His gaze locked with hers, desire making his eyes bright, as if a fire burned just beneath the surface.

Sliding his hand around her neck, he dragged her to him, lowering his mouth to hers as his large palms came up to cradle her head. He took her mouth with a passion born of longing over too many years.

Her need for him felt more like pain, so deep, so long forbidden. When he caught her lower lip between his teeth, a jolt of electricity surged through her, and when his palm closed over her breast, the sensation was so strong she wanted to cry out.

"You really need to get out of those wet clothes," he whispered against her mouth, slipping one thin silk strap off her shoulder, then the other. He lifted his lips from hers and she could feel his gaze warm the tender soft skin of her breasts as he slowly, achingly slid the wet dress down her body until it dropped to the floor, leaving her standing in only the lace bra and panties she'd put on in hopes of just such a moment.

A groan escaped him and he picked her up, carrying her to his narrow bed over the cab.

Lowering her to the bed, he climbed up beside her, and she worked frantically to free him of his wet clothing.

Kissing her slowly, torturously, he slid his hand up her waist to cup one breast. When his thumb flicked across the thin, wet lace, her nipple puckered and pushed against the cloth, a hard, aching bud stretching toward his touch. Heat licked through him as he removed the bra, then the panties, and pressed his naked body to hers. Heat to heat.

Outside, the wind rocked the motor home. Rain beat against the roof as thunder rattled the windows and lightning flickered.

Chelsea barely heard it over the beat of her heart. Her eyes locked with Jack's as he pulled her to him, hunger in his gaze, in the hardness of his body.

"Oh, Chelsea, how I've dreamed of this," he breathed against her hair.

He ran one callused finger along the line of her hip, the heat of his touch making her shiver.

"You are so beautiful," he whispered, his voice rough with emotion as she opened her lips and body to him.

The wind whistled through the cracks and the old motor home swayed as rain pounded the roof. His kisses trailed across her skin in a hot path of sensation, making her dizzy with delight, making her remember.

"Oh, Jack," she cried out. "I've dreamed of this for so long," she said, her voice desperate with need.

He wrapped her in his arms, burying his face in the hollow of her neck. "Oh, Chelsea. So have I. So have I."

Lightning lit the sky off to the west, and thunder boomed nearby. Or maybe it was just his heart thundering in his chest as slowly he began to make love to her.

JACK WOKE sometime before daylight. The storm had passed. He could hear the gentle drip of the leaves and Chelsea's soft breathing.

He rolled over, careful not to wake her. She lay curled next to him, her eyes closed, lashes dark against her creamy skin, her face composed and peaceful. The sheet was down around her waist, exposing the smooth womanly curves.

She looked vulnerable and he felt suddenly both possessive and protective of her. The emotions surprised him. He'd never thought of Chelsea needing him.

He stared at her, awed and humbled by their lovemaking, and saddened. What was that line from that Drew Barrymore movie Sam loved so much? Something to the effect that a bird and a fish could fall in love, but where would they live?

Slowly, he leaned down and kissed her bare shoulder, then pulled the sheet up over her. She turned in her sleep, curling herself against him like a spoon, and he breathed in the intoxicating scent of her as though it were his last breath.

"I'm afraid," he whispered, not sure she could hear him—hoping she couldn't, but needing to say the words. "When I left the Wishing Tree I promised myself I would make new dreams and I would accomplish them if it killed me. I have. It's *almost* killed me. But as hard as I tried, I never could forget you. I want this to work, Chelsea."

For a few seconds all he heard was rain dripping from the eaves.

"It will work, Jack, you'll see." She snuggled against him and he closed his eyes, praying she was right because he couldn't imagine going back to a life without her.

CHAPTER FIFTEEN

JACK WOKE to pounding—and Chelsea in his arms. Both took him by surprise, more like part of a dream than reality.

But the pounding didn't quit. And with Chelsea snuggled against him, her body warm, lush and silky, her skin scented with their lovemaking, the last thing he wanted to do was get up and answer the door.

"Jack? I think there's someone at the door," Chelsea said sleepily, nuzzling her face into the hollow of his neck.

No kidding. He glanced at the clock over the stove—it was 7:00 a.m. Who in the world—?

Sam? He sat up with a jerk. But why would she be knocking? Why wouldn't she just come in? There was a thought. The last thing he wanted Sam to do was catch him in bed with Chelsea. Or any other woman.

The moment his bare feet touched the floor, reality hit him between the eyes. What in the hell had he done? And how was he going to explain this to Sam? Especially after he'd told her the birds and bees didn't get "together" until they were committed to each other.

"Just a minute!" he called as he scrambled to pull on his jeans. It was way too early in the morning for Sam unless something was wrong.

Chelsea sat up in the bed, pulling the sheet over her breasts, blinking awake.

He motioned for her to stay where she was as he opened the door, blinded at first by the sunshine.

Sam? He just caught a glimpse of her and Becky disappearing around the corner of the Harpers' trailer, both running fast, leaving a trail of giggles behind them. His daughter the practical joker.

He started to close the door when he spotted the bag sitting on the step. Leaning down, he picked it up. On the side of the bag, printed in Sam's handwriting, were the words: "For Dad and Chelsea." Then in smaller print: "I hope Chelsea likes lemon-filled doughnuts. Love, Sam." He felt a rush of love for his matchmaking daughter—and a gut-wrenching worry he'd just hurt her.

"Who is it?" Chelsea whispered.

"The doughnut fairies," he said, closing the door. "Sam and Becky left us a present."

Chelsea smiled. "We should get the two of them and take them someplace fun."

"Chelsea, we need to talk," he said. "I don't know what I was thinking—"

"Yes, you do. Jack, didn't last night prove anything to you?"

"That I have no willpower when it comes to you," he said disagreeably, feeling as if he'd let them all down.

She reached to take the bag of doughnuts from him, then took his hand and pulled him onto the bed again. "I think last night was a little more than that," she said quietly, her gaze holding his.

He nodded. "But it didn't solve the problem between us."

"That I'm rich and you're just a poor rodeo cowboy?"

"It's a little more complicated than that."

"But it doesn't have to be. There *has* to be a way. I'll do whatever it takes, Jack."

God, she was beautiful, sitting propped against the pillows, the sheet pulled up over her naked body. But he knew now what was under that sheet. After last night, he knew her body as well as his own.

He wanted to tell her how much he loved her, how much he wanted her in his life, how he would do anything to make this work, but he couldn't. Not yet. Not until he figured out a way for them to be together more than a night.

Just the thought of waking up next to her every morning made him ache with longing.

She handed him a doughnut. "There's orange juice, too."

He took a bite of the pastry.

"Lemon-filled doughnuts are my favorite," she said.

"You have lemon filling—" with his tongue, he leaned over to lick the corner of her lips "—right there."

She caught her breath, her lips parting.

It was a combustible situation. Chelsea completely naked. Him only in his jeans. Their reaction was immediate—and explosive.

Her eyes darkened as if the contact had ignited a fire she couldn't put out. Hungrily, he dropped his mouth to hers, penetrating her with his tongue as he drew her to him, his hands cupping her bare bottom, pressing her into him. They made slow, sweet love again, then just held each other as if there was a storm raging inside the motor home.

Maybe there is a way, Chelsea. But it would have to wait until he took her back to San Antonio. What was another day after waiting this long?

CHELSEA'S CELL PHONE woke them both a little later. She fumbled for it, answering with a groggy, "Hello?"

"Did I wake you?" Dylan asked, sounding surprised.

She glanced at the clock over the stove. Almost ten. Geez. "No," she fibbed, sitting up. "What's going on?"

"You haven't heard then? C. J. Crocker is dead and Ace Winters is wanted for questioning by the police. I guess Crocker regained consciousness for a short period of time. Now the police are looking for Ace, but he's disappeared."

She turned to look out the window. Terri Lyn's truck and camper were gone. Ace. Had Crocker named Ace as the killer?

Jack raised a brow in question.

"Until Ace's found, lay low, okay?" Dylan hung up.

Chelsea flipped off her cell phone and told Jack what Dylan had said.

Jack looked shocked and distressed. He glanced toward the spot where Terri Lyn's truck and camper had been. "Ace. Why doesn't that surprise me?" He was silent a moment. "Let's go get Sam. I was thinking maybe we'd stop in Fort Worth on our way to San Antonio."

"Jack," Chelsea said. "Ashley Garrett is getting married Saturday and I was thinking—"

"Ashley? Not that little imp who lived on the ranch next to yours?"

"Dylan's little sister. She's twenty-four and she's marrying a lawyer named Kyle Blackstone—he lives in the same high-rise in San Antonio. It's kind of a long story, but Ashley discovered a baby on Kyle's doorstep and helped him look after it. Along the way they fell in love."

"Was it this guy's baby?" Jack asked. "Sounds like a familiar story to me."

"I thought you might relate to the situation," Chelsea said with a smile. "But no, Kyle isn't the father of the child. Nor do they know who the mother is."

"Well, whose baby is it?" Jack asked, obviously intrigued.

"A man named Mitch Barnes. I don't know much about him, other than he's an FBI agent who lived in the same building as Kyle."

Comprehension registered in Jack's eyes. "So whoever left the baby left her on the wrong doorstep." He shook his head. "What a mess."

"It gets better. When Kyle found out he wasn't the father, he asked Mitch for help, hoping he could use his FBI connections rather than turn the baby over to social services. A doll had been left with Hope—that's what Mitch renamed her—and Mitch recognized it right away. He suspected the mother was a woman he'd met in Rio." Jack's interest was promising, so she added, "It's an amazing story. Maybe we'll get to hear it when we meet Mitch at the wedding."

Jack hadn't missed the fact she'd said "we'll." "That is, if you..." She could see he was more than hesitant.

"Chelsea, you and I have a past. We can't ignore that. If we have any hope of a future together, then we have to face it. That's one reason I wanted to go to San Antonio."

"To see my brother," she said.

"Don't get your hopes up that your brother is going to accept me," he warned. "This wedding might not go like you're expecting."

She stared at him. "You don't know my brother. Or my friends."

He said nothing, but his gaze said, *We'll see about that.*

Chelsea called to have her car delivered to San Antonio while Jack took care of canceling his ride in Oklahoma City. Then he went to get Sam and thank the Harpers, and tell everyone about C.J. The clown would be missed by everyone in the rodeo community.

When they returned, Chelsea told Sam, "Thanks for the doughnuts and the orange juice."

The little girl shrugged and smiled as if it hadn't been anything, but she turned to her father, an expectant look on her face.

"I especially liked the lemon-filled doughnuts," he said. "They turned out to be Chelsea's favorite. How about that? But I was surprised to see you up so early in the morning."

"I used to get up that early every day when I went to school," Sam said. Obviously she was more interested in how things were going between her dad and Chelsea. She glanced down the hallway, saw Chelsea's overnight bag still packed from yesterday. "You aren't leaving, are you?" she asked Chelsea, sounding worried.

"You and I need to talk," Jack said.

Chelsea started to excuse herself, but Jack stopped her.

"About Chelsea and me..." he began.

"I know all about it," Sam said. "Mrs. Harper told me that you need someone to share your life with because I won't always be around to take care of you."

"Well, Chelsea and I have some things to work out," he explained.

"I know. Mrs. Harper told me about that, too," Sam replied. "But she said that if the two of you really love each other, then everything will work out."

"She did?" Jack shook his head, then seemed to give up on it. "Chelsea wants us to go to a wedding with her."

"A wedding?" Sam looked hopeful.

"It's a wedding for a friend of hers in San Antonio, so we're going to head that way today. I thought we'd stop in Six Flags if you think you'd like that."

Sam acted as if he'd just offered her the moon. Her gaze flew to Chelsea. "The three of us?"

"The three of us," Jack said.

"Great! Wait until I tell Becky," she cried.

"Hold on, now, don't go around telling people that Chelsea and I—"

"I'll just tell Becky about Six Flags!" She took off at a run with Jack calling after her to be right back since they would be leaving for Fort Worth.

When Chelsea looked at Jack, he seemed relieved. He hadn't had to try to explain their relationship. Chelsea suspected he hadn't quite decided what it was yet.

THEY DROVE to Fort Worth, but Jack insisted they get a hotel near Six Flags rather than stay in the motor home. He rented two rooms, one for his "girls" and the other for himself.

"Sam, you act as if you've never stayed in a hotel before," Jack said to his excited daughter.

"I never have!" she cried. "We even have a pool! Can we go swimming, please, please, please?"

"I have to get something to wear if we're going swimming," Chelsea said with a laugh. "There's a shop downstairs."

"I thought we'd go out to dinner," Jack suggested. "Maybe someplace nice."

She smiled at him, wondering if he was doing all of this for her? Or for Sam? She hoped it wouldn't set him back financially but knew better than to offer to pay. This was obviously something he wanted to do.

Her pleasure in their outing was clouded as she thought of the two murders. She wouldn't rest easy until Ace was found, but she refused to let it spoil this time with Jack.

Sam surprised her by wanting to come along shopping

when Chelsea asked her. Sam sashayed through the racks
of clothing, touching the different fabrics before hastily
moving on.

Chelsea watched her, wondering if she was curious
about "girl" clothes. Even as a tomboy at that age, Chelsea remembered being interested.

Luckily she'd had friends and friends' moms. Sam had
Abigail to talk to about such things, but only when their
schedules coincided. And there was Jack, but what did he
know about girl stuff?

"I didn't see any dresses in your suitcase," Chelsea
said to Sam, wading in tentatively.

Sam looked up in surprise to find Chelsea behind her.
She jerked her hand back from a dress she'd been eyeing.
"A *dress?*"

"You do own a dress, right?"

"No." Sam rolled her eyes as if to ask what she would
need a dress for.

"You'll need one for the wedding."

Sam looked torn. "Dresses are…gross. They're so…
frilly and girlie."

"They don't have to be," Chelsea said carefully.
"They can be sleek, stylish and very sophisticated."

Sam seemed to consider that.

Chelsea bought a swimming suit and a dress for dinner,
trying not to get her hopes up, and yet they floated bright
and buoyant as party balloons.

After a swim in the hotel pool, she showered and
dressed, adding a dab of perfume behind her ears and
between her breasts, taking pains with her makeup. She
wanted everything to be perfect tonight.

She glanced over in surprise to see Sam standing in the
bathroom doorway watching her apply her makeup.

The girl looked uncomfortable at being caught. Chelsea

glanced down at the perfume bottle in her hand. "Would you like some?"

Sam looked stricken.

"Just a dab? I promise it won't make you smell too much like a girl."

Sam answered with a shy smile. "Just a little dab."

Chelsea touched her fingertip to the opening, then behind Sam's ear.

"It smells good." Sam sounded surprised. She studied the array of cosmetics on the counter.

"Would you like to try, say, a little blush?" Chelsea offered.

"I don't want to look...*funny.*"

Chelsea smiled, realizing that without a mother around, Sam probably had never seen anyone put on makeup except the rodeo clowns. "Here, let me show you," she said, motioning to the toilet seat. Sam sat down and seemed to brace herself. "The trick is not to put on so much that you look...funny."

Deftly Chelsea applied a little blush, a touch of lipstick and a dab of mascara to Sam's features. "What do you think?"

Sam looked in the mirror and laughed, then moved closer. "My eyes are bigger."

"What are you trying to do?" Jack demanded, making them both jump as he came through the door connecting the two rooms. He stood glaring at them, a look of shock on his face.

"We were just playing with a little makeup," Chelsea said, surprised by his obvious disapproval.

"Wash that off at once!" he ordered his daughter.

"But, Dad!" Sam protested.

"What were you thinking?" he demanded through gritted teeth as he motioned her into the adjacent room. "She's too young for makeup."

"Of course she is. But she isn't too young to experiment with it, Jack," Chelsea said, keeping her voice down. She could hear Sam crying softly in the bathroom, the water running. "Girls play dress-up. She was just curious and we were having some fun. Why are you behaving this way?"

"She's just a child!"

"She's a nine-year-old *girl*, Jack. Of course she's going to be curious about girl stuff."

"She wasn't before you showed up," he challenged.

"She was, Jack, but you just didn't know it. Girls experiment with makeup. Occasionally, they even wear dresses. Sam told me she doesn't even have a dress."

"A dress on the rodeo circuit?"

"Jack, she's a girl. Most girls learn this stuff from their mothers. There is nothing wrong with—"

"Sam doesn't have a mother," he snapped, "and I don't want her getting hurt when this thing between us doesn't work out."

Chelsea stared at him in disbelief. "*When* this doesn't work out?" She shook her head, so angry she could spit. First he'd overreacted about the makeup, and now—

Sam came out of the bathroom, her face scrubbed clean and her eyes red from crying. Chelsea wanted to shake Jack. But instead she turned to the girl. "I'm sorry, Sam. This is all my fault."

Sam shook her head. "Can I go watch TV until we have to go?" she asked her father.

Chelsea also turned to look up at him, her gaze accusing.

Jack looked properly chastised. "Sure, honey," he said to his daughter as he brushed a lock of her hair from her damp face. "I'm sorry. I guess I don't know much about this girl stuff."

"It's okay, Dad." She slipped past him to the other room, leaving them alone.

"Don't bother to say it," Jack grumbled.

Chelsea tilted a brow.

"I'm sorry, all right?"

She could see that he *was* sorry, but the incident had spoiled their evening. Worse, it showed just how little faith Jack had in their relationship working.

JACK WISHED he could turn back the clock. He couldn't believe the way he'd overreacted. But just seeing his little girl experimenting with makeup had terrified him. How was he ever going to manage the teenage years?

To make it up, he took them to a nice steakhouse he'd heard about. Both Sam and Chelsea gave him the silent treatment. When he thought about it, he wasn't sure what had upset him the most—the idea of Sam growing up before his very eyes, or worry that he hadn't given his daughter what she really needed. A mother.

Damn it, he'd done the best he could, but what did he know about all the female stuff? Wasn't Sam too young to care about any of that? Apparently not.

After they ate, Sam went to look at the fish swimming in a large aquarium along one side of the restaurant.

"About earlier with Sam," he began.

"It's all right," Chelsea said.

"It's just that…" He shook his head.

"That as long as Sam doesn't act like a girl, you can handle it?" she guessed.

Good guess. "What do I know about what girls need?"

She smiled slowly. "Obviously nothing."

"Damn it, Chelsea, I thought taking her on the circuit

was the best thing for her. I'd considered leaving her with my mother so she could go to school and have a woman in her life, but—"

"Jack, you did the right thing," Chelsea said, reaching across the table to take his hand. "Sam has turned out beautifully. You did a great job!"

But now she needs more than I can give her, he thought. *She needs a mother.*

CHAPTER SIXTEEN

THE NEXT MORNING, after a long, lonely night alone in his king-size bed without even the sound of Sam's little-girl snores close by, Jack woke to find both females talking to him again.

To his surprise, his mistake from the night before seemed to be forgiven. Or maybe it was just the prospect of a day at Six Flags.

They spent the day going on rides, eating corn dogs and cotton candy, walking until even Sam started to get tired. Jack couldn't remember ever laughing as much as he did with Chelsea and Sam. He could see that the two had bonded. He knew if he wasn't able to work things out with Chelsea, it would break his daughter's heart. And his own.

He couldn't just keep ignoring the problem. His last ride had put him in the top world standings. Plus he'd taken home a purse of more than five thousand dollars. That might be chicken feed to Chelsea, but all he needed was a couple more good rides and he would be in the National Finals. If his luck continued, he'd bring home another world championship and then…

He dared not even think about then. He'd promised Sam a horse. That meant a ranch and leaving the circuit. But it couldn't be just any ranch. And he wasn't ready to settle for less than his dreams.

So he had to keep riding bulls. But he knew if he did,

he could lose Chelsea. And for his and Sam's sake, he couldn't let that happen. Somehow he had to find a way around the problem.

"I had a great time today," Chelsea said on the way to San Antonio that evening.

"I had a great time, too," Jack replied. He'd noticed that Chelsea seemed down tonight, as if something were bothering her. He figured it was going back to San Antonio, back to her friends and family. Surely by now she must have realized that he wouldn't fit in. That she'd made a mistake by thinking she wanted him in her life— let alone a nine-year-old girl who wasn't even hers.

"I know Sam really enjoyed it," she said distractedly. Sam was asleep in the back. She'd gone out like a light as soon as they hit the road.

"I thought we could have a talk after the wedding tomorrow night, just the two of us."

She glanced over at him, the look in her eyes so hopeful it broke his heart.

CHELSEA WAITED for him to say more. He hadn't mentioned anything about their "problem," but she wasn't foolish enough to think that just because they'd made love, their troubles were behind them.

If only they could get past what had happened ten years ago. Now that C. J. Crocker had cleared Jack's name regarding the rustling… But she knew she was only kidding herself. The heart of the problem was the Wishing Tree. Jack didn't ever want to go back to her family's ranch. There were too many awful memories for him and he could never be happy living there with her. But she couldn't bear the thought of never returning to her home.

She'd thought about nothing else last night as she had

lain alone in her queen-size bed, Sam sleeping in the ad-jacent bed, a reminder of everything she had to lose.

If she wanted Jack and Sam, she would have to pay the ultimate price. She would have to give up the Wishing Tree, but that would be like cutting out a part of her heart.

She'd turned her face into the pillow and cried, praying there was another way. She'd give up anything but the Wishing Tree. Anything but Jack and Sam.

But this morning, when she'd opened her eyes, no other answer had come to her. And as they neared San Antonio, she knew it had come down to a choice between the land and life she loved—and the man and child she loved. What kind of choice was that?

She was startled when her cell phone rang. Answering it, she hoped it was news of Ace's arrest. She didn't like the idea that he was out there somewhere.

"Let me talk to Jack," said a familiar male voice.

"Cody?"

"Jack first, then you can make me eat crow, okay, Chels?" Cody snapped.

She handed the phone to Jack with a shrug.

Jack's side of the conversation was mostly "Yes," "No" and "I understand." When he was finished he handed the phone back.

"Yes?" she asked.

"I apologized," Cody told her.

"I know how difficult that must have been for you," she said, filled with pride in her brother.

"I was wrong. Dylan told me that Crocker had named Ace and cleared Jack. I'm man enough to admit it when I'm wrong."

Any other time she might have argued that. "Thanks."

"Yeah. See you at the wedding. It sounds like you'll be there with Jack."

Chelsea realized she hadn't mentioned Sam to anyone. "Yes, Jack and I will be there, and Sam."

"Sam?" Cody asked.

"Jack's nine-year-old daughter." She hung up and gave Jack an I-told-you-so smile.

Jack nodded, smiling back at her, but she could see that he still wasn't convinced Cody Jensen would ever accept him. Unfortunately, she wasn't all that sure, either. And ultimately, that raised the bigger problem between them: the Wishing Tree Ranch.

"I NEED TO BUY a dress for the wedding," Chelsea said the next morning after breakfast and another long night of anguish.

Jack had been quiet all morning and she wondered if he regretted saying he'd go to the wedding. Sam was the only one who seemed happy. She loved the expensive hotel Jack had insisted on, the ornate rooms that overlooked the city, the mints on the pillows.

"Sam, do you want to come along?" she asked.

Sam looked to her father.

"Go with Chelsea and get something appropriate to wear for the wedding," Jack said. "I have to take care of some business, then get something to wear myself." He started to hand Chelsea a credit card.

"Would you mind if I bought Sam a dress?" she asked. "I'd really like it to be my treat since it's her first one."

He seemed to hesitate, then nodded. "That's very…nice of you."

"Coming?" Chelsea asked Sam.

"Comin'," Sam said, still looking at her dad.

"It won't take long," Chelsea assured Sam when they reached her Mercedes, which had been delivered the night before. She had a dress in mind, something that would knock Jack off his feet.

When they reached the store, Chelsea let Sam look at the dresses while she made a quick phone call.

"I'll only be a minute," she promised. She watched Sam amble uncomfortably around the store, looking out of place. Her heart went out to the girl and she promised herself that she would do whatever it took to get that look off Sam's face.

"Thank you," she said the moment her brother answered the phone.

"Chelsea, I assume?" he replied, his tone light.

"Who else would be thanking you?"

"It's just such a new occurrence. And you already thanked me last night."

"It meant a lot to Jack," she told him.

"I was wrong about him being involved with Ray Dale and rustling," Cody said.

"You were wrong about him, Cody. I'm in love with him and his daughter."

"I kind of figured," he said, not sounding happy about it.

"There's something I need from you."

She could almost hear Cody brace himself. She looked over at Sam, her courage wavering but only for a moment. "I want you to buy out my half of the ranch." Even as she said the words, she could feel her heart break.

"There must be something wrong with this phone," Cody said.

"I know you thought Jack was just after the ranch, but the truth is, the ranch and my money are the problem between us right now," she explained. "The only solution I can come up with to solve it is to do away with them."

"Chelsea, do you realize what you're saying?" Cody

asked, still sounding in shock. "Give up the ranch for…a man?"

She laughed. "I know it sounds odd—"

"Oh, it's more than odd. It's nuts. And I won't do it."

"Cody, I love this man. If giving up the Wishing Tree is the answer, then I'll do it. I've already spoken to our lawyer. He's drawing up the necessary papers. All you'll have to do at Ashley's wedding is sign them. Please."

"Sis, I know how much you love the Wishing Tree."

"Yes, but I love Jack and Sam more." There, she'd said it. It was done. She hung up and fought back the sobs that threatened inside her. Taking a deep breath, she walked over to Sam. "Want to help me find a dress?"

"I guess."

Chelsea found the dress almost at once. It was exactly what she had in mind. She took it into the dressing room while Sam opted to wait just outside.

Once she'd pulled on the dress, she looked at herself in the mirror, surprised by the woman who stared back at her. She'd changed. Grown in ways she'd least expected this week. She'd decided to give up the Wishing Tree, but would it be enough?

When she came out, she found Sam wandering through the racks of dresses, fingering a fabric here, touching a bit of lace there. Chelsea watched her for a moment, then asked the sales associate where she could find the girls' department.

"Have you ever played dress-up?" Chelsea asked as they wandered through the girls' dresses.

Sam shook her head.

"It's fun. Makes you feel like someone else."

The look Sam gave her was uncertain.

Chelsea found a dress that suited Sam and held it up. The little girl stared at the dress, then Chelsea. "Okay."

"Here, let's do something fun with your hair, too," Chelsea suggested once they were in the large dressing room together. She wound Sam's braid up on top of her head, tucking in the end to secure it. "There." Then she pulled the dress from the hanger and waited until Sam had slipped out of her shirt and jeans before handing it to her.

Sam's fingers trembled as she slid the dress over her head. Chelsea stepped over to zip it.

"It feels...funny."

"Funny ha-ha, or funny uncomfortable?" she asked.

"Just funny, different." Sam turned in a circle to let Chelsea see the dress.

Chelsea's eyes widened, a small gasp of surprise and delight escaping her lips. The transformation was magical. With her hair up and no cowboy hat shadowing her face, Sam's high cheekbones were more prominent, her eyes larger. "Sam, you look...beautiful."

Sam blushed as she glanced hesitantly toward the full-length mirror behind Chelsea.

"Are you ready?" Chelsea asked, seeing the fear in the girl's eyes as Sam nodded.

With her gaze fixed on the hem of her dress, Sam slowly stepped past Chelsea to the mirror. Her eyes widened in alarm, her expression stricken.

She hated the dress! "Sam?" Chelsea whispered behind her.

"It doesn't look like me." The words sounded awed, her eyes huge and misty.

Chelsea held her breath as she watched Sam study the girl in the mirror, turning this way and that, her gaze never leaving the image in the glass. Gone was the tomboy in her well-worn jeans, western shirts, boots and cowboy hat. In her place was a princess.

"What do you think?" Sam asked after a moment.

"I think the dress looks wonderful on you," she said.

"No, what do you think Dad will say about it?"

That was the question, wasn't it? "How could he not love it since it makes you look so beautiful?"

Sam grinned and shook her head at the idea of being beautiful, as if it had never occurred to her any more than wearing a dress. Then she bit her lower lip. "I hope Dad likes it." Her voice sounded small and scared, as if she were remembering his reaction to the makeup.

If Jack didn't like his daughter in this dress, Chelsea would wring his stupid neck. But she also remembered the makeup fiasco and began to worry a little.

"I'd better take it off," Sam said.

"Would you prefer to look for one you like better?" she asked after Sam had dressed again in her shirt, jeans and boots.

Sam seemed surprised by the question. "No, I like this one. But is it too expensive?"

Chelsea shook her head. Nothing would have been too expensive for this little girl. "It's my treat."

Without warning, Sam threw her arms around Chelsea's neck and hugged her tightly. "I love the dress."

Tears welled in Chelsea's eyes as she held the girl in her arms, knowing she'd made the right decision.

The sales associate wrapped the dress in tissue paper, then put it carefully in a box. Sam watched the process closely, as if she didn't want her dress out of her sight for fear it would disappear.

Chelsea handed Sam her box to carry out to the car. The girl clutched it to her and smiled to herself as she walked ahead of Chelsea through the store, no longer intimidated.

After they got Sam some shoes to wear with the dress,

they drove back to the hotel. The realization of what she'd done, giving up the Wishing Tree, was sinking in. Chelsea tried to imagine her future. Even if it meant living in the motor home, she knew she would do it. It wouldn't mean giving up her career—since she had a head for numbers, she could help Jack with all his scheduling and keep running stats for him.

She thought about the late-night talk Jack had suggested after the wedding. Did he have something special he wanted to tell her?

She'd wait until then to tell him about what she'd done with the ranch.

CHAPTER SEVENTEEN

"ARE YOU READY?" Sam called from the adjoining hotel room.

Ready as he'd ever be. He was anxious about the wedding. He'd be seeing people he'd hoped never to see again, people he'd resented for years. And he'd be taking Sam into the middle of it all.

"Ready," he said. Jack had vowed that even if Sam was wearing a little makeup, he wasn't going to say a word. He wasn't going to let anything spoil tonight.

"Just a minute," Chelsea called back. He heard giggling. "We're almost ready."

Several minutes later, Chelsea opened the door a crack. "You'd better sit down," she warned.

"And close your eyes, okay, Dad?" Sam called.

"Okay," he said. Sam sounded older, different. He felt a little scared as he sat down on the edge of the bed and closed his eyes. He could hear the swish of fabric and smell Chelsea's distinct perfume.

"All right, you can open your eyes," Chelsea said.

He opened his eyes, his gaze going first to Chelsea, who stood a little to his right in an electric-blue dress that looked classy and sexy at the same time.

His gaze quickly went to Sam as she came out and he caught his breath, tears rushing to his eyes. She stopped, frozen as a statue, waiting for his reaction. Her hair was wound around on top of her head and she wore a pretty white dress and white sandals. She looked taller than he remembered her being, and so pretty. So grown-up. She also looked like she might cry if he didn't say something.

"Honey, you are *beautiful*," he said, his voice breaking.

Sam burst into a smile and rushed to him, throwing her arms around his neck. "I thought you wouldn't like it."

"I love it," he said. "You look like a little lady."

She released her hold on him and brushed at the front of her dress. "Chelsea picked out one that wasn't too girlie."

"The dress is perfect. Just like you."

She blushed but looked pleased, her eyes glowing. "Don't you think Chelsea looks beautiful, too?"

"Why don't you get us an elevator?" he said, smiling at her. "We'll be right with you. I have to tell Chelsea how beautiful she looks."

Sam laughed and went racing out to get an elevator.

"You're upset with me," Chelsea said the moment Sam was gone.

He shook his head, shaken. "I just didn't expect to see her looking like that. Thank you."

"For what?"

"For helping Sam. For the dress. For…everything." He pulled her to him and slowly lowered his mouth to hers for a quick kiss. "Especially for…everything." He chuckled and, putting his arm around her, walked her to the elevator. "By the way, you look incredible!"

He felt off balance and had ever since he'd made love to her. But his heart—and the look on Sam's face when she was around Chelsea—told him he was making the right decision.

He had yet to discuss that decision with Chelsea, though, and wondered why he continued to put it off.

Tonight, after the wedding, he'd talk to her. Chelsea had said she'd do whatever it took for them to be together. He just hoped she meant it.

THE UPSCALE San Antonio restaurant had been reserved for the wedding party. Candles glowed amid an array of pretty flowers and greenery reminding Chelsea of spring.

"Wow," Sam said as they were led to their seats.

Chelsea felt the curious gazes of people she knew. No doubt everyone was wondering who Jack and Sam were. She glanced over at Jack. "Did I tell you how handsome you look in your tux?" she whispered.

He smiled. "Thank you. You remembered that blue is my favorite color on you, didn't you?" he whispered back.

She smiled with pleasure. He seemed at ease and enjoying Sam's excitement.

Once they'd found their table, Chelsea led Jack and Sam over to the head table to meet the Garretts. The ceremony itself had been held earlier that afternoon, and the bride and groom were across the room mingling with guests. Chelsea spotted Cody in conversation with Dylan. She wondered how Jack felt about seeing her brother again, but he appeared unaffected.

"Hello, Jack," Cody said, extending his hand. "It's good to see you."

Chelsea could have kissed him.

Dylan got to his feet to shake hands with Jack and make introductions. "This is my father, William Garrett, my sister Lily, her baby daughter Elizabeth and her husband Cole, Max Santana, the foreman at the Double G, and his fiancée, Rachel Blair, and Gracie Fipps, our housekeeper and the best cook in Texas."

"This is my friend Jackson Robinson and his daughter,

Sam—Samantha," Chelsea corrected, even though some of the guests had known Jack when he'd worked on their ranch.

"All the other weddings I've been to, they got married on horses," Sam announced, and everyone laughed good-naturedly.

After the usual small talk, mostly about Jack's world championship bull riding, Chelsea, Jack and Sam returned to their own table with Cody, and were introduced to Mitch Barnes and Ernie Brooks.

The wedding dinner was the best Texas could offer, and when the bride and groom came by to welcome Chelsea, she thanked her good friend Ashley for accommodating the two extra guests at such last-minute notice.

Ashley gave Chelsea a quick hug and whispered in her ear, "I'm really hoping you'll be next so I'll do anything I can to make it happen!"

If only, Chelsea thought wistfully.

After dinner, Dylan pulled Chelsea aside for a moment.

"Ace Winters still hasn't been found, but his girlfriend, a woman named Terri Lyn Kessler, has reported him missing," he told her. "She said he didn't show for his ride in Oklahoma City. He was supposed to travel with her from Kansas City, but never returned after saying he had to meet someone and would be back. No one has seen him."

"You think he's taken off?" Chelsea asked.

"It's beginning to look that way," Dylan said. "Right now he's wanted in connection with three deaths, Ray Dale's, Tucker McCray's and C. J. Crocker's. I heard from my source inside the police department that before Crocker died, he told officers that he was attacked from behind near the corrals. He named Ace as the rustler on your ranch and said Ace had threatened him if he talked to anyone. The police also found evidence at Tucker McCray's ranch that ties Ace to that death as well.''

She felt queasy just thinking about flying with Ace that day. ''He seems so...normal.''

''Often killers are just guys who screw up and commit a murder,'' Dylan said. ''In Ace's case, he tried to cover it up with more murders.''

''It just seems odd that for ten years he'd gotten away with Ray Dale's murder and now he seems to be making a lot of mistakes,'' Chelsea said.

''He just lucked out ten years ago. Now he has a lot more to lose. He's probably acting on impulse and panicking. It happens. Just be really careful until he's caught, all right?''

She smiled. ''Thanks.''

''Save me a dance later.''

As soon as she returned to the table, she told Jack what Dylan had said.

''I guess I find it easier to believe than you do,'' Jack said. ''I know Ace, and I've never trusted him.''

They saw Sam waving to them that it was time to go into an adjacent room for the dance. As they went through the formal receiving line, Ashley threw her arms around Jack's neck.

''I've forgiven you for that time you turned a hose on me,'' she teased.

''I'd forgotten about that,'' Jack said, laughing. He glanced at Chelsea. ''As I remember, you were spying on us in the barn.''

Ashley's green eyes twinkled. ''Oh, yes, I remember it well.'' She kissed Chelsea's cheek and whispered, ''I'm throwing my bouquet right to you. Don't miss it!''

Cody had saved a table for them in the reception room. Jack had expected to feel awkward around these people from his past, but it hadn't happened. They treated him like a long-lost friend, and Sam was having a great time. She'd met a couple of girls about her age and had gone off to help decorate the bride and groom's car.

He actually began to relax. What had changed? Was this Chelsea's doing—finally being cleared of all that rustling business? Or was it that *he'd* changed?

As the band struck up a tune, the conversation turned to weddings and marriage, two things Jack really didn't want to talk about just yet. But it seemed that Max Santana, the foreman at the Double G, was getting married soon.

"That just leaves you, Dylan," Max joked.

"And Dad," Dylan pointed out, indicating his father, a handsome man in his sixties.

"Yes," Lily said, teasing. "I've seen the way you look at Gracie Fipps." The Garrett housekeeper was up dancing with a nice-looking friend of the groom.

"Gracie is a great cook—and a wonderful friend," William informed them, "but that's all, so don't go getting any ideas. Some of us are just fine being single, thank you very much."

Everyone laughed.

The band broke into a tune Jack had requested. "Would you like to dance?" he asked Chelsea. It was a slow dance, a song he thought she might remember. He wanted to get away from the table before the marriage conversation turned in their direction.

Chelsea looked pleased that he'd suggested dancing as he took her hand and led her out onto the floor. "You remembered," she said.

"How can I forget?" And yet he thought he finally might be able to forget all but the good times they'd shared. He was willing to admit that he'd brought on a lot of the problems he'd had back then.

They danced to the next song as well. Then Dylan cut in and Jack went to check on Sam.

When he found his daughter, he led her out on the dance floor. "May I have this dance?" he asked.

She looked stricken. "I don't know how to dance. I'll look silly."

"Don't worry," he said. "Just move your feet back and forth like this."

Chelsea had seen them come out on the floor. She turned to smile at Sam. "Just do what your dad does. This is how we all learned to dance."

Sam didn't look convinced, but she watched Jack's feet for a moment, then followed his movements. "I feel dumb."

"You're beautiful and a quick study," he said, meaning every word of it.

She smiled shyly.

"By the way, you're dancing," he added.

She stumbled and he laughed as he got her started again. "Chelsea's right," she said. "It's not hard."

Chelsea, he realized, was right about a lot of things. He glanced over to where she was dancing with Dylan Garrett. Their conversation seemed to have turned serious, and he wondered what they were talking about.

One of Sam's new friends signaled to her. "Can I go, Dad?"

"Sure." He watched her leave, then moved toward Chelsea, unable to wait until the dance ended to have her in his arms again. He realized he'd put off talking to her about their future long enough.

"I FORGOT TO tell you, I finally got everything back on Jack," Dylan said as he and Chelsea danced. "Chelsea?"

She jerked her attention back to Dylan. "Sorry, I was just..."

"Yes," he said, smiling. "Looking at Jack dancing with his daughter."

"Yes," she admitted. "Now, what were you saying?"

"Jack. I'm impressed by what he'd done."

"His bull riding," she said with pride. "Seven world championships in eight years."

"No, I meant his net worth. It's quite impressive, especially given that he's done it in less than ten years."

"His what?"

Dylan looked puzzled. "I just assumed you knew. Jack grossed over two hundred thousand dollars most years on the circuit. He invested the bulk of the money in high-rate stocks and switched them to less risky ventures before the big drop in the market."

Her feet stopped moving to the music. "Are you telling me that Jack has money?"

"He's wealthy by most people's standards," Dylan said. "You didn't know?"

"No, I didn't." The old motor home, the tight traveling budget, the worn jeans. He let her think he was poor, while at the same time giving her a hard time about *her* money.

"Excuse me," Jack said from behind her. "Mind if I cut in?"

Chelsea smiled at Dylan. "Thank you. If you'll excuse me..." Then she turned to face Jack.

JACK KNEW at once that she was mad. He could tell by the glint in her brown eyes and the tight set of her jaw. "What's wrong?" he asked as he drew her into his arms.

"You have money."

"Yes?"

"Yes." She snapped. "You led me to believe you were *poor*."

"You came to that conclusion on your own," he defended.

"What else would I think, considering the way you live?" she demanded, obviously trying to keep her voice down.

"We live just fine, thank you."

"The point is, all this time you've been giving me a hard time about my money when you had money, a lot of money, of your own."

She had him there.

"Not as much as you by any means, but I've done all right."

When the music stopped, she stepped out of his arms. "My money was just an easy excuse, wasn't it? You've been using one excuse after another to prove you and I are wrong for each other. But you missed an obvious one. You don't love me enough to realize that it doesn't make any difference who has the money or who doesn't." With that she spun on her heel and headed toward the door.

He started after her, but had to stop to allow a waiter in with a dessert cart.

By the time he stepped out into the hall, Chelsea was gone. He couldn't leave without Sam, so he set off to find his daughter.

CHELSEA COULDN'T remember the last time she'd been so angry. Tears blinded her as she rushed out into the cool night air. She'd walked three blocks in the wrong direction before she'd realized what she was doing. Turning around, she headed back toward the restaurant and her car. She'd just rounded the dark side of the building when she saw a figure leaning against the wall out of the light. For just an instant, she thought it was Jack.

"Sis?"

Hurriedly wiping her eyes, she turned to face her brother. He'd obviously sneaked out here to get a breath of fresh air. He'd never been much for crowds.

"Are you all right?" he asked.

"Fine."

She couldn't fool Cody.

"Right. Let me guess. Jack?"

"I just found out he's made a small fortune the last ten years rodeoing."

Cody lifted a brow. "And that's a problem?"

"It is when he didn't bother to tell me about it," she snapped.

"Maybe he was worried that you'd only want him for his money," Cody said.

"Ha-ha."

"Did you tell him your plan to sell your half of the Wishing Tree to me?" her brother asked, looking concerned.

"No, it hasn't come up yet."

Cody shook his head. "It sounds to me like the two of you need to sit down and be honest with each other."

She looked at her brother in surprise.

He shrugged. "Don't get me wrong. I'm still not sure he's good enough for you, but then I can't think of any man I'd consider worthy of my little sister. The thing is, it's pretty obvious how you feel about this guy. So if Jack's the man you want..."

She threw her arms around her brother and squeezed as hard as she could. "He is, damn it."

Cody laughed. "You know, as big as the Wishing Tree

is, there's plenty of room for all of us. You don't have to sell your half.''

She'd left the papers in the glove box of her car. "Thanks. I appreciate that. But I could never get Jack to come back to the ranch. I'll get the papers. Meet you back inside?''

"There's no rush,'' Cody told her.

Chelsea shook her head. "I've made up my mind—I don't want to wait any longer.''

Cody nodded.

"If you see Jack—''

"I'll hog-tie him if I have to so the two of you can settle this once and for all,'' Cody said. "If he's going to be in this family, he's going to have to learn how to handle you.'' He grinned. "Not that you need handling, little sis.''

She shook her head, smiling, and headed for her car. That's when she saw the clown.

CHAPTER EIGHTEEN

CHELSEA WAS WRONG. Jack did love her enough. Enough to give up the one thing that had saved him ten years ago: rodeo. He'd planned to tell her tonight, after the wedding.

But now she'd stormed off. He glanced out the back door of the restaurant. Her car was still in the lot, so maybe she *hadn't* left. He went into the reception room to look for Sam, all the while facing some cold hard facts about himself.

After this week with Chelsea, he'd realized that the biggest obstacle was money. He'd been competing with her wealth and felt he had nothing to offer her. Now he saw how foolish his misplaced pride had been. He had no reason to be ashamed of his accomplishments, and the only thing that mattered was the fact that he loved her and couldn't bear facing the future without her.

He had enough money of his own to buy a nice-size ranch. Nothing as big as the Wishing Tree, but he knew of one for sale that was adjacent to Chelsea's ranch. He could almost afford it. Just a few more rides… This morning he'd made arrangements to lease it with the option to buy in the next year.

At first he'd balked at being that close to her family ranch. But he knew how much Chelsea would love being able to ride over and see her brother whenever she wanted. How much she would love being that close to the place she considered home.

It seemed like a decent compromise, but in order to afford it, he'd have to make it to the National Finals this year and win a few more large purses. He didn't want to use any of Chelsea's money to buy the ranch. Even now, he had to do this on his own. His only regret was not being honest with her about the money he'd made.

The problem was, he still didn't have much faith that she'd agree to another ranch. He knew she had her heart set on taking him and Sam back to the Wishing Tree.

"Just the man I want to see," Cody said as he almost collided with Jack.

"I take it you've seen Chelsea?" Jack said to him.

Cody grinned. "That's why you and I have to talk."

"I just need to find Sam first," Jack said, looking through the crowd for her.

"Daddy!"

They turned at Sam's cry to see her running toward them, out of breath and crying something about a clown and Chelsea.

Jack swung his daughter up into his arms. "Easy, honey," he said. "What's wrong?"

"The clown," Sam cried. "He took Chelsea."

"What clown?" Cody asked.

"A rodeo clown. He had C.J.'s face."

Jack's heart began to pound. A rodeo clown with a dead man's makeup?

Between sobs, Sam told them she'd seen the clown near Chelsea's car and went over, thinking it was C. J. Crocker. Then she remembered that he was dead. Scared, she'd dropped down beside another car to hide. She hadn't even seen Chelsea approach until the clown grabbed her and forced her into the car by putting something over her mouth. Before Sam could move, the clown jumped in and took off with Chelsea in the car.

"In her car?" Cody asked.

Sam nodded.

"Did he say anything to Chelsea?" Jack asked, his throat so dry he could barely speak.

"He said he was taking her to a wishing well."

Jack exchanged a look with Cody. The Wishing Tree. Dylan's sister Lily had approached and heard the last part of the conversation. "Samantha, why don't you stay here with me," she said quickly, exchanging an assuring look with Jack. "Your dad and Cody need to go get Chelsea."

"Is Dylan still around?" Cody asked Lily.

She shook her head. "He got a call about Lance Prescott and had to leave." Her look said the call had not been good, otherwise he would never have cut out on Ashley's wedding. "Do you want me to try to reach him or call the police?"

"Call the police," Cody said. "Tell them to head out to the ranch." He started toward the door. "My truck's right outside."

"I'm going with you," Jack said as he hugged Sam. "Stay with Lily. I'll be back with Chelsea."

"Don't worry," Lily said. "I'll take good care of her. She'll be at my house."

Jack followed Cody outside to his pickup, climbed into the passenger side and buckled up as Cody took off toward the Wishing Tree—a place Jack thought he'd never see again, but now couldn't wait to get to.

CHELSEA WOKE to a crack of thunder. She opened her eyes, at first seeing nothing but darkness, then the thin beam of a flashlight as it bobbed across the bunkhouse floor.

In the glow of the light, Chelsea realized she was lying on one of the beds in the bunkhouse at the Wishing Tree.

That surprised her. But not as much as the realization that her wrists were bound together with duct tape and the bunkhouse was being ransacked by the person with the flashlight.

She tried to sit up, but her head swam and her stomach roiled. Her mouth felt dust dry as she lay back down and tried to imagine how she'd gotten here.

"Finally awake, are you?"

The voice startled her, but not as much as the clown face that suddenly appeared in the beam of the flashlight. For just a split second, she thought it was C. J. Crocker come back from the dead.

But ghosts didn't abduct you from restaurant parking lots or drug you and tie you up with duct tape.

"Where is the evidence?" the clown demanded. "He said it was hidden in the bunkhouse."

Chelsea stared at the face in confusion. C. J. Crocker's clown face, but with the wrong voice.

"Who…?" Chelsea heard herself say, feeling groggy as the clown jerked her upright on the bed.

"Ace." The clown stepped closer, looking enough like Crocker to give her a chill. But the eyes were all wrong. Just like the voice. "Ace told me before he died. Told me the only other person who knew was you."

Ace was dead? Chelsea shook her head as she tried to understand why Roberta Crandell was standing over her with a flashlight in Crocker's costume.

The older woman went into the bathroom and came back with a wet towel. "Snap out of it," she said, squeezing the cold water over Chelsea's face. "I want that evidence. Now."

Chelsea shivered and sat up, still woozy. She glanced around the bunkhouse, trying to make sense of what Roberta was saying. "Evidence?"

"The evidence that proves Ray Dale was murdered?"

She blinked at Roberta. "Ace left evidence that he murdered Ray Dale?"

"Don't play dumb with me, Chelsea," Roberta snapped. "You know Ace didn't kill Ray Dale or we wouldn't be here right now and Ace wouldn't have been blackmailing me for the last ten years. If I'd known it was that little weasel, I'd have killed him years ago. The negatives. Where did he hide them?"

Ace had witnessed Ray Dale's murder and been black-mailing Roberta?

But then that meant Roberta— "You killed Ray Dale?"

"Just like you kill any rank animal that turns on you," she said with disgust.

"But I thought Ace—"

"The little weasel upped the ante, demanding more blackmail money," Roberta said with disgust. "You had to go and offer that ten-thousand-dollar reward. Ace knew it was just a matter of time before one of those cowhands came forward and told you that Ace hadn't been in the bunkhouse the night Ray Dale was killed. Then I would know who'd been squeezing me dry for ten years." Her clown smile was frightening. "Ace knew his life wasn't worth dust when that happened. He was already a black-mailer. Stepping up to murder wasn't hard, not when he had no choice but to keep those cowhands from talking. With that plane of his, he could fly in and out and no one was the wiser."

Ace had killed C.J. and Tucker and Lance. Chelsea felt sick, remembered flying with him, then realized that left only one other cowhand from that summer. "Jack?" she asked, her heart pounding.

Roberta shook her head. "I knew Jack wasn't my

blackmailer. Not the way he lived. Ace thought Jack
didn't know anything, otherwise wouldn't Jack have told
your old man the day Ryder fired him?''

Jack was all right. Chelsea felt a wave of relief.

Roberta's gaze narrowed, her clown makeup smeared
and dusty from searching the bunkhouse. ''That just
leaves you. I know Ace told you about the photos he took
that night in Box Canyon—''

Chelsea started to argue that she didn't know anything
about any photos, but Roberta grabbed her by the throat
and jerked her to her feet before she could speak. ''Believe me, I can get you to talk—just like I did Ace before
he died.''

Chelsea felt the cold steel of the knife blade at her
throat. Roberta was strong from years of ranch work. And
smart. Hadn't Chelsea's father told her that Roberta was
the one who'd gotten Lloyd involved in rodeo stock and
been a big factor in making their company a success? A
business she and Lloyd had started from scratch ten years
ago. Had it all been financed by Roberta's rustling
money?

''Ace better not have lied to me,'' Roberta said, not
sounding quite so sure now. ''You do know where the
negatives are, don't you?''

Chelsea was aware enough to realize that if she didn't
know, Roberta had no reason to keep her alive. She
glanced around the bunkhouse, wondering where Ace
could have hidden the negatives. He had obviously lied
about her knowing where they were. But why? Had he
been hoping to save his own skin? Chelsea wondered if
there really were any photos, let alone negatives.

All she could do was stall for time. Cody was bound
to be home soon. He'd be looking for her when she didn'
return with the papers on the ranch. But he wouldn't b

looking for her at the Wishing Tree, she realized with an inward groan.

The one thing Chelsea didn't doubt was that Roberta planned to kill her once she found the negatives—if they did exist. She tried to think on her feet, but the drug was still making her lightheaded.

"Cut the tape from my wrists so I can show you," Chelsea told the woman.

"Yeah right," Roberta said.

"I'm not sure exactly where they are," Chelsea told her. "I'm going to need my hands free to find them."

She must have sounded convincing.

"Just remember, I have the knife and I'll use it if you make one wrong move," Roberta warned. "If you'd ever seen me skin a rattler, you'd know that I'm a natural with a knife."

She sliced the duct tape with the sharp blade. Chelsea rubbed her wrists for a moment.

"Come on, quit stalling," Roberta snapped.

"Give me your flashlight. I'm going to have to crawl up into the attic."

Roberta looked skeptical. "I already searched up there."

"Not everywhere, obviously."

Chelsea took the flashlight and went over to the straight-back chair that Roberta had pulled up under the opening to the small attic. She could feel the fresh air coming in from the open door of the bunkhouse. Roberta was watching the main road into the ranch, no doubt worried that Cody would be returning from the wedding soon.

The Mercedes was parked out front. Even if Roberta had the keys, Chelsea had a spare in the glove box. She'd have to move fast—

She pretended to slide the chair into a better spot, then

saw her chance. With the chair still in her hands, she flung it at Roberta, then dived for the door, slamming it behind her.

What she hadn't planned on was how fast the older woman would recover and how much the drug slowed her own escape. Roberta came tearing after her, but Chelsea spun around and flung the flashlight at her, then grabbed the Mercedes door handle and jerked it open.

Roberta hit her hard, knocking her to the ground, before she could get inside. Then the woman was on her, the knife blade glinting in the moonlight.

"You are going to be very sorry for that," Roberta snarled. "Very sorry."

JACK TRIED to rein in the fear, telling himself that Ace was too smart to kill Chelsea. But three people were already dead.

Lightning lit the dark sky as another spring thunderstorm moved in. The night was black and the storm clouds low, the air thick with the scent of rain as Jack rolled down his window, fear making him sweat.

"It doesn't make any sense for Ace to take Chelsea out to the ranch," Cody said, as if thinking aloud.

Jack couldn't agree more. "Unless he's planning some type of hostage-ransom situation. Maybe he'll demand a plane to fly him out a million dollars."

Cody looked over at him, suspicion in his gaze as he barreled down the road toward the ranch. "You sound like you know the plan."

"You don't still think I'm after your money and the ranch." Jack shook his head in disgust.

"I'm not sure what you want," Cody said.

"I want to ask Chelsea to marry me, but I don't want to live on the Wishing Tree and always be the ranch hand who married the ranch owner. But how can I ask her to give up her home to marry me?''

"She already gave it up," Cody said.

"She what?''

"She insisted I buy her half of the ranch. I was to sign the papers tonight.''

Chelsea would never give up the Wishing Tree. "Why would she do something like that?''

Cody shot him a disbelieving look. "She's in love with you and believes the ranch is the problem between the two of you.''

Jack swore under his breath. He remembered his cruel words the night she showed up in Lubbock about her never having to give up anything she loved. What a fool he was. If anything happened to her, it would be his fault. His heart swelled with love for her—and terror that Ace might hurt her.

"I don't have to ask how you feel about having me in the family," Jack said.

"My sister falling in love with a damned fool? How do you think I feel?''

Jack couldn't argue that.

Cody shot him another look as he turned down a narrow dirt road that came into the back end of the ranch. "I'm not worried about you ending up in the family. I just don't think you have the good sense to ask her to marry you.''

"You wouldn't mind?" Jack's voice betrayed his skepticism.

"Hell, yes, I would mind. No man is good enough for my little sister. But if she loves you enough to give up the Wishing Tree, maybe you'll grow on me.''

Ahead, Jack spotted Chelsea's Mercedes parked in front of the bunkhouse.

THE NIGHT AIR nearly crackled with electricity, the thunderstorm so close Chelsea could almost feel the first raindrops. Thunder boomed and lightning lit the sky behind Roberta, pitching the older woman into silhouette but picking up the gleam of the knife blade as she brought it down.

Behind Roberta, a figure appeared, backlit by the lightning and shimmering as if a mirage.

Chelsea shifted and felt the blade cut into her arm, then Roberta fell back as a strong arm forced her to the ground. Jack!

As if in a dream, she watched Cody and Jack grab the knife from Roberta and use a piece of bailing twine to tie her up.

Suddenly Chelsea was in Jack's arms, and she could hear the sound of sirens in the distance.

"You're hurt," Jack cried as he pulled off his jacket and ripped a piece of his white shirt to bind the wound on her arm. "Don't worry, it's not deep."

She couldn't feel anything but his warm fingers as he wrapped the makeshift bandage around her arm. "She killed Ray Dale and Crocker and Tucker McCray. She killed them all. Even Ace."

He put his arms around her, holding her tight. "Are you all right? Really all right?"

She nodded, tears flooding her eyes as he hugged her so tightly she couldn't breathe.

"Thank God," he whispered against her hair. "Thank God."

CHAPTER NINETEEN

CHELSEA WOKE late the next morning in her own bed at the ranch to find Jack gone. She looked around the room, realizing that she didn't belong there anymore. She belonged with Jack. And somehow she had to convince him of that.

When she stumbled down to the kitchen, she found her brother sitting alone at the table. "Where's Jack?"

"He left you a message," Cody said, pointing to a folded sheet of paper at the edge of the table.

Chelsea felt her heart drop, remembering the last time he'd left her a note. Fingers shaking, she picked it up. Last night they hadn't had a chance to talk. By the time the sheriff left and Doc Branson came over to stitch up her arm, they'd all been too exhausted.

She opened the note and read the words written in Jack's neat script. "There is so much I want to say to you. Please come to the rodeo this afternoon. I thought afterward we could have that talk we planned last night. Until then... Love, Jack."

Love, Jack. "He's gone to the rodeo."

"I guess he's not ready to give it up and settle down just yet," Cody said. "I think last night scared him. You almost getting killed, finding out that you'd give up the Wishing Tree—"

"You told him?"

"Sorry, sis, but I thought the guy ought to know."

She felt tears rush her eyes. "It's all right. I planned to tell him last night myself." She still felt shaky when she thought about how close she'd come to dying. But Roberta was now in jail. Lloyd was beside himself, never suspecting that the money he'd used to start his stock business had come from rustling cattle. Or that his wife could kill.

The sheriff had searched the bunkhouse and the ranch and found no negatives. Whether or not any photos had ever existed, it appeared they'd never know.

"Are you going to the rodeo?" Cody asked.

The thought of watching Jack ride made her sick inside. "I can't ask him to give up something he loves so much."

"You gave up something you loved for him," Cody said. "I think you'd better tell him how you feel."

At one time she'd thought she could follow him on the circuit, that she could support his career as a bull rider and learn to live with the fear. But the last thing she wanted to do was see him ride again. She couldn't bear the thought that something would happen to him this time. Or the next.

She glanced at her watch. She had to talk to Jack, though, and right away. If she hurried she could catch him before he rode.

SEBASTIAN COOPER passed Chelsea on the highway into San Antonio. Chelsea didn't see him. She seemed lost in her own world. He'd read all about her abduction in the morning papers. It didn't surprise him about Roberta Crandell. He'd always admired her. Everyone knew Lloyd wouldn't have a pot to pee in if it hadn't been for Roberta. Too bad she got caught, though. Now she'd spend the rest of her life in prison—just like J. B. Crowe, if Sebastian had anything to do with it.

He put Chelsea and Roberta out of his mind. He had bigger things to concern himself with—like finding his wife.

But he finally had a lead. He'd searched Julie's files on the computer and found the article she'd done on Hattie Devereaux, the Louisiana midwife.

He'd read the column twice, feeling more certain each time. Hattie had come to San Antonio for a few months in 1998 to help train midwives in the Mexican community. While there, she'd been featured in one of Julie's columns.

Back in Louisiana, the woman lived in an old cabin with one room and no indoor plumbing. Even more interesting, she had several small cabins on the property for expectant mothers with nowhere to go.

A black midwife do-gooder—just the kind of person Julie might run to. He knew the type. And he knew his wife. All he had to do now was get one of his men to find this Hattie Devereaux and do whatever it took to make her tell them where Julie was.

"I MISSED YOU this morning," Chelsea said when she found Jack by the chutes.

"I had some business I had to take care of," he said. "How's your arm?"

"Fine."

He seemed nervous, unsure. "Cody told me about you selling your half of the Wishing Tree to him," he said after a moment. "Chelsea, I can't believe you'd do that."

"Jack," she said, her voice softening. "When are you going to realize that you mean more to me than anything else on this earth? You and Sam."

"Chelsea, do you realize what you're getting yourself into with me? I have so little to offer you compared to what you've always had. I can't afford a ranch house like the one you've been living in all your life or—''

"Jack.'' She silenced him with her finger on his lips. "The only thing keeping us apart is your pride. And this need you have to prove something to yourself. You don't have to prove anything to me. Or to Sam. We love you.''

"Why do I feel like there is a 'but' coming?'' he asked.

"I can't watch you ride. It's too hard, knowing this might be the time you get gored or stomped to death. I'm sorry, Jack.''

"You're up, Jack,'' one of the cowboys yelled from the chutes.

"Good luck with your ride.'' She turned and walked away, refusing to look back, praying Jack didn't end up killing himself. But she wouldn't be there to watch. It seemed he couldn't let go of this need to compete, and not just in the arena, but with her money, her family, her ranch.

"You keep going in this direction, you're going to miss Jack's ride,'' Rowdy said, catching up to her.

"I'm leaving,'' she said, and kept walking. "There's nothing more I can do or say to talk him out of it.''

The cowboy fell in step beside her. "I don't blame you. The guy's spent years convincing himself of all the reasons the two of you are wrong for each other. A guy like Jackson isn't afraid to get on two-ton bulls day after day, but he's scared to death of loving a woman like you.''

She stopped walking and turned to look at him.

"What's one more rodeo?'' Rowdy asked.

JACK CLIMBED UP the side of the chute as the Widow Maker slammed around inside. But he paid little attention to the movements of the bull. It was something he'd long become accustomed to. He tried to clear his mind. Everything hinged on his ride here today. He was on the edge that would put him in the running for the National Finals Rodeo. He'd worked so hard this year to get there and he couldn't afford to let anything keep him from it.

Why couldn't Chelsea understand that? He needed this purse. And the next one and the next one in order to buy the ranch next to the Wishing Tree. He was doing this for her. And Sam. He was ready to quit the rodeo. He didn't have that many more years he could ride, and Chelsea was right. It was time to settle down and give Sam a home.

She'd sold her share of the Wishing Tree. Cody had signed the papers that morning. It was inconceivable. She'd also almost gotten herself killed trying to clear his name. He felt sick inside, overwhelmed by her love—just as he'd been by her money.

Chelsea had proved she could survive in his world. But she'd turned that world upside down. She had him questioning the last ten years of his life. Wondering what he was doing perched on top of this chute, about to drop down on the back of this rank bull.

"Fool woman," he muttered to himself as he straddled the bull and leaned down to work the rope around his gloved hand.

"Here," Rowdy said, bending over the edge of the chute to tighten the rope for him.

Jack looked up at his friend. "Thanks."

"Don't thank me, I think you're the dumbest cowboy I've ever met."

"Why aren't you in the announcing booth where you belong?" Jack asked.

"Got someone to fill in for me so I could come down here and try to talk some sense into your hard head," Rowdy said.

"If this is about Chelsea, I don't want to hear it."

"I'm sure you don't." Rowdy tightened the rope around Jack's gloved hand. "But I'm your best friend so I guess it's up to me to say it. You've had a chip on your shoulder for years, Jack. You've had some hard knocks—no one is arguing that. But you know what your problem is?"

"I'm sure you're going to tell me."

"You don't think you're good enough for her and you're wrong. You're the best damned man I've ever known. Don't be a fool. You let her go this time, Jack, and you'll regret it as long as you live. Except this time, you'll have only yourself to blame."

"Are you finished?" he snapped. "You might not have noticed, but I've got a bull to ride."

"Yeah, I can see that," Rowdy said. "And riding this bull means everything to you, doesn't it? I hope it's worth it. By the way, this bull likes fences and stomping cowboys. Have a good ride, bud." He moved away.

Jack settled down on the bull, telling himself Rowdy didn't know a damned thing about women—or bulls.

CHELSEA WATCHED Jack and Rowdy by the chutes, wondering why she'd let Rowdy talk her into this. Did Rowdy really think her staying could change anything? She'd done all she could do. It was up to Jack now. And as she watched him get ready for his ride, she knew this would be her last rodeo. Even if—no, when—Jack made it to the National Finals, she wouldn't be there. Nor would she watch on television.

Once she left here, she'd be starting a new life. She wouldn't be going back to the Wishing Tree. As much as she loved the ranch, she knew it would never feel like home again. Not after this week with Jack and Sam.

That would be the hard part. Forgetting.

She glanced over in surprise as Sam slid in next to her.

"Hi," the girl said. Her face was still blotchy from crying, her hat pulled low, her expression sad.

"What's wrong?" Chelsea asked in concern.

"Dad said we're leaving for El Paso tonight," the girl said. "And you aren't coming with us, are you?"

Chelsea shook her head.

"Dad said he has to make it to the National Finals or we can't get the ranch he wants."

"But once you have a ranch, you can get that horse—your own Sam's Star." Her voice broke at the realization she wouldn't be there the first time Sam rode her very own horse.

"I don't want to go without you." Tears filled the girl's eyes. "I want us to be a family. I want—" a sob escaped "—I want you to be my mother."

"Oh, Sam." Chelsea pulled the girl into her arms. "That's what I want to be, too."

"And now in chute three, Texas-born and raised Jackson Robinson on the Widow Maker!"

"If Dad gets a good score, we'll be going to the National Finals Rodeo," she said, but Chelsea could hear the change in her voice. The magic had gone out of her words, out of the dream.

JACK SAID a little prayer and looked up to where Sam always sat, hoping she would be there, needing her there more than ever before.

He spotted her western hat and caught a glimpse of her face. Then his throat tightened as he saw Chelsea sitting next to her. He'd just assumed Chelsea was miles down the road by now.

He lifted his left hand and nodded to the gatekeeper.

The Widow Maker was known for high kicks and then turning back hard, trying to hook his riders. Jack didn't know where Rowdy got the idea that the bull had taken to fences.

The snorting creature came out of the chute in one explosive jump and began to buck.

"Did ya'll see that one?" the announcer hollered. "Birds could have built a nest in that cowboy's hat, that bull bucked so high."

But suddenly, instead of kicking and twisting and trying to drop him in the well, the Widow Maker headed for the fence at a dead run.

Jack could see what the bull had in mind but couldn't move quickly enough to prevent it.

The Widow Maker sideswiped the fence, slamming Jack into it. The right side of his chest hit the wooden post, knocking the breath out of him. Then the bull began to buck and jump and twist and turn, but it was too late.

"Looks like Jack Shane is going to get a reride," the announcer said.

Jack held on until the pickup boys came alongside, then grabbed one of the riders and pulled himself off the angry bull. But before his feet touched earth, he knew he was hurt.

CHELSEA SAW the way Jack grabbed his ribs. She looked over at Sam, who was watching Jack closely.

"I'm going to go talk to your father," Chelsea said, starting to get to her feet.

"It won't do any good," Sam said quietly. "You'll just make him mad, make him ride again even if he hadn't planned to." It seemed Sam knew her father. "Anyway, he's ridden hurt before. A lot of bull riders ride hurt."

Chelsea sat back down, thinking she would never understand men and their constant drive to prove themselves. She had actually come to understand Jack's need to ride bulls. He had a talent for it and he'd found something he could excel at. She knew he needed that after her father had hurt him.

But how many world championships did he have to win? How much money did he have to earn before he bought that ranch he'd always dreamed of? The ranch his daughter wanted so desperately.

But she knew the answer to that. He wanted a ranch larger than the Wishing Tree. Had she done this to Jack? Or was it just his damned pride?

She feared Sam was right. If she went down in the chutes, she would only make matters worse. It wasn't as if this was the last bull Jack planned to ride.

"Yep, the judges say they're going to give Jackson a reride," the announcer was saying. "Let's give him a big hand, because he's going to be coming back out on a bull called Dead Eye Joe. Friends, this bull has got a forty-thousand dollar bounty on him because he has yet to be ridden! But if anyone can do it, it's Jackson Robinson!"

She closed her eyes and reached over to take Sam's hand.

Sam squeezed back. "Dad can do it. He can do anything he sets his mind to."

Chelsea opened her eyes and smiled over at the girl. She prayed Sam was right.

JACK CLIMBED the metal chute and looked down on the bull. Dead Eye Joe. He'd wanted to ride this bull for a very long time. It wasn't just the bounty on this beast. No man had ridden him, and Jack wanted to be the first.

He could feel the bull moving the sides of the chute with his massive weight. A good ride on Dead Eye Joe would do a lot more than secure his slot in Las Vegas. And, of course, there was the forty-thousand-dollar bounty.

The stands were full. Jack breathed in the familiar scents, a combination of leather, dust, rough stock and concession food. He tried to focus, but he kept hearing Chelsea's voice. "Jack, the only thing keeping us apart now is your pride. And this need you have to prove something to yourself. You don't have to prove anything to me. Or to Sam."

Yes, he thought, he did. He still did. But it wasn't just about proving himself. It was about doing something he was good at, being his own man, doing it his own way. And yes, damn it, it was about pride—and money. How did you explain that to a woman? Especially this woman.

"It's about winning, damn it," he muttered to himself as he straddled the bull and leaned down to wrap the rope around his gloved hand. His ribs hurt bad and he was having trouble breathing, but with a little luck he could ride this damn bull the full eight seconds.

"Here," Rowdy said, bending over the edge of the chute to tighten the rope for him.

"You still here?" Jack said.

Rowdy grinned. "Didn't want to miss seeing you kill yourself to prove a point. Not a chance."

"Don't listen to him, Jack," Terri Lyn called as she scrambled up the side of the chute. "You can ride this bull." It seemed she'd quickly forgotten Ace and set her sights on Jack again.

"The snake was the wrong move," Jack said. "It wasn't Roberta's style. It was the kind of prank that had your name written all over it."

She pretended innocence, but only for a moment. "I play to win, Jack. You and I are alike that way. That's what makes us such a great match. We know what's important and we go after it, any way we can.''

He looked at her hard for a long moment. She thought she'd won. That she'd chased off Chelsea. He'd done that all on his own.

"Yeah, it's about winning, but it's also how you play the game."

She snorted at that. "No one gives a damn about you unless you take home the belt buckle, Jack, and you know it."

"It looks like Jackson Robinson is about to try his luck on Dead Eye Joe," the announcer informed the crowd. "This is one rank bull, folks. He looks like he could eat cowboys for breakfast."

"Good luck," Terri Lyn said as she climbed down.

Jack glanced to where Rowdy was hanging on the fence, watching him with interest. They'd been friends since Jack first got into bull riding. Rowdy was rodeo. He knew how much this meant, getting to the finals.

"I think he's about ready, folks," the announcer said.

Jack glanced up into the grandstands. Chelsea had her arm around Sam, both of them watching him, waiting.

"You going to ride that bull, Jack, or just sit on it?" Rowdy hollered at him. "You're never going to get to the NFR at this rate, bud."

Jack looked at his friend. "You're at least right about that."

"Wait a minute," the announcer said. "Looks like there might be a problem here."

With a certainty Jack hadn't felt in a very long time, he called to one of the pickup men as he quickly unwrapped the rope from his gloved hand. "Borrow your horse a minute?"

The cowboy seemed surprised, but slid off the horse to hand him up the reins.

"Folks, I'm not sure what's going on," the announcer said as Jack climbed over the chute and dropped into the saddle.

He spurred the horse and galloped across the arena toward Chelsea and Sam, barely feeling his cracked ribs. He could hear the voices of the crowd and the announcer, a dull roar over the pounding of his heart. Everyone in the stands rose to their feet.

He rode over to Chelsea and Sam, bringing the horse up to a dust-whirling halt in front of them.

"I have almost enough money for a ranch, nothing as grand as the one you just gave away, but still a fine ranch adjacent to the Wishing Tree," he called up. "But I'm going to need your help if we hope to make anything of it. It will mean a lot of hard work and, if you still have a few bucks, some of your money." The words hadn't been as hard to say as he thought they would be.

For a brief moment he was afraid she might be going to faint. But the next instant a wide smile lit up her entire face.

"Does that mean you'll marry me?" he shouted up to her. "That is, if Sam agrees."

Sam let out a very unladylike whoop of approval.

"Well?" he asked Chelsea.

"Oh, yes," she cried, climbing down from the stands and over the railing.

Jack leaned over and pulled her in front of him onto the horse, just as the crowd broke into a large cheer.

"Jack, the bull is back over here!" Rowdy called from the announcer's booth, and everyone laughed.

Sam hopped up on the back of the horse and Jack rode around the arena, stopping at the announcer's booth.

"She's going to marry me!" he yelled, and tossed his hat into the air.

The crowd went wild as he kissed his future bride. The cheers and applause were louder than any he'd ever gotten bull riding.

EPILOGUE

CHELSEA LEANED against the corral fence, watching Sam ride around the ring on Sam's Star, marveling at the beautiful summer day and her own happiness.

She just wished her father was here to see how it had all turned out. He would have been happy for her and Jack, and delighted to have a granddaughter like Sam and another one on the way, Chelsea thought, resting her hand on her swollen stomach.

She looked up to see Jack come riding toward her with Cody. It had been Cody's idea to combine the two ranches and run them as one, with Chelsea doing the books. It did her heart good to see how her brother and Jack had become friends. Jack had insisted they get married at the Wishing Tree, with Sam as her maid of honor. All of Jack's rodeo family and friends had come, as well as her own friends. Jack had asked Cody to be his best man.

"Are you sure you won't regret giving up rodeoing?" she'd asked him the night before the wedding.

"My dream was always to have a ranch with you and our children," Jack said. "I just kept putting it off because I thought I had to do it all on my own."

"Daddy, look!" Sam cried now as she prodded the colt and trotted around inside the corral.

Jack swung out of his saddle to join Chelsea on the fence, putting one arm around her, the other hand going to her stomach. "How are you feeling?"

"Great." She smiled at him. "The Garrett clan is coming over for dinner. I'm making my killer enchiladas."

Jack laughed as Cody joined them. "She's even got Sam liking Tex-Mex now." He put his cheek against hers. "Would you look at that girl ride."

Chelsea thought her heart couldn't possibly hold any more joy than she felt at this moment.

"Mind if I bring a date to dinner?" Cody asked, almost sheepishly.

A date? Cody? He never took the time to date. And he'd certainly never brought anyone home to dinner.

"Of course," Chelsea said, trying to keep a straight face. "Anyone I know?"

"She's the vet's new assistant," Cody said, watching Sam. "Her name's Megan. And don't try to make anything out of it, all right?"

"I wouldn't dream of it," she said, grinning to herself. She'd caught that sparkle in her brother's eye and recognized it only too well. She'd known it had been in her own eye every time she looked at Jack.

She snuggled into her husband's warm body, letting him envelop her with his love as they watched Sam ride around the corral. Life just didn't get any better than this.

TRUEBLOOD, TEXAS *continues*
next month with
THE RANCHER'S BRIDE
by Tara Taylor Quinn

Librarian Rachel Blair was finally about to marry the man of her dreams. Max Santana, foreman at the Garrett ranch, was shifting restlessly, waiting for the Reverend Blair to give the signal for the "Wedding March" to start. But suddenly, Rachel couldn't come to terms with the events of a fateful night in a co-ed dorm at the University of Texas. With one last, tearful glance back, she disappeared into the warm May sunshine, leaving her beloved groom standing at the makeshift altar, the solid gold band they'd chosen together nestled in his pocket.

Here's a preview!

CHAPTER ONE

OH, GOD. She wasn't going to be able to do it.

She'd really thought she could.

Her wedding day had finally arrived. The day she was to marry Max Santana. Though for years he'd done nothing more than humor her, she'd been in love with the man since puberty. Her wildest dream, her most fantastic hope was about to come true.

And she couldn't do it.

Hands shaking, Rachel Blair reached up to unhook the lacy white veil from her hair. Her father, the Reverend Donald Blair, was going over last-minute details outside on the acre of green lawn in back of the First Trueblood Presbyterian Church, where he was scheduled, in less than an hour, to perform the ceremony for the wedding of his only daughter. Guests would be arriving soon. As would Max. If he hadn't already.

Rachel's long red hair tumbled around her shoulders and down her back as she removed the pins the hairdresser had put in earlier that morning. Even that little freedom was a relief. And an ache.

She wanted, more than anything else in life, to marry Max. To live side by side with him, share the aches and joys of daily life, to eat with him every day and sleep with him every night...

The hairpins hardly made a sound as they slipped from Rachel's fingers to the tile floor of the choir changing room, which was serving double duty as the bride's dressing room this Saturday morning.

Jumping up from her stool in front of the mirror that her father's secretary had set up specifically for the bride earlier that morning, Rachel glanced around frantically. She had to get changed, get out of here, before it was too late. Before anyone came in and tried to stop her. Ashley Garrett Blackstone, the youngest daughter of the Trueblood Garrett, was already a couple of minutes late and would be running in any moment in typical Ashley fashion, strong, sure, ready to go. Pregnancy hadn't changed her a bit. And with her take-charge friend there, Rachel wouldn't stand a chance.

Rachel and Ashley hadn't seen each other all that much since leaving Trueblood for college. She knew nothing about that fateful year in Rachel's life.

And Rachel couldn't seem to tell her. Couldn't bring herself to tell anyone. Not even Max.

Only her father knew the truth. But it wasn't something they talked about. That long, debilitating year of Rachel's life was too painful for both of them.

Her father. He'd had such hopes for today. Hopes for her. And her future. Hopes that she'd finally be happy, truly happy, again.

She had to get out.

SILHOUETTE Romance

Escape to a place where a kiss is still a kiss...
Feel the breathless connection...
Fall in love as though it were
the very first time...
Experience the power of love!

Come to where favorite authors——such as
**Diana Palmer, Stella Bagwell,
Marie Ferrarella** and many more——
deliver heart-warming romance and genuine
emotion, time after time after time....

*Silhouette Romance——
stories straight from the heart!*

Silhouette®
Where love comes alive™

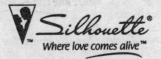

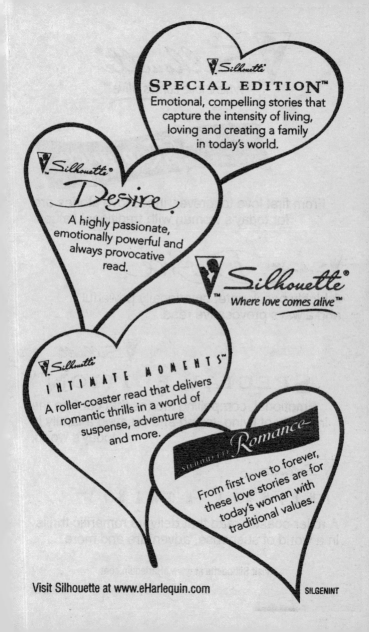